The Desire Path

A novel by
Diane Vogel Ferri

Diane Vogel Ferri

ISBN 978-0-9772245-1-7
Library of Congress Control Number 2010940377

Song lyrics on page 101 from the hymn "Come Thou Fount of Every Blessing."
Lyrics by Robert Robinson (1735-1790)

Cover photo by Diane Vogel Ferri
with thanks to Kate and Olivia.

FOR LOU
who loves me just as I am,

and Kate
who inspired so much of the beauty in this story,

and Ryan
who has made my life *better*.

And then the day came when the risk to remain tight in a bud was more painful than the risk it took to blossom.
Anais Nin

. . . desire paths . . . the imprints of 'foot anarchists', individuals who had trodden their own routes into the landscape, regardless of the intentions of government, planners and engineers. A desire path could be a short cut through waste ground, across a corner of a civic garden or down an embankment. They were expressions of free will, 'paths with a passion', an alternative to the strictures of railings, fences and walls that turned individuals into powerless, apathetic automatons. On desire paths you could break out, explore, 'feel your way across the landscape.' Nick Crane
From "Two Degrees West" (Viking 1999)

PART 1

1993

Lavender

Everyone slept as I escaped out the back door and through my dad's perfect garage. The tree frogs sang, and my dangling earrings made tiny clicking sounds with each step as I ran down the footpath, cutting through the neighbors' backyards. I wondered how many scuffling feet it had taken to make the path, and why so many had left the sidewalk to follow it. I sniffed out the sweetness of the sycamores. When I was a little girl I'd thought the fragrance came from Lake Erie, the massive, moody body of water at the end of my street.

Now the sound of the soft, lapping waves guided me through the humid Ohio night air to my favorite spot at the edge of a precarious cliff. Sitting on a mossy rock, I pulled out my last cigarette and listened to the hum of air conditioners. I sensed the soothing bedroom lights shining from the houses surrounding me.

I would miss the lake. At times it gave me my only sense of belonging, the only reassuring sound in a home of silence and discomfort. I would miss autumn in Ohio, too; the acorns and buckeyes in crowded piles, a random crocus blooming in October, the early snow resting on red leaves.

My cigarette burned down to a stub as I felt sudden tears slide down my neck and onto my shirt. The back of my head ached as if something was pushing me away from everything familiar, everything in the world I understood, but at the same time I wanted to keep walking, to keep moving away, to go towards whatever was beyond the street of colonial houses, beyond the bucolic, pretentious life my parents had chosen for me. My mother's words rang between my ears – *no daughter of mine.*

George and Roberta could have their constipated life. I would be free. I didn't even want to be their daughter anymore. I wouldn't go out into the world as Christine May. My favorite color and fragrance was lavender. The color of my hair. Lavender.

The sweaty July night made my clothes stick to my skin. I wore the jeans I had cut off at mid-thigh with a pair of scissors, and a black t-shirt with *Anarchy*! scrawled across the front in red letters - as misfit as a 17 year-old girl could be in our Ohio suburb, and in my own home. Sometimes I fantasized I was adopted. My real mother loved me unconditionally and didn't expect me to be her little clone. Maybe she was a contemporary of Warhol or a punk rocker from the seventies, out there waiting for me to find her.

A crunching sound in the dark made me turn.

"Chrissie, is that you?" Amber swatted mosquitoes and tree branches out of her way and sat next to me on the mossy rock.

"Yeah, it's me. Who else would sit here getting gnawed on by a trillion bugs just to have a smoke?" Amber had a heart-shaped face and heart-shaped mouth. The vertical crease in her lower lip made her mouth look like a little bow. Everything about her was sweet and I always felt caustic and unappealing in her presence. She insisted on being my friend anyway.

"Did something happen at home again?" she asked, smacking a bug off her leg.

"Nothing unusual, just my parents talking about me behind my back. I overheard them talking about how they're not going to let me go to college until I straighten up and fly right – whatever that means."

"And you were counting on college to get you out of Lake Village – and away from them, right?" I sensed

Amber staring at me, truly interested, waiting for an answer. I looked her in the eyes, hoping she'd sense my gratitude.

"And I definitely can't go to college without my dad's money, so I guess I'll just continue to be the town loser. What am I going to do here – help my mom bake cookies for the church rummage sale or let her teach me how to cross-stitch – her one true love?"

"Yeah," she laughed, "How many cross-stitch pictures can one place have? Come over to my house," she said, standing up, "At least you can watch MTV there for awhile since your dad won't let you have it at your house. That'll make you feel better. Do you want to call Sean? You can use the phone in my bedroom."

"No, thanks, I don't ever want to speak to that jerk again."

"I thought you two were together. What hap . . ."

"I said I don't want to talk to him, see him, smell him, or touch him ever again!"

"Sorry, you seemed so cool together," Amber said, brushing detritus off her pretty white pants.

"No, I'm sorry, I didn't mean to freak out on you. It just didn't work out with him."

"Did he do something to you? I mean, did he hurt you?" Amber touched my shoulder.

Amber was a virgin. One more thing my mother would want me to emulate if she had proof I wasn't one. I didn't know if I could explain to this innocent girl that sometimes you don't want to have sex but it happens anyway. I still wasn't sure if Sean had forced himself on me or I'd actually let him have his way because he was so cute and cool. I remember realizing we were at the point of no return and I'd tried to enjoy it, but at the same time feeling a keen sense of doom at my impulsive decision.

"I'll tell you later, if you promise not to tell anyone"

~~~~~~~

My parents knocked on my bedroom door and then just walked in.

"You're supposed to be asked in after you knock on a door," I said, shutting off my Nirvana tape.

"Christine, we'd like to talk to you about this boy you've been seeing," Dad said. My mother stood straight-backed, so much taller than me in her navy blue skirt, pantyhose and baby blue twin set, even though it was 80 degrees out. Her common, colorless hair was clipped around her ears and up the back of her neck. My dad wore belted khaki pants, a golf shirt and sneakers. His gray comb-over made him look older, but his face held a gentleness for me to cling to.

"Do you remember our discussion about premarital sex? We have tried to teach you right from wrong at home and at church," Mother said, glancing around the room with a look of disgust on her face. Her gaze turned to me and softened a bit since I wore some pink pajamas she'd made me for Christmas, but there was no light in her eyes.

"Just because I might finally have a boyfriend doesn't mean I'm having sex. Why do you always think the worst of me?" I sat on my black and white checkered bedspread and pulled a purple pillow onto my lap, clutching handfuls of it to my chest.

"We think the worst because you've shown us over and over again that you are not to be trusted. You are already grounded for dying your hair. It's illegal for you to be getting tattoos. You are not old enough to make those types of decisions. Your clothing is an embarrassment to me . . . to us."

"I'm an embarrassment to you, that's all I am, right Mom?" Tears almost forced their way out of my eyes, but then burned back in anger. I stood up, but Dad gently pressed me back down on the bed by my shoulder.

"No, of course you are not just an embarrassment, but if there was an unwed pregnancy . . ." Mom said clasping her hands together at waist level, "Well, we do not believe in abortion. The Bible teaches us the sanctity of life. The child would be given away."

"Doesn't it also teach us compassion and forgiveness for each other?" I asked.

"Of course, anyone knows that, but *no daughter of mine* would ever shame this family by getting pregnant. You know what happened to that girl down the street." I wanted the words to end, but it was like trying to stop a roller coaster with your feet.

"What about the girl down the street? She didn't have an abortion. She had her baby and she's taking care of it," I said, "and she's still going to school!"

"Yes, but with the help of her parents. She couldn't do it without them. It's changed all of their lives," my mother said, as she straightened up a pile of books on my desk. I tried to visualize my mother changing a smelly, messy diaper or cleaning up vomit from her perfect carpets. I couldn't imagine it.

"Mom, you know, I've been to the Cogan's house. They all love that little boy. They enjoy having him there. Everybody plays with him, and he's so cute."

"You don't know what you're talking about. A baby is a huge responsibility," Roberta said, "I don't know why we're even talking about this."

"You brought it up." I murmured. Looking down at my hands I noticed I'd peeled away part of my thumb cuticle with my index finger. I grabbed my guitar and placed it in front of me as a comforting shield.

"Christine, the tattoo and the purple hair are a great disappointment to us. There can be no more . . . ."

"No more what, Dad? Three strikes and I'm out? Should I just leave now?"

"Let's not be melodramatic." My mother turned towards the door.

I stood up. "The tattoo, the barbed wire?" I pulled up my sleeve to reveal the new ink on my upper arm; the symbol burned into me with all my savings and a fake ID. "You're just proving what it means to me! That this is a prison! Don't you get it?"

My mother turned back to me. "There is nothing to get, young lady. We've had enough of your teenage rebellion. Look at this room. It's disgusting. Nothing even matches. And your hair - it's ridiculous." Then she averted her eyes out the window as if her view of me was too sickening to behold.

"You're the ridiculous ones!" I felt small and childish as I sat back down on the bed. I watched George take Roberta's arm and lead her out of the room.

"Good night, Chrissie," Dad looked back at me and quietly closed the door.

In that moment I was a poker player holding cards that burned like briquettes in my hand. *I see you. I raise you. I have no idea if you are bluffing.*

My mother's words - *No daughter of mine - give the child away* - floated like miniature ghosts before my eyes. I looked around the safe haven of my punk-bedecked bedroom and wondered what would happen to my little brother John if I disappeared for a while - or forever. I needed a plan.

Going to church on Sunday morning was non-negotiable. I didn't even try to fight it anymore. Yet, as much as I despised the hypocrisy of what I heard compared to the reality of what I lived at home, it often comforted and calmed me to be in the light-filled white sanctuary; beams of sun tunneling through the colored glass onto shoulders of people I'd known all my life, the routine of the services, the sense of safety, the hope that God actually loved me as I was, not as my mother desired me to be.

As a little girl, nothing my mother said made sense to me. I had no interest in the things she wanted me to love. The dreams she forced into my world were not my dreams and I felt her displeasure in me every day of my life - as if all her hopes lay in a pile of rubble at every doorway of our home, reminding us all of the great disappointment of Christine.

My father sometimes defended my right to be Christine, but his efforts became erratic as I grew older. I'd occasionally catch a tender look from his eyes or see him stare out a window as my mother berated me for my latest hairstyle or choice of clothing. He never participated in the belittling, but he did nothing to stop it, either.

I'd slept without waking for over ten hours that night after crying until I could no longer lift my head off the pillow, but I still felt weary and lacking any fight on Sunday morning. I opened my closet and searched for the least offensive outfit I could put together to avoid further confrontation from my mother – something she never seemed to tire of.

In the car John chattered in his clueless way about his baseball game the night before and the party at his coach's house afterwards. My parents always timed their attacks on me when Johnny wasn't around to hear them.

"That's wonderful, John, I'm glad you had so much fun last night," my mother turned her head to smile at John sitting next to me in the back seat, avoiding looking at me altogether. She had not spoken to me once all morning.

"And Mom, guess what else? If we win tomorrow night our team will be in the play-offs!" John threw his arms upwards in a sort of victory gesture.

"Good for you, John! I'm so proud of you. You really worked hard this season and now all your hard work is paying off," my mother smiled at him again.

"Good job, son," Dad glanced at me through the rearview mirror and said, "Christine, are you working on any new music in your guitar lessons?"

"Sure Dad, every week I get new songs, but you probably wouldn't know any of them."

"Well, maybe you could play them for your mother and I sometime anyway, even if they're not our kind of music."

We sat in our usual pew in our usual order and listened to a sermon on how some Christians use religion and religious practices to make themselves feel like better people instead of using their faith to actually become better people, to react to difficult situations in life by the example Jesus set for us. I could see a frown set upon my mother's face during the message from my place three seats away from her. She preferred sermons giving clearly articulated rules and a list of don'ts as her inspiration each week.

My parents made me join the church youth group when I started middle school. I didn't want to go, but after attending for awhile I met some cool kids and a couple nice adult leaders. I made it pretty hard for them to accept me. My favorite pastime was alienating people by acting and dressing weird. It was the only defense I had, the only thing that worked for me. This, of course, embarrassed my mother and sometimes she even discouraged me from going after we'd had a particularly difficult week.

In the church foyer after the service the new pastor shook my hand.

"Christine, I've been wanting to call you. We're going to be starting a new service with more contemporary music using guitars and drums. I know you play a heck of a guitar. Would you like to join us?"

"Oh, I don't know, I'm not that good." I said, even though I felt a twinge of glee at his statement.

"You know," he pulled me closer to his face with our still clasped hands. "We are happiest when we are using the gifts God gave us." He grinned mischievously at me.

"We'll let you know, Pastor." My mother butted in, once again taking away the opportunity for me to decide for myself.

Driving down our street on the way home I looked at our white colonial house standing in a row of other identical white colonial houses. The only difference was the other houses looked like human beings lived there, with basketball hoops mounted on garages, swing-sets for screaming kids, and dogs barking and crapping in the yard.

George and Roberta's house lacked what makes a house a home. It was an imitation of a life, like a movie set, full of perfect things and imperfect people pretending to be perfect. The china cabinet held unused snow-white dishes and glistening crystal. The living room was a shrine to my mother's huge collection of Lladro figurines. She received one from my dad at every holiday even though they always claimed they couldn't afford to buy me a cheap acoustic guitar.

In the spring the tulips popped up in perfect rows in the front yard in a red-yellow-red-yellow pattern. In the back yard the weed-free grass existed starkly without a tree or toy ruining its perfection.

My parents often told my brother and I how much money we cost them, and we were expected to earn everything we had by doing chores and obeying their rules. We had to be good stewards of what God had given us, but to me, God hadn't given us anything. We had to work for it. There wasn't much music or laughter in our house. No roughhousing, few parties, and no sleepovers for friends, at least for me. When John turned ten he begged enough until my parents gave in. Once in awhile I earned having a friend come over, but if we got too silly or made any kind of mess my mom would send her home. No playing in a dirty sandbox or making mud pies in my childhood.

I crawled up on the couch to look out the window and saw the kids next door playing outside in the warm summer rain, splashing in puddles in their bathing suits. It looked like fun, so I slipped out the side door and stood with my arms outstretched in the gentle rainfall, my mouth open, catching raindrops on my tongue.

"Get in the house, Christine! What's wrong with you?"

As soon as I reached the doorway she yanked me inside and spanked me, still yelling.

"Your clothes are sopping wet! What were you doing out there?"

"I just wanted to know what the rain felt like, Mommy."

~~~~~~~

An escape plan began to form in my mind. I struggled with abandoning my brother to grow up in this stifled environment, yet, it did not affect him the way it did me. Something must be wrong with me. I'd understood for a long time that John was the favored child in the family, but it was more than that. How could I ever learn about myself if I constantly had to defend simply existing in their perfect world? Even amidst my angry rebellion and outward apathy, I desperately wanted to be accepted and loved. I yearned to feel comfortable and safe in my home. I just wanted what all my friends had, what other teenagers everywhere seemed to have – everyone except me.

"Can I help with anything, Mom?" Lunch after church was also sacred. No excuses, everyone was required to sit quietly or briefly comment on the morning's service.

"Yes, Christine, thank you. Would you cut these vegetables for the salad?" Mom stood at the sink in all her housewifely glory: still in her uniform church clothes -

brown skirt, white blouse and only a small gold chain around her neck. She had on a hand-sewn apron, yellow rubber gloves, and had removed her shoes and put on a pair of starkly white slippers.

"Sure, so, um, how did you like the sermon today?"

"Oh, did you actually listen for a change?" My mother said without looking at me.

My attempt at normal conversation dropped on the floor like a deflated balloon. I felt my face begin to burn and turned back to my chore.

"Christine, I asked you a question."

"Yes, I listened. I'm not stupid."

"No one said you were stupid. You have always had trouble hearing about the love of God. So ungrateful." She shoved more washed carrots in front of me.

I dropped the knife and it clattered to the floor. "The love of God? How can I believe in the love of God when my own mother doesn't love me?" I picked up the knife and turned to face my mother with the knife pointing at her. She took a step backward and put her hand over her chest for a moment and then turned away.

"Didn't I hear in a sermon that when we're loved by other people that's God loving us?" I felt my fingers clench the knife tighter. "When would I experience that?"

"Christine!" My father stood in the doorway. "Don't speak to your mother like that and put that knife down. You know we have always provided for you."

"Yes, Dad. You've given me a place to exist, but not to live. You've given me food, but not acceptance. You support everything John does, but nothing I do or care about. I've been taking guitar lessons for three years and this morning was the first time you ever asked about them! Pastor Jim knows more about what I love than you do! I was just trying to have a decent conversation with Mom, but every conversation turns into an attack on me!" I threw the knife on the counter and put my hands over my face.

"Oh, now here come the tears. *Please* Christine. You have nothing to complain about." My mother went back to washing her vegetables.

I looked up to see my dad staring at me with a crumpled face.

"At least you see me, Dad. She can't even look at me."

I ran up the stairs to my room. I heard my mother call out something about taking my guitar away from me. I sat on the bed and waited for the onslaught of my parents at the door, the threats, the punishment, but they did not come.

The door opened a crack and I was about to yell, *get out*! until I saw my little brother's face in the opening.

"Chrissie? Can I come in?"

"Sure, little dude, come on in. Sorry you had to hear all that crap – again."

He sat down on the bed next to me. "Why are you so mad all the time?"

"I don't think Mom and Dad like me as much as they like you. That makes me mad sometimes. Listen, Johnny, I want you to know that I love you, no matter what happens, OK?"

"Why? What's gonna happen?" He got up off the bed and started moving around the room picking up items and putting them back down nervously. John was almost a teenager, but my parents controlled and sheltered him to the point of immaturity I thought.

"Nothing's going to happen to you, OK?" I wanted to say goodbye, but I knew he'd tell my parents.

"I just wanted to tell you I love you and I think you're a great kid. That's all."

"OK. Are you coming down for lunch?"

"No, tell Mom and Dad I'm not hungry."

My lack of a long-range plan became a non-issue. The idea of leaving home became obsessive and somewhat illusory. In my sub-conscious the notion lingered that I might be sorry, but the whole idea was like a train already in motion – impossible to stop. I called Amber and she promised to wait up for me.

I shoved jeans and rock and roll t-shirts in a duffel bag with my Converse shoes and army boots. I threw in fishnets, thrift store mini-skirts, underwear and all the money I'd saved. I found a bag and stuffed it with my Walkman and as many tapes as I could fit. I carefully put my Yamaha guitar in its case, then opened my bottom dresser drawer and gently pulled out a forlorn, unevenly knit pastel striped scarf.

My Grandma Fiona taught me how to knit when I was nine, and I treasured the scarf we made together. Grandma was the one person who took time to see me, to know me, to teach me things. I didn't know how I would keep her in my life. I couldn't bring myself to call her because I knew I would be too honest and either worry her or let her talk me out of it. I also couldn't say goodbye.

The terror of leaving home was sucking all the fight out of me. Life had just jerked the tablecloth from under the dishes, but my dishes didn't stay on the table. I wrote a short note saying I had to leave and be my own person, so my parents wouldn't think I was kidnapped. I wrote another note to John telling him I was sorry and I'd be in touch soon, even though I didn't know if that was possible. I went to bed in my clothes, turned out the lights and waited until I heard my parents' bedroom door click shut. After midnight I got up and slowly and quietly pulled my bags from under the bed.

As I knelt at my bedside, without thinking, I started to pray. Sometimes I actually felt God's love. Somewhere in my childhood I took the Sunday school message of unconditional love and buried it deep inside of me. It gave me hope, and I desperately needed to believe in something now. My prayer was more of a giant question mark, a *God help me* moment with nothing else in my brain to say.

Before I closed my bedroom door I took one last look at the room I'd fought so hard to make my own. My mother decorated it pink and frilly until I was sixteen, and then she gradually let me add a few of the things I loved, like my posters of Kurt Cobain and The Ramones, my black and red hand-sewn curtains, a lamp with purple stars I found at a Salvation Army store, the stuffed animal collection that Grandma had given me over the years. All of the books I loved sat on the shelves, including the sexy Anais Nin titles and diaries that were hidden in fake book jackets. I grabbed one and stuffed it in my bag knowing I might need some inspiration or familiar words along the way.

At 1:13 in the morning I walked down the sidewalk of the only street I'd ever lived on. Amber waved at me from her first floor bedroom window and slid the screen up. I boosted myself up on the hose holder and fell face first onto her bed. I reached out the window and pulled my guitar in after me. She wore pink baby-doll pajamas, her blond hair was pulled back into little pigtails, and I thought of all the times my mother had asked me why I couldn't be more like Amber.

Amber hugged me tightly. She was the first and only friend I'd ever known to give hugs so easily. I'd always been a little uncomfortable with physical contact since it was unfamiliar to me, but Amber's embrace felt sincere and loving. For a minute I wouldn't let go. I let myself imagine staying there, living there, being Amber's sister – never going back to George and Roberta again.

After a comforting minute I let her go and she whispered, "I called my cousin, Raina. Remember the one I told you about in New York City?"

"Yes." We sat on Amber's unmade bed. "What did she say?"

"She is totally cool with helping you out for awhile." She handed me a small piece of paper. "Here's her phone number and address in New York." I clutched it in my hand and tipped over onto the bed, burying my face in the sheets.

Amber took out her Walkman, put the headphones on my head and turned on *Come as You Are,* my new favorite Nirvana song. She touched the top of my head and smiled at me.

"Let's try to get some sleep, OK?" She whispered as she pulled a cotton blanket over me and tucked me in like a baby.

I sobbed quietly into one of her pillows for most of the night. In the morning I tiptoed into the bathroom. In the mirror my red eyelids and the blue half-moons under my eyes made me wonder how many tears a person could cry and whether they could ever run out.

When I came back to Amber's room she was awake and pulling on a pair of jeans and a t-shirt.

"Here's all the money I saved for a new guitar." She shoved $287 in my fist and I tried to shove it back at her.

"No" she said, "this is what friends do. You can pay me back someday."

"I will, I promise." We hugged quickly.

"I'm going to tell my mom we're going to the mall and I'll drive you to the train station.

"Amber, I . . .don't know what to say."

"Come on, or we'll be late for the train," she grabbed her purse and pulled my arm towards the door. I had no choice but to follow her. I'd confided in her the night before. I needed to leave.

I was pregnant.

~~~~~

As the train pulled me through foreign landscapes and towns, I felt afraid and hopeful at the same time, and sometimes I just felt numb. Outside the window the world blurred like a watercolor painting. I dozed and then startled out of sleep repeatedly, wondering why I was moving, where I was going. I thought I was going to puke, and fought to hold it back. Once, when I opened my eyes, I saw a double rainbow in the sky. I had never seen one before and it gave me a sense of peace. Having no one else to talk to, I thought of childhood prayers and tried a few. For a brief moment I felt heard and not so alone.

I thought about Raina, this stranger that I was about to meet. I decided my fear would be silent. I would not let my heart leak out through my skin, even though my skin felt translucent, like my thin blue veins were about to burst out from beneath it. I was responsible for my situation, and I would be brave and mature about it - even if I didn't know how to be brave or mature. I tried to be the daughter George and Roberta wanted. I went to their church, did their chores, earned good grades at school, only to feel guilty knowing the girl I really was could never make them proud. I felt guilty about all the boys I had been with trying to be accepted. I felt guilty dressing like a punk just to defy and embarrass them. I was ashamed of my smoking habit and sad about how stifled I felt in the presence of my own family. Now I was playing poker for high stakes. I was risking everything to be right, to be me. The daily crucifixion of my self-image had to end. I was only seventeen, but somehow I knew that much.

A girl about my age sat across the aisle from me. Her eyes were closed and she listened to her Walkman for half of the trip as I stared out the window. When she took the earphones out she smiled at me. Her eyes scanned my outfit, but her face did not appear judgmental. My crazy hand-knit scarf fell loosely over my shoulders even though the summer sun heated the interior of the train. I didn't care. It gave me an identity and reminded me of why I'd left.

"Where are you going?" she asked.

"I'm going to New York City – well I guess that's where we're all going, aren't we?" I didn't know if she really wanted to have a conversation or if she was just being polite. I would have chatted with Hitler at this point.

Yeah, the big city. I visit my dad there every summer. My parents are divorced."

"Oh, I'm sorry. That must be hard."

"Not so much," she said smiling. "I get out of boring, rural Ohio for the summer and my dad is pretty cool. Why are you going to New York?"

"Um, well, I had to leave home."

"You're running away! Cool! Why?" She leaned forward as if fascinated by the exotic tale I was about to relay to her. "I'm Megan," and she put out her hand to shake.

"I'm Chri . . . Lavender. Well, that's my new name, 'cause of my hair color. And I left home because I needed to get away from my parents, you know?"

"Why? Did they beat you? Are they alcoholics?" Megan stared at me waiting for a story.

"Well, no, nothing like that. They just, well, my mom especially, doesn't even like me, let alone love me. She's rejected me all my life and I'm just sick of it. I figure why torture her with my presence anymore, you know?"

"Oh, that's sad." Megan sat back in her seat looking disappointed. "You don't think you could ever work things out? Maybe go to a counselor or something?"

"My mom and dad think they know what's best for everyone. They'd never bow down to taking advice from anyone else – especially not for me." Suddenly I felt my reasons weren't very compelling. Had I jumped without envisioning my landing? I doubted all the years of imaging this day – the day I would finally leave – the justification for all my pain. No one had ever starved me or hit me or gone into an alcoholic rage at me. What was I doing going to a strange city to stay with strangers?

"Listen, Megan," I leaned forward and lowered my voice. "I know it doesn't sound that bad, but I just couldn't become my own person in their house. I didn't belong there. I'm not really sure why, either."

"But they're your parents, aren't they?"

"Yes, but they don't love me," I looked away to try to dissipate yet more tears.

"Well, I understand. It's hard enough trying to grow up and know who we are and who we want to become someday. I think both of my parents have really been supportive of me, even though they're divorced."

"You're lucky I guess," I said looking out the window at a blur of Ohio greenery.

"How are you going to support yourself in New York? Do you have a job and a place to live? Aren't you going to college?"

Now Megan's mature and realistic comments started to annoy me. I didn't need to be reminded of what a weak plan and a hopeless future lay ahead of me. Her questions must have been rhetorical because she didn't wait for answers - answers I didn't have anyway.

"What was the last straw, Lavender?"

"The last straw? You mean what made me finally leave after years of thinking about it? It was . . . my mom wouldn't look at me anymore. I mean, I realized the other day that no matter what was going on she never looked at me. I'm invisible to her. Not even worth glancing at. I know she despises my wardrobe and my tattoos, and my hairstyles – but even when she speaks to me she just can't face me or acknowledge my presence."

"Wow, that does seem cruel, but is that it? I mean, that's why you're leaving a relatively safe home and family?" Megan searched my face for an answer. She was looking right at me.

"Yeah," I said aloud, but inside my head I said – that, and I'm pregnant. Pregnant with a baby they will take away from me.

A few moments passed and Megan made no more practical, adult-like comments. I thought to myself, I won't have much in New York, but at least I will have someone to love me – this baby has to love me.

One by one the tiny tokens of security, the known assurances and shelters of my world were disappearing like snow under a warming sun. As the train neared New York City I pulled out my make-up bag and tried to reapply my mascara and heavy black eyeliner while panicky tears streamed down my cheeks. I hugged my worldly possessions close. Dressed in my black boots, fishnets, mini-skirt with a studded belt, my worn-out tank top showed off the barbed wire around my upper arm. I dared Raina or anyone else to mock me. I turned up the volume on my Walkman, slung my duffel over my shoulder, grabbed my guitar and stepped off the train into the biggest and scariest place I had ever seen.

From Penn Station in midtown Manhattan I stood wide-eyed and watched people moving in all directions. Hot air swirled around me like someone had just opened an oven. An eruption of pigeons startled me, and masses of people dodged my body as I stood in the middle of a sidewalk. A world of movement and sound surrounded me, but I felt small and alone.

I'd never taken a taxi before so I observed for a while and then took a shot at it. I snuffed out my cigarette, hailed my first taxi and took a short ride to the 9th Avenue address I had been given. I knocked on the door and tried to smile casually even though my upper and lower teeth felt welded together and my arms were trembling mercilessly under the weight of all my stuff.

Raina, a tall pretty blonde in jeans and a white t-shirt, answered the door and welcomed me in. She didn't look much older than me, but when she spoke she sounded like an adult.

"Welcome to New York! Was the trip okay? What do you think of the Big Apple so far?" asked Raina. Two other pretty girls appeared. "Christine, this is Jenny and Kristin."

We all said "Nice to meet you" simultaneously and then laughed.

"Well, so far, it's big, I guess," I said stupidly.

"You know what, you're going to know this place within a week and you'll love it," said Jenny, "I gotta go to work. See you later. Maybe we should take Christine out on the town tonight, girls."

"Um, I know this is kind of weird, but I'm going by the name Lavender now."

"That's cool. Is that going to be your stage name or something?" Jenny asked as she walked out the door without waiting for an answer. Kristin said, "Glad you made it okay," and retreated to her room. Raina was very sweet and attentive and showed me around the little apartment. "I'm sorry all we can offer you is a couch to sleep on."

"I don't mind. I really appreciate your help. I'm not sure why you're being so nice to me."

"Amber told me you needed a place to stay. She didn't tell me why, but that's okay. You can tell me sometime if you want to. Jenny and Kristin and I found each other by accident a few months ago. We're all trying to get our big breaks as actresses, so we support each other. New York is kind of scary if you don't have that, you know? You'll find there's a sort of camaraderie between people trying to make it here, so we're happy to help out for a little while. Are you hoping to get into show business?"

"Me? Oh, no. I'm not sure what I'm doing just yet."

"It takes time to figure out what you want to do with your life." Raina's smile uncovered shocking blue-white teeth. She flipped her blond hair over her shoulder.

"Oh, and no smoking in the apartment, okay?"

"Sorry." I turned around looking for a way to snuff out the cigarette I just lit. "Um, where's the bathroom?"

Over the next two weeks the girls flew in and out of the apartment for work and auditions and barely seemed to notice me. I did the dishes and straightened up the apartment as much as I could to show my appreciation. Every morning I folded up the sheets and blanket from the couch and piled them in the corner with my things. A couple of times they offered me wine or beer in the evening, so I knew Amber had not told them about my condition. There were nights that I took the drinks.

~~~~~~

From the little dreary apartment building on 9th Avenue I could walk wherever I wanted to go in the city. I tried the subway and walked under towering scaffolding where men shouted out "Hey, beautiful!" I walked the avenues, letting myself move with the flow of the crowds, crossing streets with so many strangers, multiple languages in my ears. I sat in green, humid Central Park for hours and watched joggers and nannies with strollers, and dog walkers being dragged by four or five dogs at a time. I took my guitar to the park one day and boldly played and sang. People glanced at me, ignored me, or tossed a dollar into my guitar case.

A little child approached me and reached for my guitar. The mother, pushing a stroller, hurried behind saying, "No, don't touch that!"

"It's okay, little guy. You strum it like this." I took his chubby fingers and moved them across the strings, and he beamed up at me.

I watched the woman gently take a tiny baby enveloped in pink out of the stroller. "Can I ask you something?"

"Sure," she answered as she lifted the baby to her shoulder and patted it on the back.

"What's it like? To have a baby?"

"You mean actually *having* the baby? Or being a mom?"

"Well, having it first, I guess."

"It hurts like hell! You want to kill your husband for ever touching you. But then, you have this beautiful little thing and you kind of forget about your body being ripped apart."

"Your body gets ripped apart?"

"Yeah, usually they cut you and then stitch you back up though."

"They cut you?" I thought I was going to throw up right there. "Oh, my God."

"It takes a few days to heal, but by then you're so busy breastfeeding and changing diapers every hour and a half you don't have time to comb your hair, let alone worry about some stitches. It's not like you care whether you ever have sex again." The woman swayed back and forth as if dancing with the baby. "I always do this. Even when I'm not holding her I'm rocking back and forth. Do you want to hold her?"

"Can I?" I took a newborn baby into my arms for the first time. She looked up at me and I felt her soft body settle into mine. "Wow, I used to baby-sit, but I never sat for an infant. I don't even know anyone who's had a baby." The little girl sucked on her fist while her brother pulled his stubby fingers across my guitar strings. "Thanks for letting me hold her," I said handing her back as carefully as I could.

"Thanks for letting him play your guitar. We'd better get going. Good luck with your music."

I packed up my guitar and walked until I found a bookstore. I walked right past the music magazines and directly to the baby and parenting section. I didn't have a clue what was coming. I started reading and left three hours later when the store was closing.

Walking the streets of Manhattan felt like being in a tornado, but it was an organized sort of chaos. The w-a-a-a of sirens and car horns and the wind shoving itself between buildings created a constant roar. I inhaled garlic, curry and grease. At first the whoosh of hot air through the sidewalk grates coming from the subway felt like an unexpected violation, but I soon got used to it. The walkways under scaffolding displayed dozens of posters and signs to read, and as day fell into night, the neon glow attacked my eyeballs in its intensity. I would find myself standing for indefinite amounts of time on a corner just to watch the energy. Plastic bags defied gravity and rose straight up into the clouds. I studied the faces of the women in suits and running shoes, or men doing business as they walked while dodging and weaving and never touching. I would imagine where they were all going and wish I had a place to go, too. I'd never experienced anything so alien or massive, and even though I was as directionless as those plastic bags, I loved New York City.

~~~~~~

I kept seeing a girl in Raina's building wearing the same ripped fishnets, plaid kilt held together with a huge safety pin, and army boots every day. She screamed obscenities at her mother as she was leaving the apartment. One day I walked out the door with my guitar, intending to hang in the park. She walked out the same time as I did. I had nowhere to go so I followed her. After about two blocks she turned around and said, "Why are you following me, you little freak?" I stared mutely for a minute then I said, "I just wanted to meet you. I'm new around here."

"Whatever," she replied. She kept walking, but she was still talking to me. "I'm Joey."

"Joey?"

"Yeah, Joanne – Joey, okay? Come on."

"Okay. Where are we going?" I sped up to walk next to her, trying not to act excited or uncool.

"Got a light?" she asked.

"Oh, sure." So we smoked and walked on streets I had never ventured down.

"What's with the guitar? You in a band or something?" Joey asked, looking me over from hair to boots.

"Uh, no, not yet. I'd really like to be," I said as the wind whipped my hair into my mouth and stuck to my tongue and eyelashes.

Then for the first time in my life, I saw a homeless person. He was sitting on the sidewalk covered in strips of newspaper and black garbage bags. I couldn't tell if the trash was his clothing or he had possessions in them. His skin was gray and his teeth missing. His arm stretched out toward us and he started to get up, but Joey said, "Get away from us. Get a job." I looked back as we walked away and wished I had some money to give him, but by then I was almost as broke as he was. We walked until we got to a scary-looking alleyway. We stepped through an obstacle course of tipped-over trashcans and rats running for cover. I followed Joey into a dark, musty hallway. I could hear music and singing, but I didn't recognize the group. It was an all-girl band rehearsing. My fantasy come true. I wanted to jump up and down, clapping my hands like an idiot, but I stayed calm.

When the music stopped Joey said, "Can you sing?"

"Um, yeah, I can. . ." I pulled out a cigarette and my hand shook as I tried to light it.

"Do you know the song 'Rebel Girl?'

"Sure."

"Cool. This is my band, Joeygirls. Wendy, Tess and Shannon, and you are?

"Lavender."

"Cool name."

"Thanks."

"Well, get your ass up on the stage and let's hear what you can do," Joey said.

I stepped onto the stage, and my legs seemed to disappear from beneath me in a sort of floating sensation. I quickly checked out the band. Wendy was at the drums. Her hair was shaved off one side of her head, and the other side was black and hanging part-way in her face about to her shoulder. Her ears were pierced about six times, and she also had a stud through her eyebrow. Dressed completely in black, she silently nodded at me. Shannon had long platinum blond hair with black streaks. She was tiny and pretty. Tess was a huge mannish-looking girl squeezed into ripped-up jeans, black Converse shoes and a red sweater. Her brown hair looked like it hadn't been washed in weeks, but later I found out about dreadlocks.

Joey removed her black leather to reveal a sleeve of tattoos on her left arm. Later, when I asked to see it, she told me it was all dedicated to her brother Todd who had died in a motorcycle accident with his fiancé. There was a portrait of Todd on his motorcycle, his name in a heart, and a skull and crossbones with the date of his death under that, in the midst of many other images.

Joey asked if I had any. I showed her my "freedom band." Having a fake ID, I also recently had my belly button pierced, and another tattoo of a pink lotus on the back of my shoulder. I had successfully hidden that one from George and Roberta. She looked me over and seemed to approve.

"What's the flower about?"

"The lotus is a flower that grows out of muddy water, but it rises to the surface and blooms. It's also a Buddhist symbol of . . ."

"Yeah, I get it. The tatts are addictive, aren't they?"

"I know. It's such a rush to do something so permanent, so *not* what your parents would approve of."

"Revenge is sweet," Joey said, pulling up the pant leg of her jeans. "These are my commitment to *me*, not to *them.*"

"Wow," I looked at the canvas of her leg that displayed a dragon, a scorpion and a sacred heart, among others. "You mean your parents?"

"My mom, yeah, but also my fucking stepfather, the abusive son-of-a-bitch."

~~~~~~

When I was a kid I had red curly hair, some freckles, not too many. I was always the shorty in the front row for class pictures, had a squeaky, high-pitched voice and couldn't find anything I was good at. I kept hearing in Sunday school about all of God's gifts and how much He loved us. I wanted to believe it, but I didn't really feel it. I couldn't find my gifts. I might have found my ability to sing much sooner if rock music had been allowed in our house or anyone had encouraged me.

I got a lot of attention for my red hair, which fell in long ringlets down my back. Adults in the grocery store or the mall would stop and comment on how pretty it was and I liked the attention.

"Oh, what a lovely French braid, Christine. You're so lucky to have such pretty hair," my Sunday school teacher said. I beamed at the compliment. My hair made me feel special, different.

"You wouldn't think it was so pretty if you had to comb out those curls after every bath," Mother said.

As we walked away, Mother said, "That's it. It's coming off."

At home I quietly wept as my mother yanked me onto a high stool, threw a towel over my shoulders, took her sewing scissors and chopped the red off at the chin.

"Stop your crying, Christine. You're not a baby, are you? Now get the broom and sweep up all this hair."

My hair stayed in an ugly, plain bob until I was fifteen. I couldn't stand looking in the mirror anymore, so I spiked it on top and dyed it black and purple. I was grounded for two months, but it was worth it. In New York City my hair and my outfits were my calling cards. They said – these are the people I belong to. When you see my hair you will know who I am, what I like, where I want to hang out. If you come to know something about someone who decorates his or her body, you will know that same thing about the next person you meet with the same decorations. They are from the same tribe. It worked for me. Joey and the girls knew I was one of them.

Turns out I actually could sing.

And so I did. I sang and screamed and became an angry, head-banging F-you kind of girl, like Joey. Mom and Dad would have been so proud. Pretty soon I was spending all of my time with the band. We had a few gigs in little run-down dumps, and we'd each leave with $25, enough for a couple packs of smokes and some food after the show. I'd come home at all hours of the morning.

One night I ran eight blocks through the rain from the subway. Raina was still up waiting for me. My black wool cardigan stunk, and my feet were soaked since my boots weren't exactly airtight. I snuffed out my cigarette in the hallway and tried to sneak into the apartment as quietly as possible.

"Lavender," Raina said.

"Oh God, you scared the shit out of me! What's up?" I pulled my hair off the back of my neck and squeezed the water out on the floor.

"What's up is that you're probably going to have to find some place else to stay. I mean, you come in late and wake us up and your music is on all the time. We've got jobs, you know? Money is kind of tight and you're not really helping out with that."

"You sound just like my parents," I said and dropped my backpack and guitar on the floor. "I'm in a band, you know. We just need a little time to get going."

"Lavender, you seem like a bright girl. I think you can do better."

"I thought you were cooler than that, Raina, but you know what? That's fine. I'll get my stuff and get the hell out of here."

I started crying, and Raina tried to approach me, but I pushed past her and threw my few belongings into my duffle bag.

"You don't have to leave *now*. I meant sometime in the next few weeks. It's late, where are you going to go? At least stay until morning. Oh, God, I didn't mean to make you feel. . ." Raina put her hands on her pretty perfect cheeks. "Please stay."

Now we were both crying, but I ignored her and went into the bathroom and closed the door. I knelt on the floor and tried to muffle my sobs into a towel. Then I got up and washed my disgusting mascara-streaked face. I shoved the towel, some soap, shampoo, and everything else

I could find in Raina's bathroom into my duffle. I grabbed a handful of tampons, but then realized I wouldn't be needing them for a long time so I threw them on the floor, zipped up my bag, opened the bathroom door, said "Thanks for everything, Raina," and walked out. I heard her call me, and I should've gone back, but I was pissed and hurt.

In my mind I had been rejected for the last time. I didn't need these people. New York was a big place. I would just start finding what I needed elsewhere. But the fear of rejection never leaves. You live your life knowing every day that someone else can make you feel that way. You collect an arsenal of defenses to protect your heart and soul.

I headed over to Joey's and when she saw me at the door, she opened it wider to let me in saying, "Welcome to hell."

A few stoned people were draped over the furniture and barely noticed my presence. Joey introduced me to her mother and she offered me a joint, which I gladly took. During the night as I curled up in a plastic lounge chair I tried to compare this hell to the hell I'd left in Ohio, but none of it made sense anymore.

I wondered if George and Roberta worried about me. I'd been gone for over a month. I really missed John and I wrote to him regularly, sending the letters in care of his best friend Tim, but I never put a return address on the letters, not that I really had an address. I didn't want my little brother to forget me.

Hi Johnny,

How's it going? I really miss you, but New York is awesome. You would love it here, too. Guess what? I'm a singer in an all-girl band! The band is called the Joeygirls. Joey (Joanne) is the founder and lead guitarist. Wendy plays drums and Tess is the bass player. Shannon plays some percussion instruments and sings back up. Joey writes some of the tunes, but we also cover the Pretenders, Blondie, L7, and Nirvana. Of course, Mom and Dad won't let you listen to that music. I'm going to live with my new friends and I'm sorry I can't give you the address in case Mom and Dad find this. I changed my name to Lavender too, but you can still call me Chrissie if you want. I'm really sorry I had to leave you there, but I think you are more of the child George and Roberta really want and I think you'll be fine. I called Tim and he said you were okay. I really miss Grandma, but don't tell her you've heard from me because I'm not sure she could keep that secret from Dad. Please stay cool, little brother. I know we'll see each other again someday.

Love, Chrissie

The girls in the band seemed to like me. Associating with them led to meeting lots of guys, but not the sheltered little boys I knew in high school. The abyss in my heart got filled with lots of sex until I started showing. I slept on Joey's floor for a few weeks, eating her food and avoiding the cocaine floating around her apartment. Her mom joined in on the partying every night. Even if I weren't pregnant I still wouldn't be ready for coke. Maybe in my heart I still hoped to be a little bit of the daughter my parents had wanted.

Those summer months were consumed by singing for the band, sleeping with a few guys and one girl, learning that 69 isn't just a number, and smoking pot even though I knew that was a stupid thing to do. It was hard to hide my pregnancy and try to fit in with the lifestyle that surrounded me. I wanted to be accepted and appear cool and worldly. I tried to convince myself daily that I was having fun and living life to the fullest, something George and Roberta couldn't show me. But in my sober moments I felt hungry and lonely. When the smoke literally cleared, I hated myself, and my new life. I'd find another way to escape for the day, maybe a head-banging song, maybe a joint, maybe a guy, but all I got was the disintegration of my soul and spirit.

As my belly grew so did my terror. How was I going to take care of a baby? How would I even keep it safe in this environment? But sometimes when I ran my hand across my middle and felt a butterfly movement inside me none of that mattered. This baby would be mine and no one could take it away from me. It grew under my heart and the life in it kept me awake at night with its kicking – with its very existence. How could you love something you'd never seen or met? At that point I wasn't sure of anything except that I loved my baby.

Joeygirls was nothing but an opening act, a novelty display of misfit girls screaming and banging out their angst. The stoned audiences thought we were great, and the raucous cheers and wild movement of the dancing crowd sometimes made me want to be out there instead of on stage entertaining.

After we cleared the stage, caught a cigarette and peed, Joey said, "Come on, let's get out there where the fun is!"

"I don't know – it seems a little dangerous out there. What about . . .?" I pointed to my belly.

"Dancing is good exercise. Aren't you supposed to exercise when you're preggy?" Joey shouted over the din. She took my arm and pulled me into the middle of the mosh pit.

The insufficient oxygen and smoke in the overcrowded room burned my eyes and nose. The mosh pit experience that night seemed ugly and wrong. The body parts touching mine without permission felt like a violation. I wasn't used to much physical touch since George and Roberta never hugged me. Several times I pushed people away saying, *Get off of me*! The closeness and unexpected force of the crowd became demeaning and profane, the intensity of the music and movement suddenly injurious to my body and spirit. Something came flying through the air and I looked up in time to see the neck of a guitar hit me in the head. I tried to push my arms out in front of me to make a path, but no one moved or even noticed me.

Joey looked over at me. "What's wrong with you? Are you gonna hurl or something?"

"No," I screamed, "I just have to get out of here, Joey!"

In a panic I began to cry and shove the bodies with my shoulder. When I finally made it out of the club I collapsed on the sidewalk and heard my hoarse voice whimpering, *"I want to go home."* I rubbed my shins and ankles, bruised from being kicked and stepped on by oblivious moshers. I reached up and felt a small bump forming on my forehead. Joey was nowhere in sight.

That night all the girls and I came home to our pathetic little cots or sleeping bags on the floor. I placed my hand on my belly and thought about the reality of a little girl or little boy inside me, and I never felt so alone in all my life. It was like I was completely untethered from the rest of the world. Maybe, I thought, I should rename myself Tumbleweed – no roots, just blowing around aimlessly.

Joey, Shannon, Wendy and Tess really helped me through the pregnancy. We decided if we all worked together and threw the meager paychecks from our day jobs in a pot we could afford a one-bedroom apartment in the lower east side – near all the dive punk bars. It was a crappy, rundown building, and not very safe, but we looked out for each other. The tap water in the rust-stained sink was brackish and cold. In the winter we wore wool caps to keep warm all night. My knit scarf became my constant companion. The two twin beds in the bedroom consisted of broken springs and a yeasty smelling mattress so no one fought over the chance to use them. A moldy couch or some old sleeping bag worked out fine for me, but I'd often dream about my warm, soft bed on Iroquois Lane, with the sound of the Lake Erie waves just outside my bedroom window.

All five of us basically had the same pathetic story – families, teachers, and communities who didn't get us – so we struck out into the world alone and landed in NYC. But I wasn't alone anymore. I had the girls and someone snoozing inside of me. My friends seemed to understand that an accidental pregnancy could happen to any of them, and not one of them suggested I get rid of the baby. I loved them for that. It never occurred to me either, even though I was broke and only had the rights to one-fifth of a tiny apartment. I knew the little person inside of me had the potential to love me unconditionally, and that's all I really ever wanted.

I looked pretty hilarious fronting a punk rock all-girl band with a huge belly. I couldn't leap off the decrepit stages into the mosh pits, but other than that I still rocked. Shannon made sure I went to the Free Clinic every month for a check up. She wanted to be a doctor, maybe even an OB-GYN. She'd finished two years of college when her dad died unexpectedly. Her mom drowned herself in alcohol and lost her job. Shannon tried to hold it all together, but when her mom married another alcoholic on the rebound, Shannon split for the city. Shannon had learned a few basics in an EMT class, so she could check my blood pressure, and listen to our heartbeats with a medical kit she still had. The clinic provided me with prenatal vitamins, and I quit pot but couldn't seem to give up the smokes. They were like a lifeline to momentary serenity. Maybe, I told the girls, with a little help from my friends, being a mother would be something I could be good at. Of course, I had no idea what I was talking about.

After I knew my baby was coming, and having a place to belong, I wasn't as consumed with the need for self-expression. I couldn't afford all the haircuts and dye either, so I started letting my hair grow, and it grew quickly when I was pregnant. Soon my God-given curly red hair was back, although I still liked to intersperse the red with some odd colors when I could. It looked pretty freaky on stage, too. At my last concert before the baby was born, I wore an old hippie empire-waist flowery mini-dress, red knee-high boots that laced up the front, with my red and black streaked hair falling out from under a purple felt hat. The last song of the night was a cover of a Velvet Underground song called "I Found a Reason." I put my hands under my big belly, felt the unknown stranger residing there kicking away to the music and sang, *"I found a reason to keep living, oh and the reason dear, is you. I found a reason to keep singing and the reason, dear, is you."*

1995

Cole

The first time I saw Lavender she stood outside the hair salon where I worked. She caught my attention because she was hiding in a sea of hair color and all kinds of punk bravado. Her faded used-looking stroller held an adorable baby with yellow ringlets. Lavender was short and tiny, her hair a jungle of multicolored ribbons, pierced nose and eyebrow, wearing a long black skirt, saddle shoes, a black mohair sweater and a red beret, looking like she was trying very hard not to be something else. I'd stepped outside during a break.

"And who is this little doll baby?" I bent down and the little one smiled at me.

"Ah-na-eese," she said carefully, pointing to her tummy.

"Anais, what a fabulous name. The only other Anais I ever heard of was the French writer Anais Nin."

"Yeah, she's sort of named after her. I hope I haven't damaged her for life, you know?"

I looked up at Lavender, "Hi, I'm Cole. Are you coming in for a haircut?"

"Oh, no, I can't afford a hair cut, or even a good wash. I wish I could though. I need to get back to me."

The little girl, Anais, was adorable. I couldn't keep my eyes off of her. She appeared happy and healthy, but the little footie pajamas she had on were stained and worn.

"I'll tell you what, how about a wash, cut and style on me? I don't have any customers right now. It looks like a slow day. I'd love to play with all that hair of yours."

"Really? You don't have to do that. Why would you do that?"

"Come on in. It'll be fun. There are even some toys for her to play with."

I sang along with the Four Tops playing in the background *sugar pie, honey bunch, you know that I love you.* The baby babbled the whole time I was layering Lavender's hair.

"So what will you do, now that you're all dolled up tonight?" I asked while I was snipping red locks to the floor.

"I'm a singer in an all-girl band. The Joeygirls. Want to come to our show tonight at the Hook-Up Bar and Grill?" We looked at each other in the mirror across from us.

"Well, I don't have any plans. I have an idea that the Hook-Up Bar and Grill is not really my kind of place, but I can't resist coming to hear you sing, so I'd love to."

~~~~~~

I hailed a taxi in front of my dorm. When I gave the driver the address of the Hook-Up Bar and Grill he stared at me in the rearview mirror for a moment.

He stopped at a run-down building with a crowd of ornamented people of all types lingering by the front door. I noted safety pins through the ears, nose piercings, and what appeared to be whole-body tattoos, even on some faces. There were shaved heads and spiked hair of all colors. Many wore clothing with symbols unfamiliar to me or with musicians on them such as Sonic Youth, riot grrrl, Bikini Kill, and Nirvana.

A number of other similar bars were located in the area and even though it was only about a dozen blocks from NYU, it seemed like a foreign planet to me. I was aware of this subculture, but it did not exist in my hometown or in my high school. I was fascinated by these young people, so obviously creating identities, and I began to ponder Lavender's place in this lifestyle.

Inside, unpainted wooden walls were plastered with posters and graffiti. Above the stage a banner said: *Protest against the rising tide of conformity* – Bob Dylan.

I stood in the farthest corner and watched two all-male bands play before Joeygirls came out. When the girls flounced onto the stage there were screams and cat-calls as they waved and gestured to the crowd. I didn't see Lavender, but when the music started she leapt out from behind a curtain, ran to the front of the stage, knocked the microphone over and pulled it back up by the cord and started singing. A little girl with a big voice belting her heart out. I had not the faintest idea what she was singing about, but she and the girls rocked.

Lavender wore a long purple prom dress she'd found in a Goodwill store for two dollars and it clashed beautifully with her red hair. Black patent Mary Janes and argyle socks peeked out from beneath the lacy hem of the dress. She appeared gloriously comfortable on the stage and glowed with the acceptance of the crowd.

I caught Lavender's eye between songs and shouted out, "Where's the baby?" She pointed offstage and the drumbeat for the next song began. After the show I hopped up on the stage and asked again about Anais.

"Oh, she's right there!" Lavender skipped over and pulled Anais from the stroller she was strapped into offstage. Little Ani was rubbing her eyes and fussing. At least someone had put earmuffs over her little ears.

"You mean she watches and hears all this? Every night?"

"Well, not every night. We don't play every night," Lavender said, unstrapping the baby and pulling her out of her stroller.

"That's just unacceptable!" I yelled over the din of the crowd. "From now on I'll watch her!"

"I can't ask you to do that Cole. Besides we just met each other. How do I know you're not some crazy-ass person?"

"You didn't ask me. I volunteered. Ani can get some sleep while I do homework." I took Anais from her mother and she nestled into my shoulder immediately. A feeling I increasingly longed for.

"I don't know. We'll see. You're really too nice. You probably don't want to get mixed up with a needy girl like me," she said, reaching over to pat her daughter on the back.

It was a cold winter night, but the heat of the city always seemed to melt the snow before it hit the ground in New York. The random leaves inexplicably clinging to their branches looked like frozen silver dollars. Lavender took the sleeping child from me and wrapped a ratty gray blanket around Anais in preparation to walk home in the sleet and mist.

"Is that all you have to keep her warm, Lavender? It's really cold out there tonight."

"I know it is, but we'll be fine." She looked up at me, her green eyes and freckles shadowed in the wisps of red hair hanging in her face. She looked like a china doll, a waif, a lost little girl.

"You know, I'm really hungry. That was quite a long show with the two bands before you. Would you allow me to treat you and Anais to a little snack?" I asked, already sensing Lavender's pride in her independence. I didn't know what she was trying to prove by raising her little girl alone, but I hoped to find out.

"Well, I don't know . . . I am kind of hungry too and usually there's not much in the apartment to eat." She looked down at her little girl and not at me.

She started maneuvering the stroller through the clutter backstage of the Hook-Up Bar and Grill. "Well, are you coming?"

She shoved the door open with the stroller and Anais gave a little yelp. We walked several blocks in an awkward silence.

"Here's a diner that's still open. Is this all right?" I held the door open without waiting for an answer.

I ordered super-sized hamburgers and fries for all three of us, somehow intuitively knowing that Lavender wouldn't ask for much.

Lavender fed herself and Anais simultaneously and kept looking up at me somewhat suspiciously.

"I still don't get why you're being so nice to us."

"I like you and I like kids." I paused, knowing any common stalker could say the same thing. "To be honest, ever since I came to live in the city to attend NYU I've been lonely. I'm the type of person who needs to give, to please others to feel worthwhile."

"Yeah, but what's in it for you?" Lavender asked while wiping ketchup off of Anais's chin.

"As I said, it makes me feel worthwhile. I want to be a part of something. And, I know this sounds kind of crazy, but I think you and I have a lot in common."

"You think? How so? I mean, I haven't run into many people in my lifetime that I've had anything in common with. I'm a misfit. A social outcast. A bit of a freak – at least where I came from."

"Exactly." I said, ruffling the blond curls on Ani's head. Lavender looked up at me and we smiled at each other. I left money for the bill on the table and Lavender began to bundle her baby up for the night air.

"Can I continue to walk you home? Or maybe take the subway?" I asked, feeling helpless.

"Um . . . well, I don't have any money for the subway, and you've already been too generous, but we can walk from here. I usually cut through the park," she said.

"You cut through Tompkins Square Park at night?" I stopped, realizing that I had criticized another choice this young mother was making.

"Well, I love walking through a park on a crisp winter evening. It will be fun."

"Oh, yeah, it's loads of fun."

By the time we got to the park Anais was fussing and saying, "Up, up."

"May I?" I asked.

Lavender stopped and I took Anais out of the stroller. We continued walking as I sang *Heaven must have sent you from above. Heaven must have sent your precious love,* trying to keep her as warm as I could in my arms.

We walked in silence for a while and then Lavender said, "Why don't you sing *Love Child* to her?"

"You know Motown music?"

"No, not really. There wasn't much music around when I was growing up. But I do remember hearing *Love Child* on the radio someplace."

"Oh yeah, The Supremes. It's a classic." Then I stopped, realizing her reference to that particular song. "There are many more songs I'm going to have to sing to this little one. . ."

Lavender ignored that. "I usually cut through on this path. It's cool because people have made it with their feet. When you go to some parks they seem so organized and planned out. But a path like this one is here just because New Yorkers decided it should be. I wonder if there's a name for this kind of thing?"

"My guess would be that it's just called a footpath. Hey, why don't the Joeygirls walk home together? Didn't you tell me you live together?"

"They like to party all night, if you know what I mean. I used to be able to do that too, but I have to get Ani in bed."

"Oh, sure, of course," I said, still worrying about their safety in this dangerous city. "I wish I had a place of my own that you could bring Ani to. My dorm room at NYU is relatively nice, but my roommate is not. He too enjoys partying until all hours on the weekends. It's hard to get any studying done there."

"It's Saturday night, Cole! Do you study all weekend?" Lavender said as she steered the stroller up a muddy incline back onto the paved city sidewalk. Our breathing suddenly illuminated in the misty light of the city, I opened my coat and pulled Anais closer into the warmth of my body.

"Don't you ever go out and have any fun?" She took the baby from my arms to place her back in the stroller. "We're almost home, Ani," she whispered to the dozing child. It was 2 o'clock in the morning. A frigid night in a vast city. What was I doing with this waif of a girl and her baby? I wasn't sure, but I did know my arms suddenly felt hollow – just like the inside of me.

Lavender turned to me when we reached the door to her building.

"Thanks, Cole. I'm glad you walked us home. It felt good, you know? Like we weren't alone tonight." She stood on her tiptoes and kissed me on the cheek.

"How will you get home from here? It's not exactly on your way."

"It will be pretty easy to grab a taxi this time of night and I'll be back at NYU before you know it."

"A taxi? Must be nice," she said, folding up the stroller.

"My parents provide everything I need for school and to get around the city. My job at the salon is my spending money, basically. It is nice. I know I'm lucky that way," I paused, "If there's anything you need . . ."

"Nope, we're good. Thanks again, Cole. I gotta get her inside." Lavender smiled for the second time that evening.

~~~~~~

Sunday morning I arose early from only a few hours sleep and stepped into the bright new-fallen snow on campus for my usual jog. A siren interrupted the quietude as I stretched my legs. I followed my usual course, ended back at Washington Square, and sat on a cold stone wall to watch the city come to life. The pungent smell of coffee passed me by repeatedly as people began their day, reminding me of mornings at home.

I startled when I saw a young woman with a baby in a stroller, and my reaction puzzled me. My need to be a part of a something overwhelmed me. I knew I had isolated myself and used my schoolwork to distract me from the absent areas of life. Lavender and Anais had awoken something inside me and now it seemed to late to backtrack - too late not to care. It was apparent to me that Lavender's independent spirit and tough demeanor was her defense against the world, just as my solitude is to me. But solitude is like cancer – eating its way into your core, and the hunger in your middle yearns to be fed.

A message from my mother awaited me when I returned from my three-mile jog. She worried about me in the big city just as I had begun to fret over Lavender and Anais. The twice-weekly calls soothed her mind and kept us in touch since I couldn't always get upstate to see my parents.

"Cole, I don't mean to sound unkind, but what's in this for you?" My mother asked in her sweet-as-molasses voice after I told her about the night before.

"We're becoming friends, Mom. We have an awful lot in common. We're both lonely, and you know I'm still trying to get over Gavin. I thought we'd have a future together, maybe even a family . . . somehow."

"A family, Cole? Is that what you're doing? You'll have no legal ties to this baby. Lavender sounds unstable and flighty to me. What if she just takes off and you are heartbroken all over again. You're jumping in with both feet – again."

"I really don't think that's going to happen. We need each other, Mom. Why can't misfits have a life too?"

"You are not a misfit. You are my handsome, intelligent son. There is a place for you in this world, Cole. I believe that."

"Thanks Mom, I guess I need to hear that every week. Maybe someday I'll hear it from my father, too."

Lavender

The first time I met Cole Carson he made me feel so beautiful and he was so patient with Anais I thought I could fall for him; his cocoa creamy skin, short wavy brown hair, amazing green eyes. He is tall and slender with long, beautiful fingers – the fingers I wish I had for playing my guitar. Sometimes he uses words I'm not familiar with, but I pretend to understand. He loves poetry and Motown music, and always comments on the creativity of my outfits. It took a while before it occurred to me that he wasn't going to be falling in love with me. I didn't think about things like that back then, but I craved his attention and affirmation. We fit together like human puzzle pieces.

I could see through his frequent attempts to spend time with us. He'd stop over unexpectedly and offer Tess, Shannon or Joey free haircuts or styling. He'd be out jogging and end up all the way over on the lower east side. He'd say he had nothing to do when I knew he had a tight schedule with school and work. All the girls were crazy about him, including my little girl.

"Are we ready to go to the park?" Cole set the bag of snacks down and scooped Ani into his arms. The pink snowsuit from the Goodwill store made her look like a cloud of cotton candy.

"Do you think she'll be warm enough in this," Cole asked. "It's still January, you know."

"Yes, I know, *mother*, but it's going into the 40's today – and it's sunny."

The oasis of Central Park is a wonder in every season. The snow lay in blue-white patches across the Great Lawn of the park. It had melted from the pathways and the sun felt familiar and delicious.

"This reminds me of the Emerald Necklace," I said.

"The Emerald Necklace? Is that from The Wizard of Oz?" Cole said.

"No," I laughed. "It's the park system, a huge amount of park space that, on a map, looks like a necklace around Cleveland. This park is nice, but it's still in the middle of a gigantic city. The parks at home are quiet and secluded. You can walk for miles on the paths there and not see another person."

"I had no idea that your hometown would have something like that, and that you would be missing it so much. Did you spend much time in the park?"

"Yeah, I loved escaping into the woods where no one could find me – just me and my guitar."

"What else do you miss about home?" Cole asked.

"What's your point?"

"No point, just attempting to make conversation and learn more about you," he said with a grin.

"Well, there's the lake, of course. There are a few public beaches that are nice. Lots of people fish in the lake, and the walleye is supposed to be good. I've never had it though. One of the parks has an enormous heron rookery, which is really cool. A lot of streets and towns have Indian names. Like my street is Iroquois Lane, the next one is Cherokee Trail. Supposedly the Indians, well really the *Native Americans,* hung out in that area because of the lake and the Cuyahoga River. That means crooked river."

"I'd like to see where Miss Lavender grew up sometime," Cole said.

"I seriously doubt *that* will ever happen."

"Anything else you miss about home?"

"What are getting at?" I sat on a bench and suddenly I was crying, then sobbing.

"I'm sorry," Cole sat next to me, pulled Ani onto his lap, and gave her a cookie. "Lav, really. I'm sorry. I pushed you too far."

"No, you're just asking normal questions. But my life wasn't normal. How can I miss a home that wasn't mine to begin with? I miss the place because it's all I ever knew – but home? No, I don't miss home. What's wrong with me?" I wiped my coat sleeve across my dripping face.

"What I miss is what I never knew, what I never had. That's what I miss the most."

"Park, park!" squeeked Ani, her face covered in Oreo crumbs. Cole and I both laughed.

"But look what I've got here. Here in Central Park New York," and I looked up at the two most important people in my new life.

Cole

The wind blew a breeze right through the cracked and unsealed window casings as I sat at the tiny kitchen table in Lavender's shared apartment doing homework. I preferred to study in the quiet there since I had finally talked Lavender into letting me baby-sit for Anais on some nights. The peace and comfort of watching Ani sleep helped me get more writing done.

Lavender opened the door, threw her coat, scarf and hat on the floor and went directly in to check on sleeping Anais, barely acknowledging my presence. I was gathering up my books when I heard murmuring. I peeked in the other room. Lavender knelt by Ani, praying in her punk regalia; mini-skirt, fishnets, platform Mary Janes, ripped Sex Pistols t-shirt. Her hair was dyed blood red with four messy ponytails sprouting out the sides of her head. I almost laughed out loud until I saw the black-ringed eyes leaking mascara. As she gazed down at our little angel in her pink pj's and her matching pink cheeks, I heard her whisper.

"God, wherever, whoever you are, please watch over my little girl. I don't want her to go through all I've been through. Please help her find people who will accept her as you made her. I don't want her to feel like a freak of nature, or unworthy or unloved." There was a long pause and then she wiped her nose on her ratty sleeve. "I don't know why you gave me to parents who didn't even like me, but thank you for giving Anais to me. I'm doing the best I can, God, but I need your help. I really do. This is harder than I thought it would be. I don't want to mess her head up with my mistakes. Amen." She touched Anais's face and smoothed back a lock of hair from her forehead.

"Honey," I whispered, standing in the doorway. "Did something happen tonight?"

"No, well, sort of," she whispered as she closed the door halfway behind her. "It's just that there were these idiots at the show and they kept shouting that we were whores and freaks through our whole first set. It just felt like high school again, you know? When am I going to stop being called names? When will people realize that we aren't all the same? What if Anais is different in some way? What if she decides to be a conservative preppy type? What if she hates rock n' roll?" Lavender's scowl became a big smile.

"What if I can't teach her all the Motown songs before she grows up?" I asked.

We both laughed, but we also remembered the violations etched into our hearts. She easily fell into my outstretched arms in a brief moment of comfort.

"Anais has you, her mom. That's all that matters right now." I led her to sit on the couch. "I suppose every parent's prayer is that his or her child won't ever experience the pain they've had in life. My parents made every effort to accept me as I am. My childhood was a good one, despite the fact that my father is black and my mother is white. Somehow they found a suburban area upstate that prided itself on its multiculturalism."

"Your mom is white?"

"Yes, didn't I ever tell you that? You and Anais have to meet them soon. My parents are both teachers, and that counted in our neighborhood. Once the kids at school got to know me they didn't notice the skin color." I pulled a dingy crocheted afghan over both of us. "Did you ever notice the way the toddlers play together when we take Anais to the playground in Central Park? That's what the world could be. They never stop their playing to evaluate each other. They just get down to the business of having fun and making new friends."

"What about high school? God, it's cold in here! Was it as much of a nightmare for you as it was for me?"

"I never had any academic trouble in school." We both stretched the afghan up to our chins. "I loved school. And those of us who love school often become teachers so we can spend our entire lives in school, you know. My Mom and Dad were always proud of my grades and all of my creative activities. I joined all the choral and drama clubs and was editor of the yearbook in my junior and senior years."

"Wow, look at you! Mr. Big Man on Campus, huh?" You mean you weren't the school dork singing all those old '60's songs all the time?"

"Hey, Motown was a big part of my childhood. My grandparents actually knew one of the Four Tops. He visited our house several times and we'd sing around the piano."

"The Four Tops? Is that really a group? Did they spin around while they were singing?"

"You're kidding me right? The Temptations? Smoky Robinson?" Lavender kept shaking her head like she'd never heard of any of them. Then I saw a smirk under the puzzled look.

"Yeah, you know it's the greatest music ever," I said.

"Um, I beg to differ. The Sex Pistols, Blondie, Nirvana . . ."

"Ugh!" I put my finger in my mouth to indicate gagging.

"Well, it's a good thing that liking the same music isn't necessary for a great friendship," Lavender said. "Tell me more about your childhood. I want to know everything – except about your disgusting taste in music."

"I'll ignore that statement for now. Well, I had so many activities and interests in my life that it wasn't until I was about fourteen that I noticed that girls were of no interest to me. Mom and Dad were starting to tease me about girls I might like. I avoided the subject for a long time. Finally, I confided in a teacher who had been a mentor and friend to me."

"You actually told a teacher?" Lavender said.

"I sensed he could relate to my dilemma and he did. His advice was to not make a big deal of my sexuality, but to quietly observe others and I would find my way. He told me I never needed to explain myself or question my sexual identity. The sooner I accepted it the sooner everyone else would, and one day I would find someone to love and be loved by"

"What about your parents?" Lavender said putting her shoulder against mine.

"My mom never spoke to me about the issue directly, but my father had a very difficult time accepting me. He had been under the impression that sexual orientation is a choice. At first, this gave him hope that he could talk me out of it. We had many long discussions on many nights."

"How old were you?"

"That's the thing. I was only about fourteen and I didn't have the ability to articulate what I knew to be true. My dad actually convinced me for a while that I could change my mind and start being attracted to girls!"

"So, did you have a girlfriend?" Lavender lifted her head off my shoulder with a mischievous look on her face. "I'm starting to feel hopeful myself!"

"I did have a girlfriend for about two weeks. Apparently I didn't know how a fifteen year-old boy was supposed to act around girls and she got mad at me and started telling everyone in school I was gay. At that point my dad had enough of being patient with me. He spent months barely speaking to me and I heard my parents arguing about me night after night. At one point my mom kicked him out of the house."

"Well, at least you had one parent on your side. I didn't even have that." Lavender said.

"Yes, but I suffered over the fact that my reality was splitting my parents up and there was nothing I could do about it. I couldn't be something I wasn't just for them – or for anyone."

Lavender looked up at me with tears glistening on her lashes and said, "I know exactly what you mean, Cole."

"One time my dad and I got into a fist fight over it. I think I was about sixteen then and I had the gall to bring a boy home for dinner. My dad was polite during the meal, but after my friend left he yanked me outside and just started punching me."

"Oh my God, your own dad?"

"Yes, it took me a long time to get over that. I had never been afraid of my father and he and I previously had a great relationship. My mom kept telling me he needed more time, but as a teenage boy I felt dejected and lost without my father's approval and support."

"How are things now?"

"It's much better now. I am an adult and he tries his best to support me. I've almost got him convinced that those I am attracted to is not a choice." I smiled down at Lavender, seeing complete understanding in her eyes.

"What about in high school. How was that for you?" she asked.

"It doesn't take long for guys to home in on another guy who is not living and breathing for the chance to sleep with a girl. If you're not making the same jokes and crude comments in the locker room it may as well be printed on your forehead."

"What did you do?"

"Early on I'd chuckle at the comments saying, "Oh, yeah" in agreement. But it was obvious to everyone that my response was half-hearted. The first real incident was when *fag* was written on my gym locker in black marker. I was alone when I discovered it, so I sat there and cried. That was pretty tame compared to walking down the high school hallways and suddenly being pushed to the floor from behind, my books sprawled across the floor while some jock walked away saying 'You must've tripped over your wings, fairy' or some other ridiculous comment." I started biting my right index fingernail, but when I saw Lavender staring at me I stopped.

"I also got beat up several times on my way home from school. Usually some guys came from behind. One would pull a hat over my head so I couldn't see my tormentors, and then one or two of them would beat the shit out of me – at least enough to leave me lying on the ground whimpering while they ran off laughing. Once they even broke my nose."

"Oh, my God, Cole, that's horrible," Lavender touched my leg. "I received tons of nasty notes and stuff, but at least I never got beat up – at home or at school."

"My father made valiant attempts to teach me some self-defense techniques, but I never was prepared enough to really use them. I was at least as tall as most of the other boys, but I was not one to be in the weight room. I was thin and weak compared to them."

"One time I took a self-defense course because I was so sick of people trashing me and my clothes. I was determined to drop–kick the next kid that said anything about me down the school hallway. But look at me. I'm like, five foot-one, a hundred ten pounds. Luckily, I realized that I'd just be making an even bigger fool of myself."

"Did you ever confide in your Mom or Dad?"

"Are you kidding? They spent more time harassing me about my appearance and attitude than the kids at school. They would've been overjoyed to hear about it. If an incident happened I'd go home right after school and play my guitar in my room until I could forget about it. Sometimes I'd go to Amber's house. She was the only one who'd ever listen. I miss her, you know?"

"You have me. I'll always listen. I'll always understand too. When you're on the stage you are in complete control. Remember that. You're the rock star. The idiots in the audience are just showing their ignorance."

"I know, but it still hurts. I thought it would be different here."

February 1996 was a month of celebrations, especially that first February. Anais's second birthday, Lavender's twentieth, and my twenty-third. I asked my father to make a one-of-a-kind rocking chair for my girls. Shannon helped me carry it up the three floors to their tiny apartment and we wrapped it with a sheet and topped it with a big pink bow. When Ani and Lavender came through the door all the girls were there. We dramatically uncovered the rocking chair and Lavender stood expressionless for a moment, then placed Anais in my arms, covered her face and sobbed.

"Lav, are you okay?" asked Wendy. "Have a seat. Try it out, why dontcha?"

The rocking chair was made of stained dark pine with carved scrollwork and lavender flowers painted across the top. Lavender continued to cry and tried to say something. She finally took Anais from my arms and together they sat in the chair and rocked.

"I. . . I wanted a rocking chair for her. It looks almost like the one my grandma used to rock me in." She looked up at me, make-up streaking her cheeks. "Thank you, Cole. How did you know?"

"Every mama should have a rocking chair for her baby," I said.

The girls gave them a few inexpensive little gifts, and I served cake, but Lavender and Ani stayed in the rocking chair the rest of that evening. And I thought I heard her humming a Four Tops tune.

Lavender

I'd had no contact with my parents in over a year and a half, or even told John he was an uncle. I'd been too frightened to deal with it. In a way, I didn't want them back in my life because I knew they would try to take over Anais's upbringing. Either that or they'd just hate us both. George and Roberta believe they know what is best for everyone. Not just their own kids, but their nieces and nephews, neighbors, everyone. I didn't want their judgmental ways affecting my free-spirited little girl, even though I felt guilty for not letting them know they are grandparents. I figured if they ever really wanted to see me they could find a way. After all, they are the world's foremost authorities on everything.

"It's your turn Chrissie. What are you gonna do?" Grandma and I were sitting on her living room floor.
"If I move my checker there, you'll win, right?"
"Well, that's okay, honey. We both won a game. Let's play again for the checkers championship. Anyway, the fun is being together, not who wins."
"I know, Grandma. You always say that."
"I'm going to go get us a snack." Grandma left the room.
"What the hell are ya doing to my kitchen, Roberta?" I heard from the next room.
"Well, Fiona," Mom said, "The way you have your shelves set up doesn't make any sense. All the canned goods should be on this shelf."
"Who says? It's my damn kitchen," Grandma yelled.
"There's no need for swearing. This is not the most efficient use of your space as you can see by the way I've

rearranged things. George and I discussed it earlier. I was just trying to help."

"You're always trying to help where you're not wanted. I'd appreciate it if you'd allow me to arrange my own shelves in the future."

"I guess your Grandmother doesn't appreciate our help, does she, John? Why don't we go get our coats?"

"Do we have to go now, Mom? Grandma and I are about to play the championship game."

"Why should we stay when our help isn't wanted?"

Then Cole and I both found boyfriends. This guy named Chance Slater came up to me after a Joeygirls show and asked me out. I told him I had a little girl at home. He said that was cool. Joey and Tess were heading back to the apartment and they said they'd relieve Cole. So Chance and I set out for the nearest decent looking bar in the Bowery. Fog crept into the city streets, blurring the neon lights into hazy colorful clouds. A zephyr caught my peasant skirt and swirled it around my ankles. Chance's hand warmed my shoulder, pulling me towards him.

Chance was quite a bit older than me at 28, but he was hot. Average height and athletically built, he had a blond ponytail, which I was into at the time, a pierced tongue, and he seemed to really appreciate the Joeygirls' music. Sitting on two stools at a tall table, golden glasses of beer bubbling in front of us, his blue-gray eyes fixated on my face as he listened to my sorry life story. His hand moved over my forearm and he'd mutter *wow* or *oh, baby* at certain parts. I regretted blurting it all out on the first date, but he was sweet about it. His attention was more intoxicating than the beer.

Chance offered me a cigarette and I took it eagerly, even though I had been trying to quit. He yelled at a waitress to bring two more beers.

He didn't reveal too much about himself. He lived with his parents in New Jersey and worked at a computer store. He came over to Manhattan two or three times a week for the nightlife. He had seen Joeygirls one other time when we played at the opening of a music store. We talked until the bar shut down and he walked me home. He grabbed my hand as soon as we left the bar and I clutched it willingly. Once, he let it go to run his fingers through the tangled back of my hair and I trembled.

Arriving at the door to the apartment he took my shoulders and pressed me back into the bricks of the building and kissed me. I could feel the silver stud in his mouth swirl around my tongue.

"I'll call you tomorrow, Lavender – that's such a cool name." I watched him walk away with my hand on my chest, feeling the vibration of my heart.

Chance was the first man I ever fell in love with. All the twittering butterflies you read about in romance novels actually existed. At first I thought it was strictly wild sexual attraction. We couldn't wait to get naked together. Being gathered in his arms was like being wrapped in an electric blanket, warm, all-encompassing. I was high 24 hours a day. Who needed a joint? Anais would say to me, "Mommy, why are you being so silly?"

At times it was difficult for me to remember my daughter's needs since I was so enamored with my own. I'd be giving Ani a bath, and instead of playing with her I'd be daydreaming about Chance yanking open the window blinds to tell me he just wanted to look at my soft, damp body in the moonlight, or the shifting of his shoulder muscles as he moved over me in bed. The way he kissed my neck, my back, or licked concentric circles on my breasts. After our lovemaking I rested my head in the cleft of that shoulder and shed silent tears over the connection with another human being.

What Chance and I had was more than just physically satisfying. I felt accepted and alive. I started to feel like I couldn't live a day without him, without the unrehearsed rhythms of our nights together. I wasn't afraid of him or of myself when we were together. I started coming home later and later because I would go out with Chance after the shows.

"Gotta have you . . . . right now." Chance gently pushed me up against the passenger side of the car. In the glow of the streetlight he pulled me into his body, kissing and licking the lobe of my ear. When I opened my eyes the tiniest bit the neon lights from the bar we'd just come out of blurred into a moving rainbow.

"I thought you were taking me home." His arms tightened around me. I pulled back. "Chance."

"Okay, okay." He let me out of his clench and opened the car door for me.

"Thanks, you know I've got Ani . . ." The door slammed on my explanation. When we got close to the apartment he pulled over on a dark street and stopped the car.

"Let's get in the back seat."

"It's really late." But he was out of the car, opening the back door of the small compact car. I joined him, telling myself I wanted it too, although I felt a little frightened of his persistence.

In one movement, Chance reached for the lever to move the driver's seat forward and brought his hand back and up my skirt and into my panties. His fingers fumbled for a wet spot while he took the side of my face in his other hand and pressed his mouth on mine. I unzipped his pants and put my hand in, and glanced out the window, thankful the street was dark and deserted. After he put on a condom I straddled his lap with some difficulty in the small space and we both started laughing between open-mouthed kisses.

Chance tugged at his jeans. "You ready baby, 'cause I'm comin' in."

I moved up and down on him while he lifted my shirt over my head and unclasped my bra. His mouth sucking on my nipple caused me to throw my head back and I hit it on the ceiling of the car. As I yelled out "Ow!" Chance yelled "Oh, God!" and came inside me. We collapsed sideways on the seat, laughing in a noisy, wet mess.

"Fuck! That was fun! Am I crushing your leg?"

"Yeah, a little." I pulled myself up and got dressed and readjusted. "Chance, I have to get home now. Cole has been watching Ani all night. Chance?" He had passed out. I got in the front seat and drove a few more blocks to the apartment. I woke him up and made him promise to stop at the corner and get some coffee before driving back to New Jersey.

Cole stood with his arms folded facing the door when I walked in.

"I'm so, so sorry. I know it's late," I whispered.

"Yes, it's 2 a.m. I'm just glad I can sleep in tomorrow."

"You're not mad?"

"I just don't know what you're doing with this guy. Do you realize that you've been with Chance for over a month and he's never met Anais?" Cole said.

"I know, but we only get to see each other late at night after she's in bed."

"I'm sure he could find time to meet her if he wanted to. Doesn't he have any days off from the *computer* store?" He asked in what I thought was a demeaning way.

"What's that supposed to mean?" I asked.

"Just what I said, Lavender. You know I am in a relationship too. Did you ever think about that? And what about Ani? You've hardly seen her this week." Cole sat down, arms still neatly folded. Then one hand slid out and he began gnawing on a fingernail.

"Why? Did she say something?" I asked.

"Yes, in fact, tonight she kept calling out for you."

"I'll take care of it Cole, I'm sorry I've put you out." I said that, but I was pissed. Who was he to tell me how to raise my daughter?

I waited until I thought he was home, then I called Chance and talked to him about meeting Anais. I wanted to make sure he got home all right too. He said in a less than enthusiastic way he would be willing, and we decided to take her to Central Park the next day.

~~~~~~

It was a beautiful spring day and it seemed like all of New York City had come out of their winter hibernation. Hundreds of people accompanied by strollers or pets on leashes were passing each other on every pathway. We met at the IMAGINE plaque in Strawberry Fields since we both knew where it was. When Chance saw me he smiled and kissed me lovingly. He leaned down to Anais in her stroller and said, "Hi, little baby."

Anais said, "I'm not a baby!

"Ooo, a little smart ass huh?" Chance said.

"Chance!" I slapped him on the shoulder, smiling, but something hurt. "She has a name, you know," I said.

"Yeah, a weird name." He lit up a cigarette.

"Don't say that in front of her. It's a beautiful name." I said, disappointed in the way our day had started.

"Okay, sorry, little one," he said roughly patting her on the head. He handed me the cigarette he'd just lit and lit himself another one. I noticed his hand trembling slightly as he lifted the lighter to the tip of the cigarette.

The rest of the afternoon went in a similar vein. Chance kept trying to make out with me as we sat on a blanket on the Great Lawn, and Anais kept trying to get our attention and get us to play with her. Torn and uncomfortable all day, I wasn't being successful at attending to both of my loves at the same time, and they clearly did not want anything to do with each other.

"I want Cole," Anais said reaching her arms up for me to hold her.

"Hey, how about a snack?" I pulled Cheerios and juice out of my backpack for Anais.

"There's a vendor over there. What would you like?" Chance got up and thrust his hand into the pocket of his jeans looking for money.

"An iced tea would taste good." I smiled up at him.

"Be right back girls."

I felt a small sense of relief to be alone with Ani and I pulled her close to me on the blanket. I watched her chubby little fingers carefully pick Cheerios out of a plastic bowl. I put my nose into her blond ringlets and she smelled like the sky.

"These are circles, Mommy."

"Yes, they are. Yummy circles." As I turned to look for Chance I saw him pull a silver flask out of his jacket and quickly drink from it and then return it to his pocket.

"It's a really nice day, isn't it?" He handed me the iced tea and a small bag of cookies.

"You know what? I've lived in this city all this time and I've never been up in the Empire State Building," I said.

"You're shittin' me," said Chance. "Let's go, baby."

I loved Chance's ability to be spontaneous and fun loving. It was just what I needed at the time. We caught a subway to 34th Street. Chance paid for the tickets and up we went.

I couldn't believe how amazing the sight was. I had no idea what I had been missing. The past few years had been nothing but daily battles of learning to survive, learning the music business, learning to live with other girls, and learning to be a mother. In the midst of all of that I still struggled to let go of my family and my old life. I had a lot to learn about myself. Burdened with the troubles and complications of this new life I had created for myself in New York, I'd neglected to look around and discover the incredible place I lived in.

We stepped out onto the observation deck and I felt the oxygen literally sucked out of me at the sight. It was windy and I clung to Anais like she was going to float away. Chance was being kind of rude, pushing his way between people to get to the best view, while Anais and I hung back from the edge. Even though there are iron grates in front of you it's still a little scary. There are many cloudy or hazy days in New York, but this day was clear and clean.

We looked at the crude maps on each side of the building trying to decipher what we were actually looking at – Brooklyn, Staten Island, New Jersey. I pointed to midtown and told Anais that was where we lived. She looked me straight in the eyes with great seriousness and said, "That's silly, Mommy." I guess there are some concepts even a smart toddler isn't ready to grasp yet. I gazed out on the beautiful concrete forest before me and sensed a wonder and awe I had never felt before. I wanted to fall on my knees and say "Thank you God" – for the privilege of being a mother, for a true friend in Cole, for experiencing being in love with Chance, for the taste of a singing career, mostly for surviving on my own these past few years. The only thing I couldn't be thankful for was what I left behind - the parents who created me and then rejected me, who squashed my spirit and soul until I couldn't find them anymore.

"This is incredible," I said to Chance. "I can't believe I've never been up here. Can we stay all day?"

"Probably not, baby, but if you like this you should see the view from the World Trade Center."

"Can we go there next week?" My voice sounded like a little girl asking Santa for a toy.

"Anything you want, Lavender. But maybe you could leave the kid at home next week, uh, she might get scared or something."

I looked at Anais. She was giggling at trying to inhale the wind that was blowing into her face and I doubted that Chance was really concerned for her fears, but I put it out of my mind.

Later that night I had to tell someone about the experience, someone who didn't already know what standing at the top of the world was like.

Dear Johnny,

Happy 15th Birthday little brother. I'm enclosing a little cash that I saved. I hope you can buy something you want with it. I'm sorry I'm missing another one of your birthdays. I wish I could see you or have a picture of you. You're probably a lot taller now. Maybe you're shaving too. I can't send you my address because I just don't think I can let anyone find me yet. Not that they want to. I still try calling, hoping that you will answer, but I always get the machine. I guess George and Roberta screen all the calls. That's typical. How can you stand living in their prison? Sorry, I just wish I could bring you here. I am still discovering how awesome New York City is. Today I went to the top of the Empire State Building and you could see the whole city for miles and miles. It was amazing. You'd never believe how humungous this city is. There is something really beautiful about it even though it's just a massive island of buildings. I'm still in the Joeygirls, but we haven't been getting many jobs lately. Shannon dropped out and went back to school and Joey is usually high on coke. I might have to find a new group to sing for or maybe try to find another type of work. You don't realize it, but I've got a lot of responsibilities in my new life here. Someday I hope I can tell you all about it.

Love, Chrissie (Lavender)

Cole

Within a month of Lavender meeting Chance, I met Nick. It was fall semester at NYU and I was in the bookstore searching for a textbook for my "Learning Styles of High School Students" class. I saw a young man stacking books down the aisle. He had milk chocolate skin, a bald smooth head, two earrings and a compact body. When I asked him for help he looked up at me with surprisingly light brown eyes, gazed straight into mine, rose up, gently took my arm and led me to the next aisle. We smiled at each other wordlessly.

The next day I returned to the bookstore, found him in another aisle stacking textbooks. He looked up at me, lifted his curly eyelashes and said, "Yes, I'd love to." Nick was 22, and an art student at NYU in his senior year.

In the beginning Lavender seemed a little put-off by all the attention and time I was now giving to Nick. She wanted more time to be with Chance and she was getting less time out of me as a babysitter. We both understood each other's needs and predicament, but it put some space between us temporarily.

"If we both have dates Friday night, who is going to watch Anais?" I said.

"I don't know. Maybe I'll hire a sitter with all the extra money I've been making."

"No need for sarcasm, Lav. I'm serious. We need to work this out somehow. Things are changing. I can't be on call every night."

"What kind of father are you?" We stood silently for a few awkward moments.

"I'm sorry, Cole. That was just ridiculous of me to say that."

"Actually, it felt good to hear that. I want to be Ani's father."

There was another pause, then we both burst out laughing. We laughed until tears rolled down our faces. Anais toddled into the room and joined the laughter, clapping her hands and jumping up and down. At least we were making her happy.

I loved kids and hoped to have my own family some day. Being a teacher would have to suffice for a while. In reality, though, I was Anais's father. The only one she had known so far. I worried about Lavender and Chance. Chance didn't even seem to notice that Anais was alive.

Nick and I started spending more and more time together and we found that we had much in common, the same music, movies and books. He appeared to be turned on by my intelligence and I was in awe of his art talent and found his work inspiring. Nick's art encompassed many genres. He could paint in oils, do portraits, and sculpt in clay, even watercolors. Unfortunately, there is not much an artist can do with classical skills like that in the real world, so he moved into computer art and graphic design, in which he also excelled. Nick and I graduated from NYU in the same year. I was a little behind after taking a semester off in my junior year and adding education to my major in English literature.

Nick was wonderful with Anais and seemed to understand how important she was to me. He was always willing to come to wherever I was babysitting or just take Ani with us when we were doing something fun. The first Christmas we spent together I think he bought Anais more presents than I did.

"I've never really thought about being a father. I'm not sure I have the desire that you seem to have," Nick said. We were entertaining Anais with an endless game of Candyland.

"I've always felt paternal, despite the unlikely possibility of really being a father," I said. "When Anais and Lavender just sort of showed up in my life it was as natural as breathing."

Nick looked up at me and said, "What does your relationship with this little girl mean for us?"

"What do you mean?" Anais had fallen asleep on the floor and I picked her up.

"Well, it seems as though we are committed to an exclusive relationship, right? And I'm just wondering how we'll be able to pursue a life together if you're always available for Lavender and Anais. What if one of us gets a job in another city or state? Are we staying together no matter what? Or will you only consider being close by so you can be a father figure to Anais?"

"You know, all I've ever heard from Lavender is how painful the separation from her parents has been. She felt abandoned by them emotionally, not just when she left, but in all the years she felt rejected by them. I've told you all that. Would I be any better if I took off on the two of them at this point in their lives? I don't think I could add that kind of heartache to either one of them." I started swaying back and forth with Ani in my arms as Nick put game pieces in the box.

"Lavender is really struggling to make ends meet right now. The Joeygirls seem to be falling apart. The girls have had a lot less chances to play locally and Joey is usually too high to find more gigs. I think Shannon is going back to school too. If they really break up who will Lavender have then?"

"But Lavender is an adult with a child. You are not legally responsible for her or the choices she's made," Nick said.

"Nick, she's my friend. We've been best friends."

A long silence followed. I laid the sleeping Ani on the couch and covered her with a throw blanket.

"Nick," I said, touching his shoulder so he would turn my way, "We're both looking for jobs to start our

70

careers. I can't expect you to only look for jobs that are convenient to me. I know you want to be in Manhattan, but I'm not sure I can handle teaching here. I was hoping for a nice New Jersey or Long Island suburb."

"You can work there, but those aren't the kind of places I want to live, you know that. You might have a long, long commute, baby."

"Why am *I* going to be the one . . ." I paused and inhaled, trying to avoid a conflict. "Lavender's been getting more deeply involved with Chance, and she knows that I do not approve of him. Not because he appears to have no ambition to do anything but be a clerk in a computer store, but because he doesn't give a crap about Anais. Yet, she's being forced to spend more and more time with someone who treats her as if she's invisible. That's going to start wearing on her self-esteem. I can't let that happen." I looked at Nick for some kind of compassion or understanding, but he blinked his hazelnut eyes at me as if in slow motion, sat on the chair and turned on the television.

I picked Anais up in her little blanketed cocoon and took her into the bedroom and laid her on the bed. She roused slightly and I quietly sang *Baby love, my baby love.*

1997

Lavender

Anais was a little underweight at birth, so when she started growing and learning before my eyes like some kind of oracle I tried to put my mind at rest, determined not to fuck up being a mother like I had done with every other part of my life.

"Ani, let's sit down on this bench and rest for awhile." I half-ran to keep up with her in the park. "Let's read our new book together."

"No, you read it, Mommy. I'm doing my spinning," she said as she twirled around, arms outstretched, head thrown back.

"Be careful, honey. You'll get dizzy and fall."

"No, I won't. I be careful," she plopped on the grass, giggling. "The sky is crazy, Mommy!"

"I know. You're dizzy."

"I'm playing on the swings now." She ran over and I followed her, lifting her into a toddler swing. I gave a small push and she began pumping her little chubby legs the way Cole and I had taught her.

"*Baby, baby where did our love go?*" Anais sang.

"Where did you learn that song?"

"Cole teached me it."

"Cole taught me," I corrected.

"He did, Mommy?"

I just smiled at my daughter and pulled a music magazine out of my bag, and sat back on the bench, glad for the reprieve from frantically trying to keep up with her on the park paths. I hadn't slept much recently due to all the late nights with Chance, and my head started bobbing. A scream jarred me and I saw Anais lying on the ground, blood slashed across her face.

"Ani! What happened?"

A woman said, "While you were napping your little girl wiggled out of that swing, jumped off the top of that jungle gym and hit the wooden side of the swing set on the way down. You have to watch little kids you know."

I ignored her and scooped Anais into my arms. I took her back to the bench and searched for tissues in my bag to wipe the blood off. She was screaming and I became aware of a small crowd around us.

"She's okay," I said to no one in particular, "just a little bump." But as I wiped the blood away I saw a deep gash. I put the tissue over it and pressed.

"Ow, Mommy, stop that!" Ani tried to push my hand away. The amount of blood and the waves of guilt nauseated me. I was alone with a bleeding child and I had no idea what to do. It was my fault that she was hurt.

"I'm sorry, honey. I'm such a bad mother," and I began to cry. That just made my daughter cry harder in fear of her incompetent, pathetic mother.

~~~~~~

I felt completely intimidated in the presence of the pediatrician. My insecurities as a mother whirled around me like an aura.

"She is so active, and I guess, impulsive, I think. When Anais was a baby she seemed to learn things so fast. She was always very verbal, so I tried to stop worrying about my uneven prenatal care. Of course, I wasn't planning to get pregnant and so I wasn't exactly living a pristine life back then. Through the whole pregnancy I badgered my friend Shannon about all the things I might have done wrong. She had some medical classes" Flipping my hair over my shoulder, clearly, I was babbling.

"Yes, you said that Ms. May." The doctor looked up from the file folder she was holding. As she wrote I felt like a schoolgirl with bad comments being written on my permanent record. "I'm sure you did your best. There are some areas of a child's development that are medical issues and some that are environmental."

"I really missed not having a mom to help me through that time, especially because I was so unprepared and young. I've practically gone crazy thinking about the fact that I might have actually been high on pot or drunk when Ani was conceived. I quit smoking at some point during the pregnancy, but I was sure the damage was already done. Do you think that's why she can't sit still?" Ani sat on my lap with a lollipop in her mouth and red sugar smeared across her lips. The bandage across her forehead covered up four stitches.

"It's a possibility, but really *Mom*, even if that is the case, we need to focus on the here and now, don't we?"

That wasn't the last time a pediatrician would call me *Mom* and I didn't like it. It made me feel defensive and judged as a mother. I have my own name.

"My friend Shannon provided me with all the vitamins and kept track of my blood pressure and things like that."

"Mommy, let's go now," Anais said as she tried to slip off my lap.

"No, honey, just a minute more," I grabbed a tissue from the box nearby and wiped the red off of her face. I let her down and she went to a small toy box to investigate.

"It's too much sugar, isn't it?"

"Sugar certainly is not something she should have every day, but we also may be looking at some type of attention deficit hyperactivity disorder."

"What? Oh no, I don't think she's that bad," I didn't want to be a crying *Mom* in front of this formidable woman, but I knew kids in middle school that had it and they were so annoying. They'd be in trouble all the time and never shut up. A three-year-old chattering away is cute, but a thirteen-year-old who won't shut up or stop fidgeting is a pain in the ass.

"Is there some kind of test to see whether that's what it is?" I said, blinking furiously and turning my head towards Ani.

"No, not really. It's a situation where we need to look at her complete development and skills and her ability to focus based on her age. Take this questionnaire home and fill it out very carefully – and honestly." The doctor looked at me, and I knew I wasn't fooling her. "There's no need to get upset about this just yet. Anais is obviously very bright and her physical development is normal. You are right to question the attention and impulsivity issues. Children that are diagnosed early and get treatment do much better with this disorder." She handed me a folder of information.

"Thank you, doctor. Come on, Ani."

"There is an additional questionnaire in the folder. If Anais is in preschool or a church school or something along those lines I would be interested in a teacher's perspective as well."

"Okay." I took Anais's hand as we left.

"Bye, doctor," Ani said turning from me to look back at the doctor.

"Bye-bye, Anais, Bye, *Mom*."

~~~~~~

Cole got a post office box. He was thinking about moving and he wanted to be able to check for responses to jobs he'd applied for, and also responses to queries he had sent out for writing opportunities. Now I could give John a way to reach me. I ached from the fact that my mother and father had apparently done nothing to try to find me. In my heart I'd really thought that they would find a way. I continued to call Tim's house, Johnny's best friend, and I guess he'd kept my calls a secret, which I was grateful for. I hadn't told John about Anais. After three years there just didn't seem to be a way to say it. *Oh yeah, by the way, brother, I've been a mother for three years and you've been an uncle and Mom and Dad are grandparents, but I haven't bothered to tell you.*

"Cole, would you keep an eye on Ani while I run down to check the mail?" I wrapped my striped knit scarf around my neck and thought of my grandma.

"You know, my Grandma Fiona doesn't even know she's a great-grandma. She always loved and accepted me. This whole thing is my fault, isn't it? I mean, I'm the one who made the choices I knew would upset my parents. I haven't contacted them even though I could have. I still know where *they* are."

Cole looked up from his books without commenting. He'd heard it all before.

"I wonder if Anais would make a difference in our relationship. There's a remote possibility that George and Roberta could be happy to be grandparents, but I just know they would try to take over Anais's upbringing."

"Yes, you've said that many times, Lav."

"Or they might refuse to know you once they realized you're gay. I'm pretty sure that they will resent the fact that I've gone on with my life and never did come crawling back to them. They might be furious about not knowing about Anais, or ashamed of me being a single mother, or they might not even care anymore."

"I'm certain that they care. They spent seventeen years raising you, didn't they?"

"Why is it that you always make so much sense, Mr. Carson? I tangle all my thoughts up into tiny knots and you can untangle and smooth them out with a single statement." I said with my hands on my hips. "But I'm still not sure you're right - you just *sound* right."

"Teachers must always sound right. It's a requirement."

My life wasn't really going anywhere. I could have been half way through college by now, but I hadn't even finished high school. I needed to find a way to get my GED soon. I wanted to be something besides a part-time little-known punk rock singer. It was getting old, and Anais was the most important thing. There was so much I couldn't do because I was responsible for her.

I don't know what I would have done without Cole. He made me believe in the good in people. He made me believe that God really does send angels to Earth. I knew he was struggling with his relationship with Nick and I knew it was because of Ani and me. I needed to give something back to him instead of always expecting more from him. He loved Anais with all his heart, but truly he was not responsible for her. I was responsible for my little girl and for all the choices I'd made. I finally accepted that fact.

My letters to John didn't have much to say. What could I say about my life without including Anais and Cole in it? They *were* my life. So I gave him the P.O number hoping that by then George and Roberta had given up on getting any information about me through the letters that I'm sure they snooped on. I went down to the mailbox and found a letter from John.

Chrissie,

Thanks for the PO box number. I don't know what to tell you. Things haven't changed around here much. Mom and Dad have been on my case double time since you left. I wish you wouldn't have gone because I miss you and because Mom and Dad are obsessed with controlling everything I do now. Are you ever going to come home? Sometimes it's hard to remember having a sister, but I know you were a cool one and I wish you were here now.

I'm going to be getting my driver's permit soon. That is if I don't do anything to make Mom and Dad mad at me. I'm really trying not to blow it. I've been working my ass off to save money so I can buy a car and get out of here once in a while, instead of having to earn a ride everywhere I go. I've got a girlfriend, but Mom and Dad don't know it yet. Her name is Kelly and she has long red hair just like you used to, except I don't think her color is real. I don't know her well enough to ask yet.

I think Mom and Dad have pretty much given up on you coming back home, but for a long time I heard a lot of arguments between them about you. I used to hear Mom crying all the time in the bathroom after you left. But they'd never admit to themselves that any of your reasons for leaving were because of them. They tell me not to be like you and I'll be fine. Sometimes I wish I was just like you and I could get out of here. But I don't know how you make it on your own. My grades are pretty good and I'll probably get into a good college. I really need Dad to pick up the tab on that, you know? Grandma is doing okay. She brings up your name all the time. She's always telling Mom and Dad that they should be doing everything they can to find you. You should probably know that she suggests hiring a private detective to find you. They just say that it was your choice to leave. Anyways, write back soon. It was great to hear from you.
Love, John

I read and reread that letter a dozen times trying to figure out whether I should feel any hope. They wouldn't admit they were wrong, but they did argue over it. It didn't sound like they'd changed in their desire to control and dominate John, but the fact that they'd given up on me coming home meant that they must have hoped for it for a while.

"Cole, do you want to read the letter?" I asked.

"If you want me to. It's your business."

"Since when are you not in my business?" I laughed, but Cole did not laugh with me.

After he read it he said, "What are you going to do? Try going back?"

"I don't know. Do you see any reason in that letter that I should? Everyone could freak out over Anais, you know."

"What is it that you want? Do you want to reunite with your family and let Anais know her grandparents and uncle or not? Or would you rather pursue your relationship with that Chance person?" Cole said rather coldly.

"What's your problem? Do you think I'm just going to pick up and leave New York without telling you? What do *you* want? Do you want a life with Nick or with us?" I started putting dishes away in the cupboard. Silence. Then Cole started humming one of his stupid Motown songs like he always does when he gets frustrated.

"I'm sorry. You didn't deserve that. You have been so good to my daughter and me and I hardly ever even thank you for it. Maybe it's time we let you go to have the life that you want with teaching and with Nick. Let's face it Cole, I'm a bit of a burden, aren't I?" I stopped and turned to face him, but he wouldn't look at me. "We've tried to make a family here, but how can we sustain it? Joeygirls has dissolved before my eyes and I have to get a job. If your parents are going to continue to help me out with preschool I can manage, but they are not responsible to do that, especially if I am the one holding their son back from pursuing his career and a life with someone he loves."

"Hey, stop, would you?" Cole practically shouted at me. "What the hell are we talking about here? Not being friends anymore? I have to choose between you and Ani or Nick and a teaching career? Since when do you get to decide my life for me?"

"I haven't told you this yet, but Chance is moving out into his own apartment and he said Anais and I could move in with him in New Jersey. It's our opportunity to have a home of our own. Anais has spent her whole life living with wayward girls in a shitty excuse for a home, you know?" I flopped down on the couch and put my head in my hands. I looked up to see Cole staring out the window. He started humming, then I barely heard *I wish it would rain . . .* Neither one of us wanted to have this conversation.

"Joeygirls is over." I said, "Everyone is going their own way within the next month. Joey is useless. Shannon is back at school and Tess and Wendy are looking for another apartment to share. I can't just follow them to wherever they're going. The life I've made here never was the best thing for my daughter. I want her to understand what a family is like, a home that isn't overcrowded with strangers -- where there's no exposure to drugs, people coming and going all the time. It might give me the chance to go back and get my GED, make something of myself," I said looking at the floor as tears were plopping down on my shoes.

"And that's what you want? To move in with someone who can't stand your daughter? Do you need sex that badly? Do you really think that it's going to be a home? Or is that just your little girl fantasy of having the family you always wanted . . . with him? Come on Lavender," Cole said, turning towards the door.

"Cole, wait, please. I just want you to be able to choose for yourself right now and not have my needs in your way. And I really care about Chance. I think once he gets used to Anais it will be fine. He's just not used to little kids. His mom told me he used to love playing with his little cousins. Maybe he just forgot how much fun they can be."

"Do you honestly think that's what he wants from your relationship? Look at you. You're a beautiful, sexy young thing. He's a healthy twenty-eight year old straight male. He wants your little fat-free body in his bed every night, honey."

"You think I don't know what guys want? Do you have any memory of the way you found me two years ago? You think I haven't been around? And what would you know about healthy heterosexual males anyway?"

With that Cole turned dramatically and flung himself out the door slamming it behind him. I felt bad, but I picked up the phone and called Chance. I asked him if he understood that his offer included Anais and a lot of changes, and that Cole obviously would not be around all the time, or at all for all I knew, to baby-sit. He said that was no problem because his mom loved watching little kids.

"We're gonna party all the time, baby," were his exact words.

Cole

I attended the last Joeygirls show in the first place I ever saw them – at the Hook-up Bar and Grill. They still rocked with Lavender singing her heart out, her red locks flaming in the stage lights. She wore the punked-out miniskirt and Doc Marten boots, a Blondie baby tee and her hair in a million pigtails and ribbons. She looked adorable and her talent still blew me away. It was the end of the road for the girls though. Joey's drug addictions made it impossible for them to go on or to live together. Joey used to keep her partying out of the apartment for the sake of Anais, but lately she had been stoned most of the time and, even though the girls tried to help her, she was not willing to accept help yet.

Lavender and Joey never got to be very close, but Lavender was quite upset when Shannon moved out to live on the NYU campus and go back to school. Shannon tried to hang in there with the group, but she really couldn't put the Joeygirls before her education anymore. I think Lavender was a little jealous of her and she missed the only intelligent conversations she ever got to have in that tiny apartment they had all shared. Things were changing and neither of us knew which direction to take.

I prepared myself to move on to my teaching career. I was offered a high school position in a public school in suburban New Jersey, about an hour commute from Manhattan. I had to accept the offer since it was a dream job compared to starting in the NYC public schools. Nick had not found anything yet so he moved in with me in my tiny studio apartment. In a month he'd have to start paying back college loans and his parents did not want him to return home.

Lavender and Anais landed in New Jersey with Chance Slater. Chance's apartment, such as it was, was a good 30 minutes away from where I worked and even farther from my apartment in the city, so our lives changed dramatically. It became very difficult for me to spend any time with my girls. I expected Lavender to be entranced with her live-in boyfriend. Now that she was getting laid on a regular basis I figured she'd be content, but I didn't expect her to leave me out of Anais's life altogether. I wasn't working or studying on the weekends anymore and that's when I'd miss them the most. I was willing to go to them, but Lavender usually had some reason why they were busy. We often talked on the phone and she did not sound happy to me, but she continually insisted that she was. She would put Anais on the phone and we'd have funny, unintelligible conversations, but I loved them.

Lavender called to ask if they could drop Anais off at our apartment for the afternoon so she and Chance could go shopping. Nick and I were thrilled and got out all the toys and books that we'd been collecting for such an occasion. We could hear them coming up the stairs and down the hall when they got there because Lavender and Chance were arguing and Ani was crying. All I had to hear was Chance calling Lavender a bitch and I was out the door saying, "What's going on?"

"What's going on is none of your damn business, fag," shouted Chance.

"Chance!" Lavender cried,"Don't ever call Cole that . . ."

"Well that's what he is, isn't he?"

Lavender handed the tearful Anais into my arms and I held her with all my might, as if I could shield her from what I just witnessed. Lavender kissed Anais good-bye and told her to be good for Uncle Cole and Uncle Nick and then ran down the hall to catch up with Chance. I handed Anais over to Nick and tried to get her to come back, but they were gone. I felt torn between protecting Lavender and protecting little Ani.

I looked at Nick, "What are we going to do?"

Nick said, "We're just going to give Anais a delightful afternoon with her uncles. That's all we *can* do, Cole." And I knew he was right.

About three hours later Lavender showed up by herself.

"Chance took his car home and told me I should stay here unless I wanted to start giving him the respect he deserves," she said.

"The respect he deserves for what, treating you like crap?" I said.

"Crap," repeated Anais. We all started laughing and of course, she joined in the laughter, repeating crap over and over since it was so funny.

"I'm glad all I said was crap. This little one doesn't miss a thing. Did you ever notice that she seems to listen to every word said in her presence?"

"Yes, I know that. And she's heard way too many words lately," Lavender replied, flipping her red locks over her shoulder.

"Honey, tell us what's going on," Nick said in his kind, loving way.

"Just a lot of arguments. I'm not really sure what it is Chance wants. When we're alone everything is great, fantastic. But once we get out in public or go to do something he seems out of control, always angry. Then, of course, when he's had too much to drink . . . "

"Is it because you have Anais along with you? Does he get angry at her?" I said.

"Sometimes he loses patience with her, but he also doesn't want me to spend the money on a babysitter. That's why I talked him into coming in to the city today, so you two could keep an eye on her."

"You know you can do that anytime," Nick said and I grinned at him for being so sweet to my friend.

"I know, thanks, but that doesn't really solve my problem does it? We're having a hard time with money. I don't really have any marketable skills but I'm going to seriously start looking for a job on Monday, and Chance's mom said she would baby-sit for us . . . for me."

"That's great, Lav. Maybe that will reduce some of the stress for you two," Nick said. Now I felt myself glaring at him. Why was he encouraging this relationship that seemed so unhealthy for both of the girls? Was he really concerned for their well-being or did he just want Lavender and Chance to work out so the girls would be out of our hair?

"I want to be your cigarette," I said, looking at Chance light up his third in a row.

"What are you talking about?" He stared at me through smoke-squinted eyes.

"I want you to need me as much as you need *that*. Put me in your mouth every day and night, suck on me, inhale me, be addicted to me."

He put his arm around my neck and pulled me to him, "I am, baby. I let you and your kid move in with me didn't I?" Chance could articulate perfectly with a cigarette clenched between his teeth.

"Yes, you did, but now it seems like you're never here. You're out with the boys sucking on beer bottles every night instead of me."

"I need you when I get home, don't I?"

"Yes, but there's more to a relationship than that."

"Like what?"

My neck lost its strength. My chin dropped to my chest. I blinked off the tears, got up, pulled my robe over my bare shoulders and stood looking out the window into the blackness of the suburban New Jersey night as I did almost every night waiting for him to come home. I missed Cole's loving attention, and so did Ani. I wondered if this was what a relationship always turned out to be, just two people living in the same space. On the nights that Chance wasn't totally wasted, he would come home, put his hand out to me and guide me into the bedroom. Like a fish being lured and pierced by a hook, I would follow his lead, acquiesce, give myself wholly to him in hopes that he would return the devotion. I was a maraschino cherry, just there to top off his day.

"I do love you, Lav. You know that, right? Come back in bed with me."

I walked across the cold, bare floorboards, crawled into the bed and inched towards him. "Are you sure about that?"

"What the hell!" He pushed our naked bodies away from each other and got out of bed. "What do you want from me, huh?"

"I want you to care, Chance, and I want you to be nicer to Anais. She's just a little girl. She didn't choose this situation."

"That's right, but you did. I'm not her father if that's what you're looking for." He pulled on some jeans and a shirt.

"I thought you wanted us to stay together. Isn't that why we're living together?"

"I can't promise you anything for the future. I've never promised you anything, have I?"

"No." Sitting up in the bed, I pulled the sheets around me. "Please don't leave now. Please stay. We can work this out." I put my arms out hoping to lure him back to bed.

"Isn't it enough that I'm supporting you and your kid?" He slammed the door behind him. I didn't have time to cry because I heard a little voice from the next room.

"Mommy? Mommy, where are you?"

"I'm here Anais. I'm coming." I slipped my robe on and went out to the tiny living room where Ani slept on a cot in a corner alcove.

"Why did Chance slam the door? I was sleeping," she said rubbing her eyes and trying to focus on me in the dark.

"I'm sorry sweetie, sometimes he forgets that we're here."

"How can he forget? I'm right here, Mommy!"

"I know you are. You'll always be here with me, no matter what."

"I want Cole," she said as I lowered her back down and tucked the blanket around her.

"Cole's not here, honey. We'll go to see him soon, okay? Now you go back to sleep. I'll be right here."

I rocked quietly next to her in our rocking chair until she went back to sleep. I called Cole, but there was no answer. I felt a fleeting twinge of jealousy knowing he was with Nick. I had no one to talk to. No one. "I am pathetic." I said out loud as I lit a cigarette and cracked the window open. I smoked two in a row, picked up my guitar and strummed and sang softly to my daughter's pink, sleeping face across the moonlit room. I remembered the sleepless nights with Anais as a baby. I'd be walking in circles with her, bundled in as many garments as I could find, around the twelve square feet available for walking in the decrepit apartment. Ani would be wailing and I didn't know how to make her stop. Soon we'd both be crying and one of the girls would rouse from her cot and take Ani from me for a little while. On those nights I wondered whether I even had the right to keep her.

After an hour I kissed Anais on the cheek and went into the bedroom. I opened the nightstand drawer and pulled out my knit scarf. I wrapped it around my neck and pulled the covers up and over my shoulders as if they would protect me from the loneliness and fear. The last time I looked at the clock it was 3 am. Chance never did come home that night.

I had to get a job. I had been at home with Anais for the two months since we'd moved in with Chance. I'd looked through the want ads and made a few calls, but I enjoyed spending the days with her so much that I kept putting off trying to find a job. We took walks, looking for chipmunks and squirrels, and I tried to teach her the names of the trees and the flowers. I didn't have the heart to stop her when she squatted down in her little pink overalls and pulled a flower out by its roots with her chubby fingers.

Anais had a unique comfort with nature. She'd waddle ahead of me on a dirt trail and suddenly plop down in the middle of the path and start piling up pebbles and counting them – one, two, free. . . When we'd spy a chipmunk or a bird, even with her abundant energy, she would sense when to be quiet and watch. Being with my daughter on these sun-filled days was the first time I felt like a mother. How could I let them go? What if I never had this kind of time again?

Chance's parents, Lydia and Chip Slater lived about a mile away. They were incredibly kind to Anais and me. Everything on Lydia was round, from her blue-black eyes, to her soft womanly body, to her pillowy feet that seemed to just balance on her pink fuzzy slippers. Lydia's brown and gray hair was braided and wrapped into a bun on the back of her head. Her face was so sweet that I easily looked right at her when I spoke to her. I had a bad habit of looking away when I talked with people, but I noticed right away that I didn't need to do that with Lydia. The first time we met she had on high-waisted jeans and a yellow sweatshirt with chickadees on it, and a pink apron tied around her middle section. She smiled at me and her eyes seemed to disappear into her cheeks.

Chip was a stocky, muscular man, constantly in work clothes and in the middle of some never-ending chore in the garage or basement. I never saw him sit for more than a meal. He was very talkative for a man, I thought, and a toothy smile perpetually lived on his face. In fact, his mouth doubled in its width when he smiled, and the chipped front tooth just added to the charm.

"I am so glad that Chance is finally settling down. You seem good for him Lavender, and we just love little Annie," Lydia said one Sunday when we were invited over for dinner.

"Thanks, actually her name is pronounced Ah-nee, Ahna-eese," I said while setting the table with white Corelle dishes trimmed with tiny green flowers.

"Oh sure, I keep forgetting. That's a very unusual name, isn't it? Well, I guess I've heard that about Chance too, but he was our last chance to have a baby. I was almost forty when he came along, and we were sure glad that we took the chance, right honey?"she said to Chip as he walked through the kitchen door.

"Chance? I still think it's a strange name, but she was the one having the baby, so I said what the heck. Where is he anyway?"

"Oh, he's out on the back deck with that filthy habit of his. You don't smoke now do you Lavender?'

"Oh, no, well not with Anais around." I told a little lie since I was now in the habit of puffing the night away when Ani was asleep and I was waiting for Chance to come home. It took the edge off. I felt like saying – no, I wouldn't be smoking if your son treated me better.

"Well that's good. You seem like a nice girl. It's too bad that you've had to raise that baby alone though. Where exactly is the father?" She stopped stirring the gravy and looked right at me.

"I don't think that's our business, honey," Chip said, looking my way and smiling.

"That's okay. Actually I don't know where he is. Unfortunately I had to leave home when I was seventeen and I left all that behind me."

"Oh," Lydia went back to her stirring. "Well, I understand that you're going to need a babysitter when you get a job. I would be glad to help out a couple days a week."

"Lydia, that's very kind of you. I don't know. Anais is quite a handful. She's got a lot of energy."

"I've watched all my nieces and nephews at one time or another and I did just fine."

"I'm sure you'd be great. I didn't mean that. It's just that she's an unusually active three-year-old. But if you could help me out for a little while I would really appreciate it," I said folding the napkins as carefully as I could.

"Well it's all settled then," Lydia said. "Let's eat. Chance, come on in now dear. Dinner's ready."

"Okay, Mom," I heard Chance say in a voice I'd never heard before.

"Lavender, why don't you go wake up little Annie? I have a booster seat for her that I found up in the attic."

The Sunday family dinner consisted of roast beef, mashed potatoes and gravy and green beans. Chance was attentive and polite to his parents as they talked about what neighbors and family members were doing. Anais was enjoying the home-cooked meal so much that she was relatively quiet. I felt like I was in a '50's TV show and I loved every minute of it. I wanted to stay there forever. My childhood Sunday dinners were somber and quiet. Any discussion was about that morning's sermon in church, although my mother usually had plenty to criticize about the preacher's message, or would John and I adequately finish the food that was put on our plates by my mother? I already decided I would never require Anais to eat something I chose to put on her plate.

After dinner I jumped up to help clean off the table. I brought the first load of dishes into the kitchen, tripped on an area rug and the top three dishes clattered to the floor. Luckily, they were the unbreakable kind, but the leftover food and silverware noisily slid over the linoleum. Gravy everywhere.

"Oh, I'm so sorry. I'll clean it right up." I felt tears swell in my eyes and my heart started pounding, responding to the anger that messes caused in my childhood.

"It's all right, honey. No big deal," Lydia handed me a towel and knelt down on the floor next to me. An overwhelming scent filled my nose, a familiar scent. A flowery, heavy perfume. Without thinking, I turned and flung my arms around Lydia, hugging her as tightly as I could.

"My goodness," she mumbled through my shoulder that was pressed into her face.

"It's just that. . . you smell like my Grandma." Lydia held me there on the kitchen floor, both of us on our knees, while I sobbed into her warm soft shoulders.

"It's okay, darlin'. You're going to be just fine." Lydia whispered into my ear.

~~~~~~~

Chance lightly snored next to me, but his noises weren't keeping me awake. My mouth moved in questions to God. When would I stop needing other people to help me raise my own daughter, to satiate my pathetic neediness? When were people going to stop moving in and out of my life like pawns being moved and replaced on a chessboard? A secret sense in my head told me I used people to survive. I couldn't leave Chance. I was falling in love with his family. Lydia was going to be a loving presence in Anais's life. We had a home and food and shelter. I had someone who might love me someday, even if he couldn't love my daughter.

Johnny,

I wanted to let you know that the P.O. box address is gone. My friend rented it and doesn't need it anymore. I'm also moving in with my boyfriend. My band fell apart and I'm looking for a job now. I'm hoping maybe I can work at the computer store where he works as assistant manager.

I wonder if Mom and Dad ever talk about me. My life here is not one that they would be proud of. They could hardly stand me before, I'm sure they don't want to know me now. I'm worried about Grandma. I know I've let her down. She always loved me and defended me to Mom and Dad. I've paid her back by abandoning her. I wonder if even she could accept the life I've made here.

I really want to talk to you. I'm going to try to call you next Saturday. I'll call in the afternoon. I hope that's when Mom and Dad still go grocery shopping together.
I love you.
Chrissie

Cole

The town of Clairemont prides itself on its family values and the excellence of the school system. Heterogeneous groups of children of professionals and the working class walk through my classroom door every day to attend my required freshman English Lit class. I walk out that door at 3:30 knowing I have chosen the right profession. On many days it's 5:00 or later when students who had come to me for extra help leave, and I can go home to Nick.

Developing a rapport with my students is worth the long hours. Several days before school started at the end of August I set up my classroom. I found posters of classic literature that had been made into movies to capture the students' attention. I placed formidable quotes from the required reading list around the room and I ran a contest to see who could match up the most quotes with their authors. I called all the parents and introduced myself, inviting them to come and visit at any time.

On the first day at 7:45 a.m. I inhaled deeply, looked around the room and thought about how much I had done to get there. It was a great moment. My parents came at the end of the first day to see my classroom and take me out to dinner to celebrate.

Most of the teachers wear jeans or khakis, but I prefer to wear dress pants, a colorful shirt and matching tie each day. I'm a bit appalled at the way the students dress. I remember dressing in my best new school clothes at least for the first week of school. But these 14 and 15-year-olds looked like they are still on summer vacation in sweat pants and t-shirts, sneakers or flip-flops, which think should be against dress code. If there is a dress code it certainly doesn't seem to be enforced.

Fortunately this does not seem to affect my ability to develop student-teacher relationships. I keep the atmosphere light-hearted and always listened respectfully to all of their comments and opinions on what we are reading. Students stop by just to chat and it reminds me of the high school teacher I had confided in so long ago. He was my impetus to be that kind of teacher for some other confused young man or woman.

The first assigned book was <u>To Kill a Mockingbird</u> by Harper Lee, one of my favorites.

A hot, damp breeze wafted into the classroom through the windows of the fifty-year old brick school building. The students slumped over their desks, hair mashed against their skin, clothes plastered to their bodies, the study guide I labored over now substituting as a fan.

"I know it's hot ladies and gentlemen, but let's try to get through the first five questions on our study guide, shall we?" I said, fanning myself as well. "What is the theme of this novel?" Silence enveloped the room, eyes looked away from mine, heads turned down or toward the window, dreaming of the end of the day.

"Anyone? Caitlin? Jeremy?" I attempted to prompt my most vocal students. I saw Caitlin shrug her shoulders. Jeremy stared at me blankly.

"Let's start with your comments or opinions on the book. You can come up with an opinion, right? Yes, Sarah."

"It seems like it was about prejudice and how, like, you don't know who someone is until you really know them," Sarah said.

"All right, what else?" I asked. "Which characters are you referring to?"

"Tom Robinson and Boo Radley," Sarah added.

"Yes, good. How were they discriminated against?" I looked around for other volunteers.

"People thought Tom Robinson was guilty just because he was black, and they were scared of Boo Radley because he was retarded," said Jeremy.

"You think he was retarded?" I asked.

"I think he was gay," said Aaron. There was laughter and sounds of agreement.

"Why do you think he was gay?" I asked Aaron.

"He was weird and freaky and he knew he was gay and that's why he wouldn't come out of his freakin' house," Aaron answered. Most of the students laughed.

"Really? So people who are considered different should be ashamed of who they are, is that your opinion, Aaron? Should they hide themselves from the world as Boo Radley did?"

"No, Mr. Carson, they shouldn't," came a small voice from the back of the room. It was Ellen speaking from her wheelchair.

"Why is that, Ellen?" I asked.

"People think I'm different just because I can't walk. But I'm not. I like the same stuff that everyone does. I'm not different inside," Ellen said.

"Thanks, Ellen, I think we all needed to be reminded of that."

"Not being able to walk isn't the same as being gay," said Aaron.

"Why not?" I asked.

"Because people who can't walk were probably born that way or had an accident and it's not their fault, but, you know, being gay is different . . . I guess." As Aaron floundered, the rest of the class became silent. I had no idea what they were thinking, but the pounding fury in my chest felt very dangerous. I turned to my notes, searching for a way out of this discussion before it was too late. I paused and took a deep breath. I started chewing on a nail and then thought better of it.

"Thank you for your thoughts, Aaron. I think your opinion is just that. It is an opinion and you are entitled to it. Why don't we move on? Does anyone else have a comment on the book to share with us?" Of course, no one did, and so we turned to the prefabricated questions on the study guide in front of us. After class, Ellen waited patiently for the students to vacate the classroom. I heard the whir of her electric chair move towards my desk. The dejection and disappointment of our first discussion of one of my favorite books must have shown on my face.

"Mr. Carson. I just wanted to say that I think Aaron is wrong. I think everyone is born the way they are, not just normal people."

I smiled at the humor in that innocent statement. "Thank you, Ellen, I appreciate that you took the time to tell me that. Let me put those books in your backpack for you."

"Thanks, Mr. Carson. I'm glad I got you for Freshman English. You're really cool."

"So are you, Ellen."

Driving home I sang along with four or five Temptations songs before I realized it. My voice sang out the words I knew so well without any conscious thought. I turned off the music and let myself fantasize.

Nick and I had been getting along well. Once in a while one of us made a subtle reference to the future, but the words were carefully spliced together. Neither of us appeared willing to ask the bigger questions about where our relationship was going.

I couldn't stop thinking about how lovingly Nick always treated Anais. He could be very considerate. Every evening he'd ask about my day and listen patiently as I vented the inevitable frustrations of teaching. We seemed to have the same tastes in decorating, and I envisioned having our own home together, going out to shop, choosing paint colors and upholstery patterns. But that's as far as my fantasy ever took me. It stopped with an image of us happily purchasing wall paint from some unknown suburban hardware store. I couldn't picture anything further – celebrating birthdays or holidays, agreeing on where to go on vacations, growing older together.   What I really couldn't imagine was Nick staying with one person for very long, or being a part of any sort of family.

Lavender

"What kind of experience or training have you had with computers?" Mr. Ruiz looked me over from the barrettes I put in my hair to hold it in place, to my red mini-skirt, to my well-worn leopard print Creepers. His eyes slowly moved back up to my face and lingered on the silver ring through my eyebrow.

"Training? Well, Chance has been teaching me some things on his computer and I. . . I thought this job was for running a cash register. I have experience with that." I said.

"Yes, that would be a small part of the position, but customers ask a lot of questions and all of our associates need to be knowledgeable."

"I can learn. Chance will . . ."

"Miss May. Is it Miss?" I nodded my head. "Miss May, I understand that Chance is your friend and he would help you, but we really need workers who have a good understanding of our inventory," Mr. Ruiz said. I was viciously picking at the cuticles of my fingers and one of them had started to bleed. I stuck my finger in my mouth to stop the bleeding just as Mr. Ruiz looked up from my miserably deficient application. I pulled my finger out of my mouth and pressed on the cuticle with my thumb. Mr. Ruiz's eyebrows were pushed together in sympathy. I looked past him to a shelf of family photographs and sensed the absurdity of the situation.

"What would you like to be doing a year or two from now, Miss May?"

"Doing?" I gazed at my lap as if there was something fascinating in it. "I'm a mom, Mr. Ruiz. I would like to be able to provide for my daughter. But I do have a babysitter so that's no problem for working. I can start any time."

"I don't think we a have a position for you at this time, but if you should gain some solid computer experience in the future please stop by again." His ample torso rose from the comfy leather desk chair. He put his hand out and I shook it.

"Thank you for your time," I said as I tried to smile at him.

The interview only took a few discouraging minutes so I decided to take my time getting back to Lydia's to retrieve Anais. I drove slowly through a maze of quiet suburban streets, being careful to come back out on the main road each time so I wouldn't get lost.

I imagined Chance as a mischievous little boy with a messy head of blond hair under a baseball cap roaming these streets with his buddies. He never spoke of his childhood, but knowing Chip and Lydia I thought it must've been close to perfect. I could see him climbing trees in the back yard, catching frogs at the pond, and never getting yelled at for getting dirty or wandering freely. He probably helped to build dozens of projects with his dad in the basement woodshop too. I wanted a fun, loving, carefree childhood like that for Ani. The one I didn't have. I wondered what made Chance begin drinking so excessively. Maybe he'd gotten into the wrong crowd in high school.

I drove past a small white church. Something about it appeared so safe and inviting that I turned around and pulled into the parking lot. A side door was propped open, so I walked in and looked down a hallway. The sun filtered through the windows of the pastel stained glass in a sanctuary and made the room glow in a warm light. I quietly walked in. The décor was simple. Clean white walls and pews with red carpet flowing down the center aisle and matching pew cushions. Brass chandeliers hung overhead. I walked slowly to the front altar and knelt on the cushion facing a large gold cross that hung between shiny metal organ pipes.

I prayed my usual prayer – that Anais would be protected from her inept mother, that God would guide me to find my place in this world, and thanks for Cole, Chance, Chip and Lydia. Somewhere in my heart I still believed He was listening and would get around to answering all these requests in His own time.

As I stood up I heard footsteps coming down the aisle.

"Oh, I'm sorry. I didn't mean to disturb you. I can come back later."

"No, no I was just leaving . . . this is a lovely church." I didn't know what else to say. I wondered if I was trespassing.

"Yes, it is. It's very old. I love this time of day when the sun comes through the western windows." She walked up to me and extended her hand. "I'm Susan, the church organist."

"I'm Lavender. Nice to meet you. You're probably here to practice. Can I stay and listen?"

"Sure, as long as you want. I'm going to run through Sunday's hymns first. They're listed on the board over there."

"Thanks." I sat down in the front row and pulled a red hymnbook out of the pew rack as I had done so many times in my life. The tune Susan began to play sounded familiar to me and I turned to it in the book.

> *Prone to wander, Lord I feel it*
> *Prone to leave the God I love*
> *Here's my heart, oh take and seal it*
> *Seal it for Thy courts above.*

I remembered loving this tune as a child. It would sing in my head for days. Now the words lodged in my heart with a new clarity. By the time Susan finished the hymn sobs were forcing their way out of my throat. I quietly placed the hymnbook back in the rack and slid out of the pew to the side where she wouldn't see me. I hurried out the side door, got in the car and pulled out of the parking lot like a chased criminal.

I drove around aimlessly to cry myself out. I blew my nose at a stoplight, hopeful that I wouldn't look too hideous by the time I got back to Lydia's.

"How did it go, darlin'?" asked Lydia.

"Not so well. I only know computer basics. We never had one at home because my parents didn't think they were worth the money. I learned word processing at school, but computers weren't as necessary as they are now. I can't expect a store to hire me with no experience," I peeked in the guest room to see Anais sleeping on the bed covered with a gold and brown afghan.

"I thought maybe Chance would be able to have some influence there," Lydia said.

"I guess even knowing Chance doesn't make up for the fact that I'm a loser. I haven't done anything with my life. I didn't go to college. I'm a nothing." I felt tears floating on my lower eyelids and I turned away from Lydia and moved back towards the guest room door as if I'd heard Ani call me.

"That's not so. Anyone can see that you're special, Lavender. Just look at you. You have your own special style, and Chance tells me you are a very good singer and guitar player. From what I can see you are a wonderful mother, and that's not easy to do at any point in life let alone at your age. You could have done the easy thing and never had that beautiful little girl in there. But you were brave and you did the right thing."

Lydia was standing with her hands on her hips, gazing at me as if she really meant all the things she just said to me. "I believe there is a place for everyone in this world," she continued. "God wouldn't have made all of us if that weren't so." Lydia picked up her dust cloth and continued her housework.

I went to her side. "No one has ever said anything like that to me before."

"Well, it's about time someone did," she answered without missing a speck of dust on the coffee table. "You also put up with my Chance. I don't know why you do sometimes. Chip and I think he drinks too much. That's not the way we raised him, you know. I don't know where he got the idea that you have to have alcohol to have a good time. He sure didn't learn that from us." Lydia looked up at me as if she expected an answer to that puzzle. I was certain Chip and Lydia didn't know the half of it as far as Chance's drinking was concerned. I didn't think it was my place to inform them either.

"Yeah," I said, "he likes to go out with his friends two or three nights a week."

"He does, does he? And he leaves you and your little one home alone? I thought that might change once he was in his own place and had you and Anais," She put her cleaning supplies down and sat next to me.

"We're okay, Lydia. Chance has been generous to take care of us."

"I'm sure Chance is getting plenty out of this situation too." She squeezed me around the shoulder. "I'll make some tea and get some cookies for when the baby gets up."

"Thanks." I watched Lydia move into the kitchen and I realized she wasn't as oblivious as I'd thought she was.

~~~~~~

I could hear Chance coming down the apartment hallway. It was almost midnight and I got out of my rocking chair and stood by the little alcove where Anais was sleeping. When he opened the door I said, "Please don't wake her again."

"Yeah, okay. It's my apartment you know." He threw his jacket on the back of a chair.

"I know it is. You remind me of that everyday. But if she wakes up we won't have any time alone, right?" I walked over to him and unbuttoned his top three shirt buttons. I put my hands inside, caressing his chest. Putting my lips on his skin I smelled a flowery fragrance.

"Why do you smell like perfume?"

"What? I don't."

"Yes, you do!" I pushed away and put my hands over my mouth to remind me that Anais was asleep nearby.

"You're crazy! Oh, yeah, I stopped at my mom and dad's. You know my mom always has to hug me before I leave. Now come back here." He took my hands and placed them back on his bare chest. I looked straight into his eyes as my fingers automatically began to move through his blond chest hair. I could easily find out if he'd stopped at his parent's house, but I already knew I wouldn't even try.

"Ooh, that feels good. Anywhere else you want to do that?" Chance pulled his zipper down and then pushed me down on the couch.

"Not here. Let's go in the bedroom."

"Aw, that's the only place you wanna do it. Why not take a risk?"

"Ani will wake up," I said pushing him off of me.

"So, she's gotta learn sometime." He grabbed me roughly and kissed his way up my neck to my earlobes.

"I don't think three years old is the time . . . Chance, stop." But he didn't stop. He pulled at my shirt until two buttons popped off. His hand went under my skirt and yanked my panties aside. Silent tears started falling down my face. I was silent. Any protest would wake up my little girl. I whispered *stop, stop*, but he was on me, pushing himself inside me. "Please, please don't Chance, you're hurting me," I said into his ear.

"Stop!" I said louder than I'd wanted to. I pushed at his shoulders with my small hands, but it didn't make any difference. I closed my eyes and slowly opened them, hoping it was a bad dream. I had never felt this scared with a man.

I thought about pushing him off, but I knew I wasn't strong enough, and I feared his reaction. I strained to see across the room in the dark to where Anais slept while he did what he wanted. Chance's orgasms were usually loud, raucous and uninhibited, but he was drunk enough to barely make it that far. He collapsed on me. We stayed unmoving on the couch entangled in each other. Tears slid from my eyes into my ears and down my neck.

"How could you do that to me?" I whispered, but he was already asleep. I pushed him aside and went over to check on Ani. She was still sleeping. I pulled the rocking chair next to her and stayed there all night.

At the first light of day I awoke with my cheek indented with the scrollwork from the back of the chair. Chance was on the couch, his pants around his knees and his mouth open and reeking of beer and ashes.

I picked my daughter up and carried her into the bedroom. She roused briefly but it was still dawn and she fell back to sleep. I sat on the side of the bed watching her until I heard Chance get up and go to the bathroom. He looked in the bedroom and said, "Hey, baby" on his way back to the couch. He didn't remember the night before, but I did.

Later that morning all three of us were eating breakfast together. Anais chattered away happily about the creatures in her cereal bowl and Chance heartily ate the scrambled eggs and toast I put on his plate.

"Wow, I'm really hungry this morning." He smiled at me. "Today is my day off. What do you girls want to do today?" Ani immediately started bouncing up and down in her chair saying, "Park, park, park, playground!"

"The playground it is, little one. Is that okay with you, Mom?" Chance looked at me with the grin I fell in love with. I was certain that he had blacked out the night before, something that was happening more frequently. A heavy, sickening feeling welled in my gut when I thought about what he had done to me the night before, but today we were in love again. Today would be different.

"That sounds great. Just give us a few minutes to get ready." I got up to clear the table. I kissed Chance on the cheek and whispered, "Thank you."

"I'll pack the cooler." He opened the refrigerator and before the smile could fade from my lips he was pulling beer bottles out the refrigerator and setting them on the counter. I turned away and lifted Anais off the chair and wiped off her milky mouth. "Mommy, at the playground, will you go down the big slide with me?"

"Sure honey. We'll have fun today." I glanced over at Chance loading up his fun for the day. Since he was in a good mood I decided to ask if I could call Johnny.

"Chance, would it be alright if I made a quick long distance call?"

"Who to?"

"I really need to talk to my brother. I don't think my parents will be home this time of day and I wrote and told him I would try to call. Please? It won't be a long call, I promise."

"Sure, okay. But keep it short. And don't get all teary and crap when you hang up, okay?"

"Okay, I promise." I didn't want Johnny to hear Anais in the background so I plopped her in front of the television, something I really hated doing, but I knew she'd be quiet for a while and she wouldn't bother Chance. I wanted him to stay in a good mood for as long as possible.

"Johnny, is that you? Yeah, it's Chrissie. God, you sound so grown-up."

"Yeah, it's me. Mom and Dad are out at the store like you thought. What's up, Chris?"

"I really miss you, you know."

"Well, maybe you shouldn't have left home. It really sucks around here, since I'm the only one Mom has to boss around."

"I'm sorry about that. I wish I could tell you why I had to leave . . ."

"Why don't you then? What's the big secret? I know you hate Mom and Dad, but they *are* your parents. They raised you and then you just take off? I mean, sometimes they're a bitch, but they're still your parents, Chrissie."

"I … I know, it's just that . . . "

"You think you had it rougher than everyone else? You think other kids don't hate their parents sometimes? Maybe you should have appreciated what you had."

"John, you sound like Mom and Dad. I thought you'd be the only person that could understand, at least a little. I know our experiences weren't the same but . . ."

"No, they really weren't. Now that I'm older and I've thought about this, I just don't get it. I'm trying to be the child they wanted. I'm here trying to make up for one of their kids leaving. It's not easy. They're hard to make happy."

"That's exactly it, I could *never* make them happy. I never did anything right. It was like I was some kind of alien in that house, like I never belonged there in the first place!"

"I don't really know what that means, but I gotta go. I think their car is coming down the street now. I'll talk to you later, okay?"

"Okay, John, I really miss you and love you . . ."

"Yeah, later."

The silence of the phone in my hand was overwhelming. I had expected understanding and a kinship with my brother, but now I knew he was one of them. He sounded like them. He defended them. I was really alone.

Cole

"When we get to Aunt Judy's house we're going to act like we're just college friends, right?" I rubbed Nick's thigh in the subway seat next to me.

"Yeah, sure. But you know this goes against my principals. You're the wimpiest man I've ever been with. When are you going to come out to your family?" Nick asked. He looked across the aisle at a gorgeous young man reading an art book.

"My formerly unbiased parents are having enough trouble with our relationship. Somehow the reality of who their son is never sank in until they actually saw me with you. I believe I overestimated their level of tolerance. Either that or they were just kidding themselves. I can't bring myself to push it any further right now. You understand, don't you?" I tapped him on the shoulder to try to bring his gaze back to me. "I'd do it for you."

"Whatever." He waved a golden hand decorated with the ring I had given him for Christmas. "What do I get out of this situation, dear?"

Without looking at my handsome brown boyfriend I said, "Well, I guess you get to have me continue to support your lazy ass. Not such a bad deal for you, right Nick?" The dispassionate look in his eyes told me that we both already knew the last scene in this play.

He huffed and turned away from me. Our bodies toggled back and forth to the erratic movement of the subway. When our shoulders touched lightly we both made the effort to adjust ourselves in the sticky yellow seats so that it wouldn't happen again. Like magnets repelling.

Since we barely spoke at Aunt Judy's barbeque, it wasn't difficult to act like we were nothing but college acquaintances. As soon as we arrived I told my family that Nick had come for a visit, but he wasn't feeling well. I don't know why I needed to make excuses for him, or if anyone was dull enough to believe me. My extended family didn't spend much time together when I was growing up, so it didn't really matter much to me what they thought. I was starting to wonder, however, what the hell *I* was thinking.

It was a lovely spring afternoon and most of my aunts, uncles and cousins were milling about the patio and lawn, chatting, glasses of wine and beer bottles attached to their hands. I noticed Nick helping himself to his third glass of chardonnay and discussing something rather intensely with my Uncle Gordon. I felt a little of my breakfast trying to come up. Most of the family avoided anything controversial like politics, religion, and most of all sexuality to Uncle Gordon, as he viewed himself as the mouthpiece of moral rectitude in the family. Many an event had ended with him shouting his biblical platitudes while someone was backing out of the driveway as fast as possible.

"You believe in Jesus, do you not?" Nick asked.

"Yes, sir, I do and because of that I know . . ." my uncle started.

"You know what? Exactly what did Jesus have to say on the subject of homosexuality?"

"I'm sure that He was against it," Gordon replied, his back straightening in readiness for a showdown.

"In fact, He said nothing on the subject. Nothing at all." Nick calmly took a sip of his wine, looking quite confident in his pronouncement.

"Young man, it is not natural for a man to be with a man. It says that in the Bible."

"It does? What verse is that?" Nick looked up at the people who were listening. "Does anyone have a Bible on hand?" He waved his arm out to the side of his body as if he were showcasing a prize on a game show.

"I'm not sure exactly where to find the verse, but I know it's in there," Uncle Gordon said gulping down some beer.

"Let's see, what else is in there? Did you know that it says in that same book of Leviticus that whoever curses his mother or father should be put to death? Or how about the verse that says if you touch a woman having her period you are unclean all day. Have you ever touched your wife when she was having her period? Did you ask all the women here if it was their time before you hugged them? What about where it says a man should not clip the hair at the sides of his head or the edges of his beard? You look nicely clipped and shaven to me."

"Nick, Nick, come on," I grabbed his elbow, but he pushed me off.

"Or how about when Jesus said love your neighbor as yourself, no conditions on that!" I was pulling on his arm now.

"Cole, your friend is no longer welcome at this party," Gordon looked me right in the eye.

"I'm sorry for the fuss Uncle Gordon, but I don't think it's your place to ask him to leave just because you don't agree with him - with us."

I managed to calm Nick down and get him seated in the house with some family members who hadn't heard the unpleasantness outside. My mother approached me and said, "It's one thing to have this lifestyle, but it's another to start flaunting it in our faces."

"Flaunting it? Is that what I do, Mom? By bringing someone I care about to a party? Is that what everyone else here is doing, flaunting their lifestyle at me?"

My mother gazed down at the grass for a moment and then vainly looked around for my father. "Cole, we just never knew it would come to this."

"To what? That I would actually live my life the way I was meant to? What did you expect me to do, Mom? Be alone forever, so no one would have to think about it?"

"Well, you spent so much time with Lavender and Anais, we thought . . ."

"Oh my God." I quietly walked away, found Nick and said my goodbyes to my family.

In addition to this revelation by my parents, Nick's excessive hubris and lack of employment were annoying me to the point of distraction. Besides the fact that we both named "Philadelphia" as our favorite movie, there was nothing else we agreed upon anymore, nor had in common. My life revolved around my students in the surprising swiftness of my first year teaching, as well as my concerns for Lavender and Anais living with Chance Slater.

~~~~~~

"Can't you see that he's a raging alcoholic, sweetie? Is that what you want Anais to see growing up? Chance is no good for you. For either of you." I said into the phone.

"But we have a home and a family now. That is good for Ani, don't you think? Lydia and Chip are so sweet to both of us. Lydia took us to church last Sunday and the people there were so welcoming to both of us. They didn't look down on me just because I am an unwed mother. Anais went to her first Sunday school class and she loved it. She needs to be around other children. How is she going to be prepared for kindergarten if she's not spending time with other children?"

"And you think going to Sunday school once a week will fulfill that need?"

"Ani said the cutest thing last night. We were saying bedtime prayers and she said, 'and God bless everyone in the whole why world.' I said 'Don't you mean the whole wide world?' And she said, 'No Mommy, I always wonder why God made the whole world, so it's the whole why world.' Isn't she smart, Cole?"

"Of course she's smart. I wonder where she got it from?" There was silence on the other end of the phone. "I'm sorry, I'm just worried about you two and I miss you so much. Does Ani still ask for me?"

"Yes, all the time. You know, Chance doesn't drink much here at home. It's mostly out with his buddies, and then Ani and I have time for stories and games and going for walks. We're doing well. Maybe you just don't want us to be doing well. Maybe you want a reason to break up with Nick so you can take care of us again. Is that it? I'm not the stupid little teenager you met at the hair salon. There are other people that care about me now. I will always remember everything you did for Ani and me, but right now I'm doing what I think is best for her."

"All right, I hear you. I just hope it's what is best for you too. And I am thinking of breaking up with Nick. I guess you figured that out too, smarty," I said, enjoying Lavender's newfound confidence.

"Yeah, I could see from the beginning that you and he had nothing in common, but you thought you were in love and, like, I know how that feels now."

"Put Anais on the phone, would you?"

"Sure. Cole wants to say goodnight to you."

"What do I say, Mommy?" I heard a little voice in the background. Every night when we were together I would say to Anais –I'll love you until – then add something like – until the moon is square. She'd been learning to say the same back to me.

"You think of something silly just like Cole does," I heard Lavender whispering.

"Hi Cole, where are you?" Anais said when she got on the phone.

"I'm at my own house, honey."

"You come here, okay?"

"I'll see you soon, baby. You go to bed for Mommy now. I'll love you until the sun is green."

"I love you until . . . my Pooh bear can talk!"

"Wow that's a good one, sweetie. Good night."

"Bye, Cole, you come here, okay?"

"Yes, soon, baby."

That night Nick got home from God knows where at one in the morning. I had waited up.

"What are you doing up? Are you my Daddy or something?" Nick walked right past me.

"I waited up to tell you that I think you should find another place to live."

He picked up a book and threw it across the room, then plopped down on a chair, folded his arms and refused to speak to me for several minutes.

"Nick," I said, "I think it's best, don't you? Besides, we both know you weren't out looking for a job at one in the morning."

"I'm sorry, Cole, really." He started to weep.

"It's too late for that. We don't want the same things."

We sat silently for at least fifteen minutes. I played with loose strings on the fringe of a throw pillow while Nick alternately sniffled and smoothed tissues on his lap.

"I hate to inform you, but you're never going to have the perfect little family you're looking for, Cole. Men like us don't get that – ever! I don't know why you even want it. There is not a place in these great United States that is ever going to look at you as a normal person, a family man. Oh, your teaching career is a good cover-up. At least you're not a fashion designer or a hair stylist anymore." He rose from the couch, grabbed the tissue box and started walking into the bedroom. "It's never gonna happen, honey."

"I guess that's for me to figure out, isn't it? Nick, wait." He stopped but did not face me. "You can have all the time you need to find a place to live. I'm not kicking you out."

"Don't worry, dear. I already have a place to go. That's where I was tonight."

Lavender

No one wants to hire you when you have no skills or education. I couldn't go to college as I planned, but I could still learn. Chance had a surprising amount of books in his apartment. Lydia told me what a bookworm he was when he was little, and apparently he still was. We'd actually had some good conversations about books we'd read in high school.

When Anais was napping I'd educate myself. If I could read about the world maybe I could decide what my place in it could be. So I started tackling all the books in the apartment. I applied for a library card. The library was quite a hike, but still within walking distance if I put Anais in the wagon that Lydia found at a garage sale.

~~~~~

The sidewalk was polka-dotted with sunlight and scent of sycamores filled my head. I breathed in the fresh morning air and smiled as I pulled Ani along the suburban streets.

"Squirrel! Bird!" Anais exclaimed at every movement along the way.

I felt like a mom, like a stay-at-home mom, like all the moms I knew growing up. I liked the feeling, but it was illegitimate. I hadn't earned it. I had no real home, no husband, no father for Anais. I had no rights in the place I lived, or any of the places I'd lived.

Nearby a squirrel missed a branch and plopped to the ground near the sidewalk. Anais reached out and fell out of the wagon. Unhurt, she began to run towards the squirrel into someone's yard.

"Ani, get back here! No!" I shouted. I left the wagon on the sidewalk and ran, but I couldn't see her. She'd run around the corner of a house and disappeared.

"Ani! Anais! Come back to me!" I couldn't hear her – or anything. My heart lurched out of my chest and into my throat. My voice seemed to have no volume or strength. Here I was on a lovely side street on a summer day fearing for my daughter's life. It didn't make any sense, it couldn't be happening. Anais's impulsiveness and exuberance were too much for me. I was a failure at being her mother. Why did God give her to me? I stopped running and stood still to listen, trying to hear anything but chirping birds above me.

"Come here, kitty." I heard a little voice in the distance.

"Anais? Where are you?"

"Here, Mommy. I found a kitty." She was sitting on someone's front porch petting a white cat.

"Oh God, Ani. What am I going to do with you? You can't run away from mommy like that. You can't go into people's yards. Do you hear me?"

"I can hear you, Mommy." I roughly picked her up and hurried back to the waiting wagon.

"I just want to spank you, but I don't want to get arrested," I mumbled to myself. Angry tears fell from my eyes.

"Why are you crying, Mommy?

"Because you're a bad girl, Ani." She didn't say anything else and I felt horrible for what I'd said. I put her in the wagon and yanked it the rest of the way to the library. By the time we got there I'd walked out my frustration and decided to consult Lydia on how to discipline my child.

At the library I explained how we could borrow the books and bring them back when we were finished. Anais asked if we could bring them all home. She sat on the floor and gently pulled one book off the shelf. She reverently opened it and studied each picture. I expected her attention for one book to last about ten seconds, but I was wrong. She carefully previewed each page and then looked up at me and said, "Read it Mommy."

We sat cuddled on a beanbag chair most of the afternoon as she brought one book after another until I told her my voice was wearing out and she could pick some to take home. As she made her selections I browsed through the picture books myself. I picked up a book called *Peter Spier's Rain* and an inexplicable sense of warmth rushed through me. It took me a moment and then, with complete clarity, I remembered the illustrations of the boy and girl in their colorful raincoats and boots finding all sorts of ways to have fun on a rainy day. There is no text in the book, just pictures of all their adventures in the wet neighborhood, stomping through puddles, seeing the raindrops settled on a spider's web, watching the ducks splash in a pond, racing home, their umbrella turned inside out, to the warmth of a bath. And there is the mother smiling as she serves hot chocolate and cookies.

I thought it must have been my mom who sat and looked at this book over and over again, but then with equal clarity I knew it was my grandma. My Grandma Fiona, with her bleached blond hair in pin curls, her pink lipstick, her colorful Bermuda shorts. I could feel myself sitting on her soft lap, I could hear her talk me through every illustration, until the end when the brother and sister are tucked into their beds for the night, and then the last page, the sun shining on the soggy backyard full of toys and play equipment. It wasn't my mom. It was Grandma. My own mother wouldn't let me stomp through a puddle let alone look at pictures about it. I realized at that moment that it was my grandma that taught me how to be a mom to Anais, and I knew that somehow I had to thank her before it was too late.

That same night Anais brought one of her books over to Chance and asked him to read it to her. He said, "Maybe later, I'm busy."

Anais said, "You're not busy, you're just drinking your bottle."

"Hey, Lav, would you get your kid off my back?"

"Come here, Ani, Mommy will read it to you right after I finish the dishes."

"Why won't Chance read it to me, doesn't he know how to read like you?"

"Sure he does, he's a grown-up, honey. He's just busy right now."

"No, he's not."

"You girls want to go out for some ice cream? I need to get some smokes. Let's go."

"I don't know. It's getting kind of late."

"Late for what? It's only 8:00."

"It's Anais's bedtime."

"Oh yeah, the world revolves around her bedtime. Come on." Chance looked at me as he grabbed his car keys. I looked at the car keys. "I've only had a couple, if that's what you're worried about. I'm not stupid you know."

"No, I know that, it's just late is all."

"Oh, shit."

"Don't get mad, we'll come. Ani, get your pink sweater."

I belted Anais in the back seat. She had her pink sunglasses on.

"You don't need your sunglasses at night, honey."

"I know, Mommy, but they make the world look pretty."

Chance pulled out of the parking space without looking and almost hit a car going by.

"Watch out, will ya?" He yelled out the window.

"Chance do you want me to drive?"

"There you go again. Don't you trust me? I'm not gonna do anything dangerous."

"I know but . . ." He put his hand gently on my leg and smiled at me. I smiled back and glanced in the back seat at my daughter holding one of her library books in her little hands, her pink sunglasses touching the tip of her nose.

It was a humid, windless summer evening and we all enjoyed the cooling effects of the ice cream cones. I tried to get Chance engaged in a conversation about a book I was reading, but he lost interest quickly.

"You know," he blew smoke out of his nose, "I used to be into a lot of stuff. I read a lot about American history. I even thought about being a history teacher once, but I didn't want to teach a bunch of idiots like me in high school."

"Really. I know what you mean. If I ever became a teacher it would have to be preschoolers or something. I never thought I'd like being with little kids, but I've been helping your mom with her Sunday school class and it's really been fun."

"Yeah, my mom loves kids, that's for sure. Too bad she only had me. Actually I was a pretty good little guy until high school, and then I kind of got mixed up with some of the wrong people, you know?"

"Me too. I was mostly my own worst enemy, trying to be a punk in an all preppy high school. I tried to fit in sometimes, but after awhile it was just too late. Everyone knew I was a freak."

"And look at you now, the little mommy." He kissed me on the cheek.

"I guess that's all I am now – a mommy. Sometimes I really miss the Joeygirls and the singing and the rush of being in Manhattan."

"We should go over there more, Lav. You know my mom will baby-sit."

"I know, but she does so much for me, for us, already. Besides, it will only make me miss it more."

"Yeah, she's pretty cool. Too bad I let her down. They had high hopes for me, but somehow all the stuff I thought I was good at I kind of lost interest in. I just wanted to be out at the bars at night, and I was doing a lot of drugs for awhile, but I quit that shit."

"Yeah, that stuff can kill you. I'm glad we both found that out anyway." I looked over at him. His crooked half-smile, the cigarette in his hand, the breeze tousling his sun-streaked hair. I had a little disposable camera in my purse. I pulled it out and took his picture. After the flash went off he looked over and me and said, "I'm pretty handsome, huh?"

After we finished our ice cream cones Chance went into the convenience store next door to get his cigarettes and came out with a six-pack as well.

"Let's go girls. It's a good night for a ride through the park. Too hot in the apartment, right?"

I buckled Anais in and heard the crack of a can opening. I put on my seat belt but Chance did not. The night breeze was soothing and soon Anais was asleep in the back seat.

"I hope she doesn't just get a nap in and then be wide awake when I take her out of the car," I said.

"I hope not either. I need some alone time with my girl tonight," Chance looked over at me with his dimpled grin. His face was a golden tan in contrast to his blond hair. His hand moved between my legs and he leaned over for a kiss. As he leaned he brought the steering wheel with him and the car swerved off the road toward a ditch. Chance slid back towards his seat in slow motion and pressed on the brakes, but his reactions were too slow. We struck a tree and Chance and I violently fell forward. The seat belt crushed my rib cage and my forehead struck the dashboard. Chance made a horrible guttural noise. I pushed off the dashboard towards the back seat. Anais was hanging forward from her waist. The shoulder belt was off to the side and the seat belt across her abdomen had sucked the air out of her. She looked at me with eyes and mouth wide open, trying to find her breath.

The car's motor revved against the tree and I screamed, "Chance, shut off the car, we have to get out!"

Chance did not respond. His body slumped part way across the front seat. I got out of the car to open the back door, but it wouldn't open. I crawled back into the front seat, shoved Chance into an upright position and reached between the front seats to Anais. She suddenly inhaled a deep breath and started crying. I yanked her over the seat and we tumbled out of the passenger door onto the ground. I moved a few yards away and laid her down on the grass.

"Mommy, what happened?" She coughed and choked on her tears and mucus.

"We were in a car accident. Ani, are you all right? Mommy's here." She grabbed onto my arm and pulled me down to her. "It's okay, baby. We're okay. Can you wait here while I get Chance?" She nodded. "Don't move, promise?"

I ran around to the driver's door and reached in to shut the car off. I pulled on Chance's shoulder to rouse him. He didn't respond so I yelled into his ear, "Chance, wake up!" I opened the door and tried to lower him to the ground. His legs were still in the car as I tried to drag his body out. He was heavy and lifeless. My body felt small and weak and incapable. I kept pulling and looking over the roof of the car at Anais. She was sitting up, still crying, watching me struggle with Chance's body. A car stopped along the empty parkway. A man and woman got out. The man helped me pull Chance to the grass. He began to make moaning sounds.

"Geesh, how much did this guy have to drink?" the stranger said, and then I could smell it too. Chance started coughing. The man and woman were kneeling down asking him questions so I ran back to Ani and I found the strength to scoop her up in my arms.

The strangers called 911. Chance gained consciousness, and an ambulance arrived within minutes and took us to the hospital. I asked if we could stay together, and we were immediately placed in an examination room. Chance sat on the table with his head in his hands and would only say that he had a headache. I sat in the chair holding Anais on my lap. I felt all right except for a slight headache and a sore rib cage. After we were checked out the doctors told us that Chance had suffered a concussion and would need to stay for a while, but that Anais and I were free to go. I called Lydia. While waiting for her to pick us up a policeman arrived to charge Chance with a DUI. I didn't know it was his second time.

In New Jersey you receive a jail sentence for a second offense. Chance lost his license for two years, had various fines and was required to attend alcohol awareness classes. I wasn't able to find the courage to visit him in the jail until his third day.

"I'm sorry I didn't come sooner. I just didn't want to see you in a place like this I guess."

"I didn't want you to see me here, either. I'm really sorry. Is Anais doing okay?"

"Yes, she's pretty much stopped talking about it now. But she did ask me about you today. I told her you were still at the hospital getting better."

"Thanks for telling her that. Maybe at least one person won't hate me forever," he said with his head bowed, picking at a crack on the yellowing laminate counter between us.

"No one hates you. We just want you to get better. You're sick, Chance. You need help. You're so smart and you're wasting your life. I can't change my life right now, but you can." I let go of his hands and put mine in my lap.

"The other day Ani and I were watching *The Wizard of Oz*. You know the part when the tornado comes and Dorothy looks out the window and sees everything she knows flying through the air past her? That's how I feel about my life. Everything I loved and knew I just watched fly past my eyes and disappear. But you, you still have great parents and they really love you. They'll help you through this."

"And you? Are you going to be there too?"

"I don't know. I want to, but I have to protect my daughter, at least I have to do that, you know? I *have* to be successful with her. She's all that I have."

"Do you ever think about going back to your family? They probably still love you too," Chance said in almost a whisper.

"I'm still so afraid - afraid of being rejected again. Afraid of the effect they'd have on Anais. It's been so long. I don't know anything about them anymore. I know my grandmother would welcome me back, but I don't want to put her in the middle like that."

Chance looked up at me and there were tears in his eyes, "When I get out of here in a couple weeks, I hope you'll still be there. But if you're not, I understand. At this point a relationship with me gets tedious and difficult. It drags other people down. I know. It's happened before. You're a really good person, Lavender. I don't want to drag you down with me. I don't want to hurt you or your little girl. I'm sorry for how shitty I've been to both of you."

My own tears were surfacing, but I couldn't argue with him because he was right. He'd get drunk, do something rotten, apologize profusely and promise never to do it again. But within days he would. He'd promise to go to AA, but never actually got there. He'd cry and I would make love to him to make him stop. On that day, something inside me told me he wasn't ready to change, even after hearing his self-pitying speech. He wasn't in love with me. He was in love with alcohol. I feared for Chance's life, but I couldn't save it. I was watching him disappear.

"I have to go, Chance. I'll try to stop back if I can."

"Lavender, wait. Um, you know all those nights I was out with the guys?"

"Yes, all the nights I waited up for you, worrying if you were all right? All the nights you woke Ani up and I had to try to get her back to sleep?" I stood up to leave.

"Yeah, I wasn't always with the guys."

"I know Chance. I always knew. I was a fool to keep hoping that it would change. I'm so afraid of being alone again that I kept trying to convince myself you really cared about me."

As I left the jail I felt like papier-mache, like I could just break off into tiny fragments and disintegrate. I wanted to run to Lydia, but Lydia was Chance's mother, not mine.

1999

Cole

My girls moved in to my new apartment in New Jersey. There was a lot of paraphernalia that came with a little girl and her mother. Toys, books and the rocking chair took up all the extra space in my tiny living room, but the two of them also filled up the empty space inside of me. Chip and Lydia Slater helped them move. Lavender crumbled into Lydia's arms crying as they left that day.

"You're doing the right thing, honey. You have to do what is best for you and your girl. I know this young man here will take good care of you, won't you Cole?"

Lavender looked over at me, "He always has." Turning back to Lydia she said, "What's going to happen to Chance?"

"We're going to make sure he gets the help he needs," Chip said. "At least he seems to know he needs help this time. I don't think he'll ever forgive himself for putting you two in danger like that. We never did believe he was prepared to have a ready-made family. He needs to grow up some."

"We are going to miss you so much." Lavender wiped tears off of her chin.

"We're only a half hour away! How about if I come and take you and Anais to lunch next week after you're settled here?"

"Yes, yes!" Anais shouted, jumping up and down.

"It's all settled then, we'll see you next week. Bye now, honey. You take care. We love you both." Lydia patted Lavender's shoulder, gave Ani a hug and turned to leave.

Lavender stood by the window watching their car pull out of the parking lot. Anais walked over and put her arms around Lavender's waist. "It's okay, Mommy, Cole will take good care of us."

"I know. We always need someone to take care of us, don't we?" Lavender stared out the window with tears falling off her face. "That's it, Cole," she said turning to me. "I need to call home."

I watched her hand shake as she dialed the number.

"Johnny, it's Chrissie," she whispered into the phone as if someone on the other side would hear her.

"Is that Mom? Who's yelling in the background? Oh, God, I'm sorry if I'm causing you a problem again . . . Johnny, are you there?" She stood unmoving for a moment.

"He hung up on me! I heard my mom yelling in the background and he must have put his hand over the receiver to answer her – and then he hung up!"

"He probably didn't know what else to do, honey. Just let it go for now."

Lavender's nose was turning red and she pulled a tissue from her pocket and turned away from me.

"No one cares, Cole. No one in my family cares about me, or where I am, of if I'm even alive."

"What about your grandmother?" It was the only thing I could think to say that might comfort her. "Why don't you give her a call?"

"Should I? Okay."

"Grandma, it's me, Chrissie. Yes, Chrissie" She yelled into the phone.

"Yes, really!" Lavender's face started to redden again and she turned away from me.

"I know, Grandma, I'm so sorry. I live in New Jersey now." I handed her another tissue and left the room so she could speak freely. I don't know how much information she conveyed to her grandmother or whether it was understood. She didn't know what to make of it and just cried herself to sleep on the couch that night.

~~~~~~

I live in the same school district that I work in. It's a good school system so I felt confident enrolling Anais in kindergarten there. Anais loved being with the other children, something that was sorely lacking in her first five years. Lavender had done the best she could, but the two of them had been overly isolated and hooked to each other like two attached train cars going down the same track of life together. Anais was in an all-day kindergarten, which gave Lavender the chance to start looking for some income without needing a babysitter. She owed almost all the Joeygirls money as well as loans she wanted to pay back to the Slaters.

The day of her first interview for a sales position at the Gap, she got out of bed and fell on the floor. I heard the thump from the kitchen and knocked on the door.

"Are you okay?" I pushed the door slightly ajar and saw her sitting on the floor rubbing her leg.

"I guess so. I went to get out of bed and my left leg collapsed. It's kind of numb. That's weird. I wonder if it's some kind of after-effect of the accident?"

"Probably so. I can't think what else it could be. Did you hurt yourself?"

"No, I'm okay now." She stood up, leaning on the edge of the bed. Anais was still fast asleep in the cot on the other side of the room. "I need to get her up and get ready for my interview. Any coffee?"

"Coming right up," I said.

Lavender's first job interview did not go well. She's smart and well read, but her only real experience is being a punk rock singer and being a mom. She went to the Gap in her typical punkish outfit, hoping they would think her stylish. She still wears these clunky platform shoes called Creepers that apparently never wear out year after year. She had on a striped mini-skirt, black tights and a red, rather nice T-shirt. I'd just helped her dye her hair a little brighter red than her natural color with just a few tiny streaks of black winding around the curls like the stripes in a candy cane. She had a few earrings in her left ear and had taken out the pierced eyebrow a while back. She looked presentable, a little funky. No tattoos showing. But when the interview bombed she decided it was because of the way she looked, and she spent the evening pouting about being rejected again.

"Maybe I should look like THIS!" She shoved a fashion magazine at me. The cover photo was of the latest hot starlet, straight long blond hair in a sequined cocktail dress.

"Or how about this!" She flipped a few more pages and pointed to a six-foot tall woman in a black and white fur coat, carrying a designer bag.

"She looks like a skunk," I commented.

"Or how about this one!" Another eveningwear photo. Then a gray wool suited model.

"Lav, I don't think wearing a designer gown to the Gap would've improved your employment opportunities."

"Yes, but what's wrong with me? The way I am. Right now. Why do I have to be judged everywhere I go?"

"Maybe it's not your style. Maybe they think you're too short to reach the cash register."

"Very funny." The magazine came flapping and flying at me from across the room and landed in my lap.

Lavender

I finally got a job at a most unlikely place, a plant nursery.
It was right down the road, and having no car, I could walk
there. I went in and the owner Lizzie, was this older hippie-
type woman wearing a long denim skirt and Birkenstocks.
Her long hair, gray, and wildly frizzy. She wore no makeup
on her open friendly face. She even had round frameless
glasses. I told her I didn't know much about plants but I
was a hard worker and willing to learn. She looked me
over, smiled, and said it would be very cool to have
someone named Lavender working there. She asked me
when I could start. Immediately.

The greenhouse and the attached storefront smelled
of wet soil and flowery fragrances. The place looked
disorganized with piles of pots in every color and size
leaned against all the walls. Stacks of potting soil, mulch
and plant food sat haphazardly on shelves. The floor
littered with plant leaves and petals. Lizzy frantically
moved about creating a floral centerpiece. As she squatted
to retrieve a pot her skirt lifted and I could see her
unshaven legs. I felt a sort of kinship with her.

I began with the challenging job of watering all the
plants in the greenhouse for six bucks an hour. Lizzy said I
could leave whenever I was finished and to come back the
next day wearing sunscreen or a hat because she had
something to show me. I still had my old purple felt hat
and I had a goofy derby hat I used to wear to shows, but
those didn't seem like they'd be helpful in the sun.

The next day I slathered on the sunscreen. I hate
the millions of freckles on my arms and face that darken in
the sun every summer anyway. I burn like toast set on high
too. Lizzy greeted me with a sudden hug and said, "Let's
take a walk." We walked past the greenhouse and out into a
field that I was surprised to see since it wasn't visible from

the road. White daisies, brown-eyed Susans and a whole lot of other colorful flowers decorated the rows of other plants that I did not know the names of. Towards the back of the property she stopped.

"Well, here it is," she announced. I stood there mutely looking at some greenish gray plants with slender purple stalks and I smelled something amazing.

"Here is what? Sorry, I'm clueless."

"I thought so. It's lavender! Don't you even know what you're named after?"

"Actually I named myself that after my hair color," I said weakly.

"Your hair color. Okay. That's cool. I guess that was a while back, huh?"

"Yeah, but I still like my name."

"Well, it's my favorite plant and my specialty here at the nursery, so I'm going to teach you all about lavender, Lavender, how's that?"

"That makes sense." I inhaled the aroma. "Is that what I'm smelling?"

"Sure is. Rub your hands over the leaves and then smell."

I did and it was delicious. "I can't believe I've never seen or smelled lavender before. It was just a color to me."

"I sell most of it to a lady down the road who turns it into potpourri and soap and lotion and all sort of things." She bent down to pull off a branch to sniff.

"Wow. I had no idea."

For the next few weeks Lizzy patiently and lovingly guided me through the world of flowers, plants, shrubbery and small trees. She spent hours explaining things to me. I began to love the peacefulness of the fields and the renewing aromas that filled the air everyday. And I wondered why God was visiting me once again, this time in the form of a hippie named Lizzy.

I was supposed to be sweeping the storeroom floor but I stopped and took the photo of Chance out of my wallet. It was the picture I took of him right before the accident. It perfectly caught the charm of his smile and a moment of the spontaneous nature I loved so much about him.

"Who's that?" Lizzy came up behind me.

"Oh, sorry." I grabbed the broom.

"Relax! You're allowed to take a break once in a while. Especially to look at that hot little number. Who is he?"

"That's Chance. My former boyfriend. He could be a real jerk and he hurt me, but I still miss him, you know?"

"Been there, done that, honey. Men can be pissers. I married one that was just as big an idiot as my father. I've know more women who look for their daddy, good or bad."

"Chance is nothing like my father. My dad, well, he's kind of a pussy. My mom was the boss when I was growing up."

"Where're you from?"

"Ohio. A suburb of Cleveland. I left home because I was pregnant and I didn't think my parents could handle it. I had to make my own decision for the first time in my life. I couldn't let them dictate that one for me."

"God, you've been on your own all this time? Do you ever visit?"

"No, they've never looked for me and I've never tried to be found. It's a sad story – for me and my daughter. She's like a little vagabond, just going wherever I go with no family, no roots or stability."

"I think you're amazing, sweetheart."

"What's so amazing about running away from home and giving my daughter this kind of crazy life?"

"It's amazing that you've done it all on your own. You have made a ton of good decisions for her, you just don't realize it yet. It's a mother's instinct. Kids can see that and feel that. Even getting away from this gorgeous hunk of man. You did the right thing. I'm sure you did, and your little girl gave you the courage to do it. Some women just stay and let themselves be abused and miserable. You're moving forward."

"Well, I guess so. I'm just sweeping floors at the moment. No offense. I appreciate the job."

"None taken, honey. Someday you'll see what all this was for."

"Okay, if you say so, Lizzy." I went back to sweeping.

"You're on your desire path, that's all."

"My desire path?" I looked up from the dustpan of leaves and dirt I'd collected.

"You've taken your own path to get where you are now and you will continue until you find your peace, honey. We all have to do that in our own ways. A desire path is a landscape term for a path that's worn off the planned sidewalks by people walking their own way. That's all you've done here. It's okay, really. We're not all the same in this life. We each have to find our own way."

"My desire path. Thanks, Lizzie. I never thought of it that way." I felt myself smiling down at my dustpan of debris, remembering walking home from the Joeygirl's show through Tompkins Square Park with Cole and Anais. I had been cutting through the park on a desire path all that time. I just hadn't known it.

I missed Chance and the relationship with a man. To me, the two greatest experiences in life are being someone's mother and being someone's lover and I have experienced both. Neither have been ideal situations, yet, I have grown from them. Anais surprises me with joy everyday. The more joy and wonder she brings me, the less I understand my own mother. How could she have rejected everything about her own child? How could her heart have been so rigid that she could not enjoy the unique treasures of my childhood? Why, I still ask myself, did she always want me to be someone I was not?

People like to say that children are resilient, but they are not. How many children are damaged by one incident, one careless comment by an adult in their world? The terrible weight of rejection has changed who I am and will always be with me. Every day I verge on overindulging Ani with assurances that she is wonderful and special and unique. I'm so afraid she will feel like a misfit because of the unconventional life I have provided for her.

My daughter has her share of challenges with no father, and a mother only 18 years older than she. The pediatrician diagnosed her with attention-deficit-hyperactivity-disorder and I know she will deal with that her whole life. She has no grandparents or cousins to make memories with, no place to really call home. I tried to make up for all of that with Chance and especially with Lydia and Chip, but they didn't belong to me and I knew it the whole time that we were together. There's a difference between facing a challenge head on and pretending that it is something it never will be. I know that now about Chance and me.

When I look at Ani I search for myself in her. Is there something in her eyes that reflects mine? A gesture, the tone of her voice, something she laughs at? Did my mother ever see herself in me? Was it something she despised? How can you blame a child for that? Since the moment of her birth my daughter and I have been spliced together like one being. She is the only perfect thing I will ever do, and I sensed that the first time I saw her little face in the curve of my arm.

I said to Shannon that February night, "I have an urge to create." Shannon took me to the hospital and tried to prepare me for what was coming. I remember her saying,

"Lav, you probably screamed when something went there -- feel free to scream while something's coming ou.. And I did. I had no idea it would hurt that much and I was scared shitless. My body felt completely ravaged by the pain and pushing. Anais was face-up, which made things more difficult. Now I realize that Anais will never do anything in a typical fashion and that began at her birth.

Then there was that perfect moment when earth connected to heaven and when it detached -- she was mine. The fear vanished and love was all I felt that day. Her tears became my tears, her blood, my blood and all the years since are only marked by her presence in my world. Did Roberta ever feel that way about me?

Now I wish for a frozen moment, a static day, so that she will never grow up. I want to keep her as she is today at age five, and at the same time I want her to experience everything I never have, all of life, the good and bad, every adventure waiting for her. The only constancy in my life has been her steady breathing at night nearby. But I know, even now, that I will not hear that forever. She will grow beyond me - she will be more than me.

Cole

Lavender at the lavender farm. It's beautiful, really. I love my girls, but they can be a handful sometimes. September came and Anais was off to kindergarten and Lavender was off wallowing in the lavender fields, and the entire world was at peace until one sticky, sunny fall day. During second period sophomore Literature class there was a call into my classroom. We were in the middle of an excruciating discussion of Romeo and Juliet and I gladly asked the class to read the next scene silently and try to glean something – anything - out of it. I took the call and it was Lizzy.

"Cole? I'm a little concerned about Lavender. She was working out in the field and she fainted. I wouldn't have even known it if I hadn't called out to see if she wanted a glass of iced tea. It is awfully humid out there, and she stayed out in the sun longer than she should have. But now she wants to walk home and I'm not sure that's such a good idea. What do you think? I mean, no one is there to see that she gets there safely and I can't leave the storefront right now."

"Yes, yes, Lizzy. I agree. I'll tell you what. I have a free period in about twenty minutes and then I'll come and pick her up. How's that?"

"That would be fine, Cole. Thanks."

When I arrived at Lizzy's, Lavender looked flushed and tired. She argued about me having to leave work, but I was already there so I took her arm and led her to the car. She pulled her arm away from my grasp and said, "What the hell are you doing? I can walk!" That took me aback some, but I figured she was just tired. I got her settled at home and just as I opened to door to leave, the phone rang. This time it was Mr. Marsh, the principal at Anais's school.

"Mr. May?"

"No this is Cole Carson. Can I help you?"

"This is Frank Marsh at the school. Is Mrs. May there?"

"Yes, Ms. May is here. Just a moment." I whispered, "It's the school." as I handed the phone to Lavender.

"Yes? Is Anais all right?" After a pause, "We'll be right there."

"What now?" I asked.

"We have to go get Ani. She was running around the room hitting kids and laughing and she wouldn't stop and when her teacher put her in time-out she ran out the door and out of the building! She's just out of control, Cole! What are we going to do?"

"First, I need to call my school and tell them I'll be back after lunch. I think one of my colleagues can take my next class and then I'll make it up to him later."

"I don't care about your frickin' class! Let's go!"

"Hey, calm down. I've got a life to lead here, too, you know."

"Don't you care about Anais? I thought you were going to be her father now!"

One of us had to be in a rational state of mind, so I decided to ignore all that and we left immediately. By the time we got to the school, Anais was sitting in the principal's office eating a cup of ice cream. I'm not sure about the logic in that consequence, but I guess they just wanted her to calm down.

"Hi, Mommy! Hi, Cole! I got ice cream!"

"Yes, we see that. Were you naughty today? Why did Cole and I have to come to get you?"

"I was just having fun with the kids, but Miss Kay said I was bad."

"Ani, you must listen to Miss Kay. You aren't bad, but you did a bad thing by running away. Do you understand?"

"Yes, Mommy. Sorry. Can I go back to my room now? I'll say sorry to Miss Kay."

Lavender looked up at Mr. Marsh and he nodded his head. "That's fine for now, but I think we need to set up a conference to discuss some concerns Miss Kay has about this young lady." That would be the first of many times we were to hear that statement.

Lavender

At the end of following school year I didn't argue when Mr. Marsh informed me that the Intervention Assistance Team recommended that Anais repeat first grade. It wasn't because she wasn't smart. It was that she hadn't paid attention to enough of the lessons to grasp all the concepts she needed to understand to be successful in second grade. She also seemed to be socially immature and was having trouble sharing and cooperating with other children. Her reading was above average and I worried that she would be bored with another year of the same reading material, but they assured me she would be challenged in a special reading group for above average readers.

It was the math concepts and writing skills that were behind. Anais was bright enough, however, to know what was going on and she was quite upset to learn that she would be in first grade again. But once the year started and she made some new friends she adjusted. Her impulsiveness and talkative nature continued to challenge even the most patient teachers, but they always started out conferences telling me how much they enjoyed her in the class – most of the time. The team urged me to seek medication for her, but I kept putting it off, saying I would check into it.

I regularly contacted my brother John and he had become a young man since I'd left. I regretted not knowing him during those years, but I still had hopes that we would reunite. Roberta could not stop John from calling me anymore. He was 18.

"There's something I've never told you. It's something big."

"What? You're married? You're getting married? What is it?"

"No, neither of those, unfortunately, I guess. It's just that. Well, I think I needed to get to know you again, as more of an adult. I'm really sorry I never told you before."

There was silence at John's end of the phone.

"It's not bad, or anything. It's just kind of – a big deal."

"What is it, Chrissie. Tell me."

"Well, I have a daughter. You're an uncle."

"You have a baby?"

"Not exactly a baby, no. She's six years old."

"Six? You have a six-year-old daughter? When? I mean how . . . ?

There was a long pause. "John, are you there?"

"Yes, I'm still here."

"I can't tell if you're happy or shocked or you think I'm crazy. I wish I could see your face."

"I'm definitely shocked. I don't really know what to say. I'm an uncle and Mom and Dad are. . . "

"Yeah, grandparents and they don't even know it."

"Oh my God."

"Yeah, I know. I think the longer time went on the more impossible it seemed to tell them, you know?"

"How could you not tell us?"

"You sound mad. Are you mad? I mean, I just . . . I just didn't think anyone would care after a while."

"Oh, I think everyone will care. What's her name? What's she like?"

"Her name is Anais, like the writer? Sometimes I call her Ani. I know it's kind of unusual but it suits her. She's really smart. She's a good reader and she's funny. . . She's got blond hair, little curly ringlets of blond hair."

"Where'd she get . . . oh, sorry."

"That's okay. I can't say I'm proud of this, but I'm not absolutely sure who her father is. I don't really care. She's mine. Sometimes she's been the only person in the world that loved me. Well, you know what I mean."

"So he, I mean, you were here?" John paused and I let him think it out.

"That's why I really left. Mom and Dad gave me this big lecture about premarital sex and unwed pregnancy and I was already pregnant. I was younger than you are now, Johnny. I didn't know what else to do." There was another long, difficult pause.

"Are you ever going to come back here? Because if you're not, I am going to find a way to get to New Jersey to meet my niece. I don't have a lot of mad money since Mom and Dad are expecting me to pay tuition for my first year in college. Then, if I meet their expectations, they said they would pay for the rest. Last year I sunk all my savings into an old beater of a car, but I don't think it would make it there and back, and I can't afford airfare."

"I would love to see you and I would love for Ani to know at least one of her relatives. But, I don't know, John. You haven't told me anything that makes me think that Mom could accept us. Since I've been a mother I've thought a lot about it and I don't understand how she could have treated me the way she did when I was growing up. I was just a child. How could I ever have lived up to her expectations and her standards?"

There was silence for a few awkward seconds. "I can't promise anything. She's so off-the-wall most of the time. I don't know how she'd react. Dad doesn't even hang around the house much anymore. He's found a whole lot of reasons to be out most nights. And even then I think he's afraid to come home. She's bitter."

"That doesn't make me feel any better. What about Grandma? I finally got up the nerve to call her a couple months ago, but every time I call her, by the end of the conversation she seems a little confused and sometimes she starts to cry. Then I feel bad that I've upset her. I want so much to tell her about Anais, but I don't think she could keep the secret, do you?"

"Probably not, she forgets a lot of things now and she does get confused sometimes, but I don't think it's too bad. I don't know much about these things with older people."

"I've lost all these years with Grandma. She won't be here forever."

"I know. She seems like the one really together person in this family. She tries to be supportive of Dad, but I think even she's had enough of Mom. She blames Mom totally for you leaving. She says she'll never forgive her for that. She says when you were little she knew that was going to happen someday. That you'd have to leave as soon as you had a chance to be your own person."

"Wow. I didn't know all that. That's why I'm afraid to put Grandma in the middle of all this. I've made a pretty decent life here with my friend Cole. He takes good care of us and we're like a family."

"It must be awesome living by New York City. I've always wanted to see it."

"It is an amazing place. The big drawback is that it's so expensive here. But we get to take Anais to lots of places on the weekend. We can drive to the station and get a subway into the city in about 45 minutes. We've been to most of the museums and sometimes we just hang out in Central Park. This weekend we're going to the World Trade Center. You can go all the way to the top and look out over the city. I haven't done that yet, so that should be cool."

"That sounds great, Chrissie."

"You mean Lavender."

"No, I meant you, Chrissie."

~~~~~~

It was an October day so unblemished that from 107 floors up every building in Manhattan seemed as if it was outlined in fine black ink. The sky was chicory blue, the air sweet compared to the myriad odors on the sidewalks of New York. The quietude was tranquilizing. You could see the chaos and noise below, but you could not hear it. Anais was spinning like a top from one spot to another trying to take it all in, her mouth never still, her questions never-ending.

"Her fearlessness is admirable," said Cole while trying to keep up with her everywhere she moved.

"She's not going to fly off the edge you know." I laughed at his overprotective efforts.

"Well, I never know what this child is going to do."

Even though all three of us were tired and hungry we decided to stay until closing. My daughter finally quieted and ran out of questions and the three of us - my family - stood awestruck at the sight.

"Can we come back here again, Mom?"

"Definitely. Let's come every season and see how different the city looks from up here."

And we did just that until the fall of 2001.

2001

Cole

When you think back to that day you can still feel the fear like a riptide rushing through your being. You remember you couldn't stop crying and it didn't seem strange that no one around you could stop either. You remember not being able to look away from the television as your mind tried to comprehend the fact that it was not a Hollywood movie. You remember the urgency to physically be in the presence of those you loved, that a phone call saying they were all right was just not enough that day.

You remember days, weeks of speculation, conversation, and obsession at all the ways the world had changed forever. It was walking in a haze of collective grief and knowing that there was not a soul in America that was not damaged by that day. Every morning you sensed confusion and something new and unnamable as soon as you awoke. You asked God for forgiveness for all the years of your life that you took safety and peace for granted, never imagining it could be taken from you.

Anais could not be protected from it. She watched and cried but for a while I think her tears were more a result of seeing Lavender and me suffering. Her gaze focused on us as much as the television. We were exhausted, as all Americans were that day, but there was a point in the evening when Anais seemed to suddenly understand that she had stood at the top of those glorious towers.

"Cole? I'll love you until there are no more bad people in the world." She collapsed into sobbing so deep that she soon fell fast asleep in her mother's arms, holding her Winnie the Pooh. Lavender put her to bed and came back to the couch.

"It's not safe here anymore. I want to go home. I really want to go home. I need to see my family. I need to hug my brother and my Grandma. Will you take me home, Cole?"

"We'll talk about it in the morning." We leaned against each other on the couch, with the TV still on, and in the morning we were still there, tissues clutched in our hands.

The next day held more of the same, the television, the questions, the tears. We eventually contacted everyone we knew, and all were unharmed. Lavender did not bring up going home again and so I let it rest. I had no idea if she had really thought it through or it was just an emotional reaction to all that had transpired in the world and in our beloved city. She and Anais spent several days that week visiting Lydia and being comforted by her loving reassurances.

But the world had not come to an end, and soon we had to return to the normalcy of jobs and chores and living. Some nights we watched the continuing coverage on the television, but other nights we left it off and played games with Ani, or just sat quietly reading to focus on something else and give our hearts a rest. When a few channels started running regular programming we attempted to find some humorous child-appropriate programs to lighten the mood.

"Cole," Lavender called me in from the kitchen. "What's wrong with the television? Does it look blurry to you? Just that one spot on the side?"

"It looks fine to me. What do you think, honey?"

"I think it's okay," Anais looked up from her coloring book.

"Oh," Lavender stared up at me with a confused expression on her face. She slowly turned her head as if scanning the room for something lost. "Oh, maybe I have something in my eyes." She rubbed her eyes and blinked. "I think it's okay now."

"It's probably from smoking your yucky cigarettes, Mom."

She looked up at me with eyes so wide and blue that if I didn't know better I'd think she was still seventeen. For some reason I didn't believe her.

Lavender

Pumpkins and multi-colored leaves are usually enough to bring back a few happy memories of autumn in Ohio. The smell of burning leaves takes me back to a time when neighbors made campfires in the backyards, even though it was against city ordinances, and I could smell the sweet smoke drifting through my bedroom window.

Once in a while our family was invited to a neighborhood clambake or cookout and I had the chance to play with the other kids, roasting marshmallows and hot dogs over the fire, catching lightning bugs and tearing around by the light of the moon. I remember laughter and music.

Halloween was a big event at school and every year there was a Halloween parade around the school grounds. My costume was usually boring and benign, a hobo or a gypsy. The opportunity to go out trick-or-treating varied from year to year, depending on whether I was being punished for something or not. I wanted to make Halloween a good memory for Anais, especially this year. The on-going coverage of September 11th had worn away our spirits and left me with more confusion than ever. My desire to go home became overwhelming at times and Cole continued to patiently support my wavering convictions.

Anais had dressed up as her beloved Winnie the Pooh for two years straight, but now, sadly had grown out of her pooh bear stage. She had moved on to princesses and movie characters. Cole was totally into Halloween costumes, so he purchased her an elaborate Little Mermaid costume, complete with a long red wig.

"I look like you Mommy! I have red hair!" Anais exclaimed coming out of the bedroom in her Ariel regalia.

"Oh, you're much prettier than Mommy, Ani . . . I mean, Ariel."

Ani giggled and twirled as Cole took some pictures of her. It was a warm Indian summer evening. Cole offered to take her out trick or treating. I hated to miss the experience but, I had been fatigued and achy all week. After they left, I put the television on and began searching for anything that did not show walls covered with photographs of missing persons or people searching for loved ones. My heart couldn't take anymore. I lay down on the couch, and drifted in and out of sleep, grateful for the respite. I couldn't believe I allowed myself to miss a Halloween night with my daughter, but I was so tired.

Crinkling candy wrappers woke me up. My little girl was quietly placing all my favorites on the couch next to my head – M&M's, Tootsie rolls, and Snickers.

"How was trick-or-treating?" My head felt like lead trying to lift it from the arm of the couch.

"We had fun, Mommy! I gave you candy!" Anais dumped the rest of her goodies on the floor and plopped down next to them. She had chosen the ones to give me first.

"Thank you honey, you are very generous." I looked up at Cole and saw a father's beaming face full of pride. Who would Anais be without him? He taught her so much.

"Thank you for taking her. I feel so bad that I missed it. We're there lots of little princesses out there tonight?"

"No," Cole said, "I'd say there were more Statue of Liberties and American flags and more patriotic costumes than I've ever seen in my life."

"Getting attacked will do that to a country I guess. I wonder how long the patriotism will last?"

"Can I watch TV, Mommy?"

"Sure, you've had a busy night." I laid back on the couch and watched my daughter stuff more candy in her mouth than she could chew at one time.

"Hey, slow down, Ani, you'll get a tummy ache."

"Boo Radley," she said, "Look. Cole, Boo Radley!"

"Oh, it's *To Kill a Mockingbird*!" he said turning the sound up.

"Hold on, how does Ani know who Boo Radley is?"

"Cole is reading it to me."

"You're reading *To Kill a Mockingbird*" to a seven-year old?"

"Mockingbirds don't do one thing but make music for us to enjoy – but sing their hearts out for us. That's why it's a sin to kill a mockingbird," Ani announced.

"So there!" Cole folded his arms in front of him defiantly. "It's never too soon to memorize this book."

"You never really understand a person until you consider things from his point of view," Ani said while gnawing on a caramel.

"Or understand the wisdom of Atticus," he added.

Cole

The weeks following the horrific tragedy in New York City and elsewhere had a similar effect on most Americans. Everyone needed to be near loved ones, and I was no exception. My parents and I were not as close as I wished to be, but in light of my "lifestyle" as they so bluntly put it, I had no choice but to keep my distance in an attempt to make life easier for them. Our phone conversations were distant and polite in their nature. I felt greatly disappointed in my formerly open-minded mother and father. Ultimately, their liberal thinking did not extend to their son's sexual orientation. Nevertheless I felt a strong desire to spend a weekend visiting my childhood home about an hour upstate from the city.

I found my parents in the living room of their three-bedroom ranch house watching television interviews of people who had been witnesses to the falling towers in New York. We shared a polite greeting, but it seemed to me that my mother was uncomfortable embracing me. We had never been a particularly demonstrative family, and yet, I had always believed us to be loving and close.

"How are the girls doing, Cole?" My mother inquired as she brought mugs of coffee into the living room.

"I think all this coverage on television has been difficult for all of us. Lavender is considering a way to return to Ohio, and Ani sometimes cries when she recalls our visits to the top of the World Trade Center. It's so hard for anyone to understand, let alone a child."

"Yes, of course. And how are you doing with all this?"

"Living so close to the city certainly is disconcerting at times. We're a little wary of even going in to visit now," I answered.

"Your father and I do not intend to go down there again – at least not to do our Christmas shopping as we used to," my mother replied.

My father settled back onto his leather recliner. "How's the job? Thinking of getting out of the high school scene yet?"

"No, Dad, I still enjoy the young people. I hope I can have a positive impact on their lives in some way, not just teaching them about Shakespeare."

"Well, if you ever want to move on to administration or something at the college level, you know that your mother and I have many contacts."

"Yes, I know, Dad. But right now the girls and I are pretty content together. I just have to wait and see what Lavender decides to do."

"Lavender is not your family, dear. You don't need to wait for her decisions. You should be doing what's best for your career and your own personal life right now. Sometimes we worry about you being so attached to Lavender and her little girl. You have no legal rights to that child, and yet you act like you're her father," my mother said.

"I *am* her father. At least the only one she's ever known. I know Lavender would never leave me out of their lives completely, no matter what decisions she makes."

"How else is the boy going to experience fatherhood?" My dad added, shrugging his shoulders at my mother.

I didn't know whether to be angry or relieved at that statement so I excused myself to take a walk in my old neighborhood. The tree-lined street ended in a small park where they had torn down my old elementary school. I moved slowly down the cracked sidewalks and remembered the days of life when I didn't feel different, didn't know I would be rejected by so many of those friendly neighbors whose homes I now passed. Many of them still lived there just as my parents did. Their lives were safe and uneventful. Nothing much had changed for most of them. They had raised their children, retired and enjoyed their grandchildren. I was an only child and would never give my parents grandchildren – something they now suddenly could not get over.

The contrast of living in the massive, never-ending chaos of New York and this familiar placid place took me by surprise. Instead of being comforted by the memories and knowledge that once my life had been carefree and wonderful – I felt angry at the way my life had turned out. As much as I loved Lavender and Anais, they would never be mine. It would never be completely safe or even real.

I reached the one-acre park at the end of the street and imagined the little boy I had been in that spot for so many years – before life took a slice out of my spirit, before the world I lived in became dangerous and unforgiving.

"Cole? Is that you?" I turned and saw a familiar face.

"Mark? How are you? What are you doing here?" It was Mark Bowden, my best friend in elementary school.

"Visiting my parents, just like you, no doubt." He reached out to shake my hand.

Neither of us seemed to know what to say after that so we both turned towards the space that used to hold our elementary school.

"It's weird that the old place is gone, isn't it?" Mark said.

"It is. I was just thinking about how different life feels now. So what's been happening with you?

"My wife just had a baby. We had a baby girl, named her Annie." My stomach lurched slightly.

"We're here so Granny and Granpop can have some time with her. Can you believe it?" Mark pulled a photograph out of his wallet and handed it to me.

"Oh, she's lovely, Mark. You're going to love every minute of raising this little beauty. Make sure you appreciate it." I handed the photograph back to him.

"Sounds like you're speaking from experience, buddy."

"Well, I am, but the little girl is my friend's daughter. We're raising her together."

" Oh, that's nice, I guess. Yeah, I had a chat with your parents awhile back . . ."

Mark suddenly became visibly uncomfortable and moved away from me.

"Gotta get back to the family. It was great seeing you Cole. God bless."

We shook hands again and Mark was gone.

I noticed a dirt path that had been created by children taking a short-cut to the swing-set instead of following the paved sidewalk, and remembered Lavender's fascination with that type of unplanned pathway on the night when I first heard her sing. What was so wrong about a different path? We already had memories and a past together. We were actively raising Anais together. Why did I not have the privilege of pride in my life, in bragging about my girls? We were a family. Why couldn't the rest of the world accept that?

Lavender

Winter is my favorite season. I look forward to feeling cozy and warm and safe, snuggling up to my daughter on the couch with a book. Winter is quiet. The windows closed, the traffic mute, the snow peaceful in its descent to the ground.

Lizzy's floral shop was in business year-round, and very close to a cemetery, so people came in for seasonal wreaths and holiday centerpieces. With the extra hours at Lizzy's, I'd earned enough to pay back some of my debts and save some money for Christmas. For the first time I'd be able to give something to the people I loved instead of just taking from them. I mailed Amber half of what I owed her in a Christmas card with a photo of Anais and me, knowing she would not show anyone.

In my childhood, Christmas was never a holiday I looked forward to. My parents put up a fake Christmas tree that looked the same every year with its theme of red and green glass balls and silver tinsel. They brought it out exactly one week before Christmas and it was down before New Year's Day. A small wreath hung on the door and a nativity set perched on the fireplace mantel.

"Daddy, will you make a fire in the fireplace?"

"Sure, it's Christmas morning. That seems like a special enough occasion, doesn't it?"

"You and Johnny will have to clean out the fireplace tomorrow if that's what you want your father to do. I don't like ashes smelling up the house." Mother said.

"Let's open our presents now!"

"John, you are such an impatient little boy. What do you think George?"

"I think Santa came last night and these two have waited long enough."

There were always four presents for each of us. Two of them clothing, a toy and a book.

"Thank you Mom and Dad. This is the book I wanted."

"You can read that over Christmas vacation, Christine. Now, clean up all this wrapping paper and go get dressed. Your Grandmother is expecting us for lunch."

My best Christmas memory was when I was nine and Grandma Fiona gave me the knitting needles and skeins of neon-colored yarn, which my mother pronounced hideous. But the best present was the time Fiona spent teaching me how to knit. Her patience and gentleness always made me yearn for more time alone with her. I didn't knit very much after that first striped scarf we'd made together, but the memory is all I have ever needed.

When I was with Chance we would take trips into the city and soak up the lights and beauty of the season. The displays in the city put my daughter on sensory overload and she would practically explode in her excitement. Sometimes just the three of us traveled into Manhattan, and several times with Lydia and Chip. In toy stores Chance's parents would watch Anais to see what she wanted for Christmas and there it would be on Christmas morning. I could never thank them enough for that. Visiting Lydia and Chip at the holidays was a scene from a Norman Rockwell painting: cookies baking, homemade ornaments dangling from piney tree branches, haphazardly wrapped presents under the tree, colorful lights decorating all the shrubbery outside.

After September 11th everyone wanted to hibernate a little closer with family in an effort to feel safe and protected. I wanted it to be a Christmas that Anais would always remember. It turned out to be one I will never forget.

Anais knew she was allowed to see what was in her stocking on Christmas morning, so around 6:30am I began hearing little squeals of delight. I quietly put my robe on and stepped around the corner to see her plopped on the floor in her Little Mermaid pajamas, empty chocolate candy wrappers strewn around her.

"Is that good?" I leaned up against the hallway wall, my arms folded in front of me, aware that there wouldn't be many more Christmases with Santa. I doubted if she still believed in Santa now, but we all played along.

"Yes! Look at what Santa brought me!" She dumped the rest of the contents of her stocking on the floor and I sat down with her to look over the goodies.

"Here, Mom, have some." She held out some chocolate balls to share with me.

"Ooh, I love chocolate for breakfast."

"Hey, where's mine?" Cole stood in the hallway.

Without a moment hesitation she scooped up the rest of the chocolate candy and ran over to give it to Cole. "Here, you have it, Cole. Can we open presents now?"

"Sure," Cole said, "I have nothing else to do at 7:00 in the morning."

After all the presents were unveiled, and wrapping paper and ribbons carpeted the floor, I went into the kitchen to make coffee. It was then that I realized that Cole hadn't given me a gift. Maybe, I thought, he'd spent all his money on Ani, which was all right with me.

I turned on the tree lights and put on some Christmas carols. We ate a light breakfast because we were going to Cole's parents in the afternoon for dinner. I dried the last dish and put it in the cupboard when there was a knock at the door. I peeked out of the kitchen and standing next to Cole in the open doorway was a handsome young man. My brother.

"Johnny? Johnny!" I ran across the room and threw my arms around him. Cole stood there grinning knowingly and I reached out an arm and pulled him into the hug.

The next thing I remember is Anais standing next to me saying, "Who is it, Mommy?"

"It's your Uncle John. It's my brother, Johnny. This is Anais," I said, not taking my eyes off the brother I hadn't seen in so many years. I finally turned to Cole, who was handing me a tissue, "Merry Christmas, honey." He had given me the best Christmas present ever.

My arms barely reached to Cole's shoulders. I pulled him down to my level and put my mouth next to his ear, but I couldn't speak to say thank you. The words seemed so small anyway. I turned back to John, noisily blowing my nose.

"How did you get here?"

"Your friend, Cole, arranged everything. He paid for everything. I went home for a couple weeks from college and then I told Mom and Dad that I was spending Christmas Day with my girlfriend. They were a little mad, but they'll get over it. So here I am!"

"Johnny, you're so. . . tall!" We all laughed as I gazed at someone I hardly recognized. "Come in, sit down."

We sat on the couch facing each other and I couldn't stop gawking at my brother's grown-up face. I reached over and touched his cheek, rough with unshaven whiskers.

"Is it really you?" I hugged him again. "This is my brother, Ani."

"I know, Mom, you said that!"

"Thank you, Cole!"

"You said that too," Cole said smiling at us.

"Yes, thank you again, Cole" John said looking Cole's way. "I don't even know you and you've given *me* the best Christmas present ever. I can see why Chrissie has told me so many great things about you."

"You want to see what I got for Christmas?" Anais tugged at his coat sleeve.

"Sure, little lady, let's see what you got. You must have been a good girl this year." John took off his coat, threw it on the chair and sat down on the floor with his niece. I just stared at the scene as if it was happening in some other dimension.

"Do you drink coffee, little brother?"

"That would be great.Black, please."

On the way out of the kitchen the mug of hot coffee wavered in my hand and I dropped it on the floor. I jumped backwards out of the way.

"Hey, a little excited?" Cole stood there, still glowing.

"I guess so. I don't really know how that happened." I bent down with some paper towels. I looked up, "How long can he stay? What about this afternoon?"

"Everything is arranged. My parents know he's coming with us and they are glad to have him. I reserved a room at the Stratford Hotel in town since we don't really have room for one more person here. I believe he'll be staying until New Year's Day. He wants to see some of the city. Is that all right with you?"

"Much more than all right. How can I thank you? This must be costing you a fortune."

"Like I said, Merry Christmas, honey."

I made some fresh coffee and the four of us spent all morning trying to get to know each other. It was almost eleven by the time Cole, Ani and I got showered and dressed. We packed up Cole's car with gifts and goodies and took the hour and a half trip into upstate New York to Cole's parents, chattering all the way.

On the way John said, "Oh, I almost forgot, Grandma gave this to me a while back. She made me promise to give it to you." He handed me a large envelope with a letter and small package inside.

"She knows that you're here? Isn't she going to tell Mom and Dad?"

"I don't think so, at least not intentionally." I saw the smile he was trying to hide.

I sensed certain things in my life breaking down, going away. The secrets didn't seem so shocking anymore. The strain of protecting the life I'd made didn't seem so urgent now that John was here. He didn't hate me for leaving. I felt a turning, a new direction, a lessening of the fear that I had carried with me for over seven years.

My Dear Christine,

I sure am thankful for your recent phone calls, but some things are hard to say on the phone. My mind works kind of slow now so I decided to write some of my thoughts down. I don't know all the reasons that you left us, but I can damn sure guess at some of them. I never understood the way your mother treated you and sometimes I do not understand why my son even married her. I am a person who believes in keeping promises and there are things your mother and father went through early in their marriage that I promised never to tell you or John. I will keep that promise as long as my mind allows me to. But I am pretty sure that some of those events would explain your mother to you.

I used to try talking to her about sharing herself with you, opening up, being more loving and forgiving, but I believe her emotions shut down a long time ago. It was never your fault, Christine. You were a perfectly delightful, inquisitive child and you had the right to become the person you wanted to be. I know you were some trouble as a teenager, but who isn't? Your father was no angel back then either. I don't remember a lot, but I remember that. I don't think he's been happy with your mother. I think she sucks all the joy out of life, but I raised him to keep promises too, and a marriage vow is a promise, for better or worse. I'm proud of him for that. I am not proud of the fact that he didn't take charge and stick up for you.

Sometimes mothers expect an awful lot from daughters. I remember wanting your Aunt Kathy to be just about perfect. It wasn't until my second child came along that I realized I was being too hard on her. I let up and just tried to enjoy the little people that God had given me to raise. I decided to let Him do the hard part because He knew better. I can't speak for your mother, but I know your father misses you terribly. I know for a fact that he regrets agreeing to go along with Roberta on some of the things that happened. I know this is a lot to ask, and I'm sure you've made a successful life for yourself wherever you are, but I do wish you'd give your dad another chance. I'm an old lady and one thing I've learned in life is that people can change and there are always second chances. Then there's forgiveness, too. It's a miraculous thing. It's something you do for yourself, not the other person.

I'm giving you the gold cross your grandfather gave me as a young woman. I've worn it most of my life, not to shout out what a good Christian woman I am, because mostly I'm not. I wore it to remind me that I need to be saved. Not in the way most people think, though. I need God to save me from myself mostly. I pray for you, honey and hope we'll meet again soon.

Love, Your Grandma Fiona

I opened the small package and saw a worn golden cross on a chain. I put it around my neck and have never taken it off.

Cole

"While Lavender is getting ready can I speak frankly with you, John?"

"Sure, is everything all right?"

"Oh, yes. It's just that, well, I've never seen Lavender this happy. Something unnamable has begun to change within her the past few months. I loved seeing the expression on her face this morning, but I have an ulterior motive in inviting you here."

"I thought that you might," John said.

"Lavender needs to reunite with her family. She will never have any peace until she does. Having you here is the first step. I hope it will break down a barrier inside of her. She has emotionally dug herself into a very deep hole and I don't think she knows how to begin to come out."

"Well, it's been a long time. I didn't really know how I felt about coming here when you first called. I've been angry with Christine for a long time. I felt abandoned by her. I was so young when she left, and I couldn't understand how someone could just leave home. I'm hoping for some type of explanation eventually."

"I appreciate you putting your own feelings aside to give the girls such a great Christmas surprise." I became aware of biting the nail off of my index finger when it began to bleed. I pressed my thumb against it.

"This is difficult to admit, but I have allowed my illusion of a family with Lavender and Anais to fulfill me. We've created a safe and somewhat sheltered existence with each other. Maybe I've been unfair to the girls. Maybe it's time for me to let them go, let them find their own life with their own family."

John didn't respond. He glanced around the room as if taking it all in, all that Lavender and I had created and lived through.

"John? I know this is all sudden . . . "

"I don't know. I just don't know what to think right now."

When we arrived at my parent's house that Christmas afternoon I felt the irony of bringing another handsome young man along, but not one that my parents would have to concern themselves with this time. I'd only been in one serious relationship. There had been plenty of dates and introductions from friends that went nowhere. At this point I could see why my mother and father were still holding out hope for a different outcome in my personal life.

My parents grilled John on all the particulars of his education and plans for the future. Then came the *piece de resistance*.

"Do you have a girlfriend, John?" My mother asked quietly.

"Yes, I do. We met last year at school. We both are majoring in business." John looked up from his apple pie with a curious expression on his face.

"Oh, that's lovely. We're still hoping Cole will find a special someone."

"Let's not start that now, please," my father glared at my mother.

"Yes, Mom, please." I added.

Everyone was quiet for a moment and then John spoke up.

"You know, I think things have changed a lot in this generation. People don't have to be married to have happy, fulfilling lives. There is so much more available to us to keep us satisfied with life, to be creative. I personally know many people who don't intend to marry or even if they do they may choose not to have children. Careers are more demanding. Take Cole, for instance. Teaching is a much more demanding career than it was a couple decades ago. Students need much more guidance and the competition to get into college is much more stringent. A 4.00 GPA is just average now. That gives Cole a real challenge to prepare his students for any type of success in their lives. I'm sure he's very consumed by that challenge."

John quietly bowed his head and returned to focusing on his pie. Lavender was looking at her plate, but peeked up at me through her eyelashes and grinned. My mother started collecting plates and took them into the kitchen. My father arose and moved into the living room and turned on the television.

"Why isn't anyone talking?" Ani said, and the three of us couldn't hold the laughter back any longer.

We packed up the car late that night with more presents and leftover dinner that mother insisted we take. After being on the road for ten minutes little Ani was fast asleep. All four of us were exhausted from the holiday festivities and the excitement of this new person in our midst.

"John, what do you think would happen if Anais and I came home?"

"It's hard for me to say. After a couple years Mom and Dad didn't really talk about you much anymore. In the beginning I remember them just being angry and pretty self-righteous about the whole mess. They were sure you'd come crawling back, that you'd be sorry and claim to have learned your lesson and never disobey them again. Since I was so young I remember being scared to death that if I did one bad thing they'd disown me. I mean, I was just a kid. I didn't understand what happened. Some of your letters and calls helped me sort it all out."

"I'm so sorry for that. It must have freaked you out to have something like that happen when you were so young. I felt terrible about leaving you there with them, but at the time I didn't think I had a choice. Now you understand that it wasn't just the punk lifestyle and the boys and the tattoos. I was already pregnant with Anais. I felt so alone in the world. I believed I had already done so many bad things that I couldn't bear the thought of letting go of something, or someone who might love me unconditionally. I suffered over you and Grandma, but I was too frightened to do anything about it."

"I can't pretend that you would be welcomed with open arms. I really don't think that much has changed. Maybe Dad, I don't know," John said quietly.

"It doesn't matter. I've made a life here with Cole. He's a father to Ani. And she's in school here. She has friends, and we are, strangely enough, still a part of my ex-boyfriend's family. She's had some struggles in school but she's doing better in second grade this year. This is my home now. The good thing is you are grown up and we can get to know each other again, right?"

"Right." John said. "Maybe after I get my MBA I'll be a big-shot businessman in New York City."

"I have no doubt that you could do that," Lavender said staring lovingly at her brother.

Lavender

It's Lydia Day. That's what Anais calls it when we get the chance to see the Slaters. I don't have a car and Cole uses his for work during the school year, but it's President's Day and Lydia asked us over for lunch. Cole said he had plenty of essays to grade and he would be at home working, so I could borrow his car. Snow had fallen the night before turning dirty New Jersey and its barren trees into a wonderland as delicate as crystalline spider webs. The roads were snow covered, but not slick.

I drove slowly so we could take in the beauty and Ani had enough time for all of her questions. We imagined the fat flakes floating to the earth were little fairies, just freefalling. A cardinal flew in front of the car like a streak of red lightning. And when the sun moved from behind the clouds we both inhaled in a moment of amazement as we saw every snow-laden branch glisten. Once in a while the unexpected brown spot of a squirrel would race across our path and we'd giggle at his struggle to leap the mountains of white on the roadside.

I don't think I could live without the snow, the peacefulness, the white beauty. It's the one thing here that is just like Ohio - one thing that hasn't changed from my childhood. It brings happy memories of staring out my bedroom window at night. Lying in bed I could see the dancing of the flakes under the streetlight or the Christmas lights on the neighbor's houses and shrubs. On snowy days Dad would help Johnny and me make a snowman, with maybe an old hat, pipe or scarf from the basement.

"Christine! What are you doing out there?" Mother shouted out the front door.

"I'm making a snowman with Dad and Johnny!" I yelled through the blowing snowflakes. John threw a snowball at me, but he missed.

"Hey, cut it out!" I laughed and scooped up some snow to throw back.

"Christine! Get in here!"

"Why Mom? I'm having fun."

"You are thirteen years old. Too old for playing in the snow. Come in now!"

"Christine, listen to your mother," Dad said.

"But Johnny gets to play outside with you."

"I know, honey, but your mom needs you in the house."

"John gets to do everything he wants. You must love him more than me," I said stomping my boots on the driveway.

In the house, Roberta directed me in what to do with every piece of wet clothing and my boots.

"I told you we were going to repack the items I purchased for your hope chest," Mother said.

"Mom, nobody has a hope chest. It's stupid. My friends don't even know what a hope chest is! I'm never getting married and even if I do I'm not gonna use that stuff. Why can't you ever buy me something that I want?"

"Here are my girls!" Lydia cried opening the back door. "Come in. Don't worry about the snow, it's clean, for heaven's sake."

Anais and I stomped our feet on a flowery welcome mat and handed our coats to Chip who was standing nearby with his arms out for them. "Look at you, little one. Have you grown since Christmas?"

"I think she has, Chip," said Lydia. "Maybe you'll be tall someday." Then Lydia looked up at me awkwardly.

After all, whom would she get height from? Not me, that's for sure.

"Well, she might be, look how tall my little brother turned out to be," I said turning to Ani, "Are you going to take after Uncle Johnny?"

"No, I want to be little like you, Mommy."

"Well, that's just fine, isn't it? Your Mommy is a lovely lady," Lydia said. "Are you girls hungry for some of my homemade vegetable soup?"

We had a delicious lunch of homemade food. Lydia, Chip and I sat at the table with mugs of hot tea while Anais went to the spare room for the basket of toys they kept for her.

"How's Chance doing?" I asked.

"We thought this last bout of rehab would be successful, but he doesn't seem to be able to stay sober for more than a couple months. We're very worried about him. He always convinces himself that he can just cut back on the drinking and it will be enough. We all know the disease doesn't allow that," Chip said, his elbows on the table and his hands massaging each other furiously.

"It just doesn't work that way. But I believe one day he will face that. He's lost too much with his drinking. He lost you, and he finally lost his job at the store. Bill put up with the time it took away to go for rehab for as long as he could, and we thank him for that."

"What's he going to do now?" I asked.

"We don't know. We told him he's welcome to come home, but of course, no drinking. He's not taken us up on that yet, but eventually he'll have to, unless something changes," Lydia said, now dabbing the sides of her eyes with a tissue.

"I'm sorry it's been so hard for you. Is there anything I can do?"

"No, you did the right thing by moving on with your life. You can't get involved for the sake of your daughter," Lydia said. "Let's talk about something else. How was the visit with your brother? I want to hear all about it."

"It was the best thing anyone has ever done for me. I don't know what I'd do without Cole. He thinks I don't know why he did it, though. I'm sure he's trying to get me to reunite with my family."

"Is that something you're considering?" said Chip.

"I don't want to disrupt Anais's life right now. Cole and I have worked hard to create some stability. But remember how I've been telling you I haven't been feeling well for quite awhile? I feel like I'm in the wrong body sometimes. It's made me wonder about the medical history of my family. I remember my grandfather on my mother's side died of a rare disease at a fairly young age. I don't remember now what it was. And I also remember some sort of sickness my dad had as a teenager, but I don't know what that was either. It just makes me wonder, you know?"

"Of course, that information can be valuable." Lydia started clearing dishes off the table. "Is there a way you can find out?"

"I'm afraid of everything having to do with contacting family. It's been so long."

"You met John, and that went just fine, didn't it? He didn't hold a grudge, did he?"

"No, you're right about that, and in fact, we got along great. He turned out to be a good guy, although I can still sense some anger at me, some holding back, I guess. Here are some pictures from Christmas. That's him there." I felt so proud to have a picture of my brother to show someone. He was the something good that rose above it all. Something I wasn't able to do. Something I'd been running from all these years.

"He's quite handsome, isn't he," said Lydia. "Look at that fine suit and all."

"Yeah, he's something. I can see my mother's fingerprints all over him. I mean, he's very particular and neat – of course, nothing like me," I said.

Chip said, "I'll leave you ladies to your girl-talk. I have some work to finish in the basement."

I automatically began to dry the dishes that Lydia was gently placing in the plastic rack.

"I hope you don't mind me saying so, but honey, someday I think you're going to have to face your past. I'll bet your family would love to see you and meet Anais. You're a grown-up now, and before you know it she'll be all grown up too. Sometimes you just have to take charge of your life and believe that God is guiding you and helping you along the best that you'll let Him."

"I keep waiting to feel like a grown-up woman. Waiting for someone to tell me I'm an adult now. I feel stuck at seventeen. Look at me, Lydia. I persist wearing the same styles of my punk rock days, and no one questions it. Lizzie thinks it's cool, but that's because she's just an old hippie" I looked down at my clunky old Doc Marten boots, my ragged jeans with the studded belt and my same old red wool cardigan held together with safety pins.

"I'm starting to wonder if I've stunted myself. Or maybe I'm waiting for another chance at my youth, to catch up on what I missed since I had Ani. I know in my head that I'm old enough to make adult decisions and follow through on them, but I don't *feel* that way. Cole lets me depend on him because he wants to be needed, and boy, he couldn't have found a better candidate than me." I put a stack of dishes in the cupboard and turned to face Lydia waiting for her response.

"We don't ever feel that we have arrived. It's a process, it's life. Sometimes you go out on a limb. You just go for it and have the faith that it won't be nearly as scary as you're imagining. Do you know that in the Bible it says *do not be afraid* 365 times? That's once for each day of the year. It sure seems like that's God's main message for us." She stopped what she was doing and put her hands on my shoulders. "What do you really have to lose?"

"I have never thought about my parents that way. What *do* I have to lose? We are already lost to each other. We couldn't be more disappointed in each other than we already are," I said putting the last pot away. "These past few years I think Cole and I have led a life of solitude and protection. We share an innermost fear of rejection and we have both sheltered ourselves from that possibility, using Anais as a reason for everything we do."

"Well, that's understandable. A child *is* a reason for most of the things we do. But you are a person too, honey. You need to be able to stand alone, apart from Cole and eventually even from your daughter. I'm speaking from experience here. Since Chance was my only child, I devoted myself to him completely, and then he grew up," Lydia threw her arms up in the air as if she were shouting out 'surprise!' "He left me and I was lost. I became so depressed because I didn't know who I was anymore."

"That doesn't sound like you, Lydia. I can't imagine you depressed."

"Oh, it happens to the best of us mothers. My knees were bruised many a time from falling on them. But God helped me through and he'll help you, too."

"I wonder if I depressed my mother."

She patted my shoulder as we walked into the living room to see Anais balancing on one shoeless foot on the back of the couch, putting another block on a wavering Lego tower.

Lydia whispered, "Don't be afraid of everything, your daughter certainly isn't."

Cole

"If you spill one more thing or trip one more time I'm going to drag your little ass to a doctor," I said after a year of hounding and unsuccessful persuasive techniques.

"I'm just clumsy. I've always been, ask John the next time we see him. Besides, with no health insurance I can't afford it. You know that. They always want to give you every test known to man and then charge thousands of dollars for them." Lavender was rubbing her shin after ramming it into the coffee table. "I can barely afford Anais's doctor visits, although he does charge less because I don't have insurance."

"Maybe another doctor would do the same for you."

"I'm fine, really. Why won't you believe me? I know I was complaining about some things, but that was almost a year ago. It was probably some kind of virus or something."

"I still think you should investigate your family medical history."

"I don't know how to do that without involving my parents, and if I ask Grandma, I'm afraid she'll either tell them or she'll get worried about me."

"I'm afraid, I'm afraid," I used a mocking tone. "When are you going to do something even if it is a little frightening?"

"Shut up, Cole! You're a fine one to talk. When was the last time you asked someone out on a date? When are you going to come out to your co-workers? When are you going to go for that Master's Degree in Administration you keep talking about? What are *you* afraid of?" Lavender pushed herself off of the couch and stomped out of the room, tripping over some toys on the floor. "I just didn't see them, okay?" She yelled from the hallway. She doesn't see a lot of things lately.

"Maybe you need glasses!" I shouted back. We were like two horses wearing blinders, unwilling to see any life but the one we had today. Looking back was sad, looking forward was daunting, and muddling through was all we recognized or knew anymore.

Lavender repeatedly berated herself for not having a college education. She loved Lizzy and the nursery, but it would not ever get her ahead or provide her with any independence. I had been teaching English at JFK High School for five years already. I loved teaching and the students, but there had been plenty of unpleasant incidents. Anonymous notes, parental threats and once a short administrative leave while the superintendent put out a fire over an innocent relationship I had with a student. I viewed these teenagers as students, as children, just as any other teacher did. I often felt angered over the fact that I had to question my decision to teach high school students and try to hide my nature to avoid controversy.

I am a good teacher. I inspire students to reach goals they didn't know they could achieve. I bring stale, required literature to life for them, and I care about them as individuals. The seniors have voted me favorite male teacher three out of my five years there. It is usually the other teachers, the administrators, and the parents who have made my career uncomfortable for me. It's like walking on cracked ice and waiting for the cold splash.

Another summer came to an end and a new batch of freshman arrived at 8:15 on that first Tuesday morning. After first period was over a young man approached my desk.

"Is that your wife and daughter?" Antonio asked pointing at a picture of Ani and Lavender on my desk.

"Yes, that's my family," I said as I always do.

"That's funny because I thought you used to live with a guy named Nick."

I shuffled papers around on my desk and did not look up, "I used to have a friend named Nick, yes. That was quite a while ago." I looked up, "How do you know that?"

"Because he's my fag cousin. Are you one, too?"

"Antonio, there is no need for us to discuss my personal life, but Nick was just a friend of mine." I heard myself lying out loud.

"Yeah, right," Antonio walked away, but the next day he returned to my desk after class with two other boys.

"Nick wants to know if you still love him."

"Nick and I are no longer friends, now you boys need to move on to your next class," I said with as much authority and calmness as I could. The boys left but they returned each day that week with questions and comments, laughing on their way out the door.

On Monday morning Len Johnson, the principal, called me into his office.

"Cole, we've had another complaint from a parent that you've been inappropriate with a male student. I'm sure it's unfounded, but I need to deal with it and I wanted to hear your side."

"Let me guess - Antonio La Matta. He and his friends basically harassed me all last week. I used to have a relationship with his cousin, Nick. I try to end each conversation as quickly as possible, but he isn't going to let it go, I can see that. What do you want me to do, Len? I'm just doing my job and you know I'm a good teacher. I do absolutely nothing to bring this type of thing on."

"I know that. I am one hundred percent on your side, but we can't let this thing get out of control either." Len looked out the window at the hundreds of students arriving. "I'll call Antonio in and have a talk with him. We'll try that first. If that doesn't help I'll request a meeting with his parents, how's that?"

"That's fine, Len. I'll just be on the second floor doing what I'm paid to do around here." I walked out, slamming the door, even though Len didn't deserve any of my anger.

Whatever Len did worked and I heard no more from Mr. LaMatta, but I knew it was just a matter of time until something else happened. I thought about getting that Master's Degree and moving on to another job or school system. My discomfort in the area, the instability after September 11th, Lavender's odd behavior and need to eventually reunite with her family brought some clarity to my thinking at last. I already had a few graduate classes completed and I signed up for two more the next day.

Lavender

Cole took my challenge and fell knee-deep in schoolwork again, working for a Master's Degree in educational administration. Anais began doing a little better in school. I finally realized getting her some help had been one more thing I'd avoided because of my fears. How many things I had let Ani down on because I was afraid to try them? We found a doctor that would charge us the minimum and work with us on a low dose of Ritalin for Anais. I heard Lydia saying *what have you got to lose?* I realized that my guilt about drugs possibly kept my daughter from something she needed. It wasn't a miracle, but she had less problems getting along with her classmates, her math skills improved gradually, and it made her feel better about herself. It was trial period and I wanted to give it a chance, but if she ever didn't seem like my quirky, lovable Ani she'd be off the stuff in a heartbeat.

Now can I take a challenge and break out of the non-person I've morphed into? There's nothing in my life that is for me. No music, no hobbies, no friends -- except Lydia and Lizzy. I gravitate towards older, wiser women.

I have dreams about the Joeygirls, the rush of being on the stage, the partying after the shows, the friendships with the girls -- and the guys. God, how I miss sex. Lydia keeps urging me to get out and meet a "nice young man" as she calls it, or some girlfriends, but where am I going to do that around here? I work all day with plants and an old hippie. Cole and I don't exactly want to hang out in the same type of places and it's hard to venture out alone. I was never very good at making friends anyway. I love my daughter to death, but I'm going crazy in this little town I thought would be so perfect for us, and I can't afford the excitement and nightlife of Manhattan. I really believe I'm holding Cole back as well. As much as we love each other, we both need more than this. With Chance I had passion and excitement, even though it wasn't always the good kind. His spontaneity and sensuality sparked life into me, and now I feel dull and inanimate.

I live for the contact with John. He actually has a life and a future. I wonder what kind of life I'd have now if I'd stayed. I know I'd be a college graduate. I feel ashamed that I have never been to college. I think I am an intelligent person, but no one believes that when you don't have a degree. I spend a lot of time on the Internet reading about colleges and majors and careers. I look through Cole's textbooks and graduate school catalogs, and wish they were mine.

On the bookshelf is a picture of me with the Joeygirls. We're all punked out and we've got our arms around each other's shoulders taking a bow after a show. Cole took the picture shortly after we'd met. The photo brings back feelings of belonging and adventure, but also the terror and loneliness that was a part of that time in my life. Right next to it is a photo of Anais at about three years old. She has a red skirt on, her arms are out at her side and the skirt is flying away from her body. I remember that moment. I asked her what she was doing and she said, *Sometimes I have to twirl, Mommy.* That's me right now. I have to start twirling.

"Cole, can you take a break from your schoolwork tonight so we can talk?"

"Sure, this paper isn't due until next week. What's up?"

"Let's wait until Anais is in bed." I put a big bowl of spaghetti on the table. "Ani, come and eat," I shouted into the hallway.

Ani did a cartwheel into the room and flopped down in her seat. "Guess what? I got an A on my facts time-test today!"

"Wow! That's excellent, sweetie," I said.

Cole looked up at me smiling as if to say *I told you so.* He had urged me to try the Ritalin for quite a while. "That's my girl," he added.

"What do I get?"

"What do you mean, what do you get?"

"A reward, a prize, what?"

"You get a big fat kiss from me," Cole leaned over and kissed her on the cheek.

"That's it? Crap!"

"Excuse me?" I said.

"Sorry. I know, I know, my reward is using my brain and being smart, right?"

"That's right," Cole and I said in unison.

Later when Anais was in bed, I felt a fluttery feeling in the core of my stomach. It surprised me, but made me realize I was at a turning point.

"So what do we need to discuss?" Cole said in his matter-of-fact way. He sat on the couch, his body angled to face me in my rocking chair, and to show his complete attention, as he always does.

"I think we need a change . . . I mean, I know Ani is doing pretty well at school right now, but . . ." I looked at my hands. I was peeling some of the cuticle away from my thumb with my forefinger and hadn't even realized it. "Is this the life you really want?"

"I'm not sure what you're getting at."

"Don't you want more than this? You've given up a lot for my daughter and me. And I . . . I've given up everything for her." I paused. "I don't mean that I regret that, but, is this it? I mean, is this all I'm ever going to be? You have a career that you are proud of and you should be,

Cole. You make a difference in the world. I don't. I'm nobody."

"Honey, you're . . . "

"I know, being a mother is something, but you know what I mean. I have no family, no career, I don't own anything, I can't afford hobbies, no friends . . ." I started crying and got up to find a tissue.

"I do know what you mean, and I'm not surprised at all that you feel this way,"

"You're not?" I blew my nose and looked over at him. He put his hand on my knee.

"It's time, Lavender."

"I know, but how?" The chair beneath me rocked so far back that it hit the wall.

"We'll figure something out together. We always have."

Cole

I set a goal to finish my degree by the summer and begin applying for elementary school principal positions. Len allowed me to intern with him while I was teaching. There was some extra time involved, but it was manageable.

"I have a friend who is an administrator up in Paterson. I could put in a good word for you if you like," Len said during our last internship conference.

"What are you saying? You don't think I have a chance in this school system, do you?"

"It's not that. You've been an excellent teacher. It's just that some of the incidents that have occurred have been fairly well known. I wouldn't want them to haunt you."

"They already haunt me. I've never been inappropriate once. I didn't deserve any of those so-called incidents. Just because . . ."

"I know," Len put his hand up, "You're just another dedicated teacher to me. I think you'd have a fresh start somewhere else. I'm just being honest with you. I hate to lose you as a teacher, but it looks like that might happen anyway if you've got your eye on being a principal." Len got out of his seat.

"I appreciate all of your help, Len, I really do. I'm sure I'd be gone already if it weren't for your support." I reached out my arm and we firmly shook hands. "You don't need to talk to your friend though. I think I may be moving out of state soon."

"Oh? Where are you off to?" Len asked opening the office door.

"Ohio. I think we'll be moving to Ohio."

"Well, let me know if I can be of any help. I'll write up that letter of recommendation and have it to you by Monday."

"Thanks. I appreciate that, Len. Goodbye."

The long conversations into the night revealed that all roads led to Ohio. What did we have to lose? John was working behind the scenes to locate job opportunities for us, as well as housing and schools. Grandma Fiona was in on it and had offered her home if we needed a temporary place to stay. Lavender was twirling furiously and more hopeful than I had ever seen her. Neither of us knew what was awaiting us in Ohio, but we were ready for the change.

PART 2

2003

Anais Fiona May – age 9

I came into this world face-up. My mom says I was ready to see the world, no looking at the floor or some doctor's shoes for me. She's always telling me that face-up is not normal, that it's a harder delivery. At one point the doctor reached in there and tried to turn me over, but I wouldn't comply. I've been non-compliant ever since.

I wish I could remember that moment when I came screaming into the light and saw my mom's face as she gazed at me for the first time. Of course, she constantly reminds me how my birth destroyed her body, including her face. Her eyes were all swollen with blood vessels bursting from all that pushing. That's gross. Okay, maybe I don't want to see it.

Then my mother, having no one to compromise with, named me after her favorite writer Anais Nin. Right there you've got a problem. So my name is Anais Fiona May.

So this is my story. I am born. Good beginning, huh? I am born to a punk rock mama named Lavender, and I have a list of aberrations (I love that word). I just recently found out that I'm SLD, which means I have a specific learning disability and ADHD, which is short for attention deficit hyperactivity disorder, so I'm kind of weird. But who knows? I think all those words are just stupid names for stuff that's a part of me, of who I really am, the way God made me – a non-compliant, impulsive, quirky social

181

outcast who is really bad at math. But I do love words, and I love to drive my mom crazy. I think we're growing up together. She hates when I say that, but I know it's true.

My Uncle Cole is awesome. I call him Colette sometimes and it cracks him up. He's like the best dad ever. I can't remember him not being in our lives. I've never met my real father. That's okay. I figure you take love wherever you can in this world. Lavender taught me that. And I've always got God. She loves me just the way I am. When I talk to her there are no labels like LD, ADHD. I'm just Anais.

I think we must have gotten some funny looks back when I was little. Me with my curly yellow hair in my stroller, my mom all pierced and punked out, and Cole, our handsome half-black best friend all out for a walk. In New York we'd go to Central Park almost every weekend and we were just a family. The thing I remember the most about Central Park is that you can walk into the park and you can't see a building or hear a siren or horns honking.

Cole has been reading me poetry since I was two-years old. When I was little he would be at our apartment when it was bedtime. He'd tuck me in and read me grown-up poetry. I had no clue what it was about, but I loved the sound of his voice and all the big beautiful words. I'd interrupt him all the time asking what this word or that word meant. He'd always say, "Listen to the whole poem first, doll baby, and then I'll answer your questions."

Even though I'm 9 now I still can't wait to have my questions answered. I interrupt everybody. I can't help it. It's like my mouth works before my brain. Cole and Mom are always telling me it's rude. I really get that. Sometimes I just do stuff I don't want to do.

When I was little and Cole would tuck me in at bedtime we had a thing we always did. He would say something like; "I'll love you until the moon is square." And then I would say one like; "I'll love you until fishies fly." I had to think of a good one almost every night. Then we would say bedtime prayers.

It's funny how kids can understand there is a God, even though we can't see her. If the people who love you tell you about God I guess you just believe them. You have no reason not to. God is more of something you feel. Something you just know no matter what anyone else says. You look around and know that the world is still spinning, and there is the sun every morning and you wonder how does that happen? How does my body grow a little every day even though I can't see it?

I believe in Godlove. That's my religion. If there really is a God, then she's the creator of all of us. And if she created all of us then why wouldn't she love all of us? Why would a creator want everyone to be the same? An artist doesn't paint only the same subject.

I think I like the idea of Godlove because at school there are a lot of kids and teachers that don't like me. Even in stores, strangers get annoyed with me. I usually don't know why until my mom says something like "Ani, you're talking too loud or Ani, you just interrupted the salesperson or Ani, say excuse me when you bump into someone – why are you in such a hurry?" I don't realize that I'm being so loud or impatient. I know I have to learn. When I was little I was in time-out constantly, but I was so antsy I usually couldn't stay there as long as I was told to. Then I'd get in trouble for that! It was confusing!

We came to Ohio, where my mom grew up, because Cole had a job interview. Ohio looked just like New Jersey to me, no big deal. The roads were mostly flat and straight. Sometimes there were farms with big, old smelly cows and then all of a sudden you'd see a town like Clairemont or a medium-sized city. But the best thing about that trip was that I got to meet Grandma Fiona. As we drove down her street Mom started to cry and she said how much she loved this place as a little girl. She acted like a little kid too. She was like, "There it is! There it is! Slow down the car, Cole!" Pointing and crying.

It was a little white house with a garden in front that had those goofy gnomes all lined up in front. There was a flag waving from the porch and a rusty basketball hoop on the garage. The front yard was really big and the grass was really long. As we pulled into the driveway this little old lady came running out the door, her arms waving all crazy and she had a huge smile on her face. I liked Grandma Fiona right away. I remember her yellow hair was pulled back with little black bows on either side. She had on a flowery t-shirt, baggy shorts, brown knee socks and some sneakers.

Mom practically fell out of the car and they started hugging and crying. Cole told me to stay put with him in the car for a little while. And then I saw Uncle John standing by the front door and he looked like he was about to start crying too. Mom waved for me and Cole to get out of the car and Mom took my hand and said, "This is your great-grand daughter, Anais."

Grandma Fiona didn't say anything. She just grabbed me and hugged me so tight I thought she was going to squish me. Then I heard her whispering *Thank you, God.* After about an hour she let go of me and looked me over.

"Anais, what a beautiful name for a beautiful girl. Why, you have blond curly hair just like I had as a child. I hardly know what to say. I just found out that I have a great-grand daughter a few days ago, so it's going to take a little getting used to, isn't it?"

I thought I should say something so I said, "I've always wanted a grandma." That was kind of dumb, but she said, "I'll bet you have, dear."

Then we all hugged Uncle John and everything and went inside. The house reminded me of Lydia and Chip's house. It had lots of family pictures and little knick-knacks and potted plants on every table. There was a yellow canary singing real loud on the screened in back porch. It was really nice. I mostly played with Cookie, Grandma Fiona's old beagle, while the grown-ups all talked their heads off the rest of that day.

It turned out that my other grandparents only lived ten miles away from Grandma Fiona, but I wasn't allowed to meet them on that trip. They didn't even know I existed. I kept wondering *why am I such a big secret?*

Lavender

Seeing my Grandma again gave me hope and gave me a family. I felt full having John and Grandma in my life again. Introducing my daughter to my grandmother was one of the most joyful moments of my life. I felt so proud of Anais, and for the first time I felt proud I had raised her by myself - with Cole's help, of course. All the good memories of Grandma temporarily erased the bad memories and the fear of how close we were to my parents, logistically and in the realm of new possibilities.

As soon as she bounded out the door that day I saw the same Grandma I'd always known. The same little black bows in her hair, the same shorts and knee socks that she favored three seasons of the year. The same yellow hair, pink cheeks and red lipstick on her mouth. The only thing that was different was her memory. A couple times during our two-day stay there she would walk into the living room and seem surprised we were there. She'd look at Anais for a moment, not saying anything and then you could see the recognition spread across her face. She got some family names mixed up a few times and asked John about college, forgetting that he had just graduated. But she was still Fiona through and through - loving, kind, funny, and most of all accepting of anyone who crossed her path in life. She and Cole had some lively conversations about the state of education since she had been a teacher back in the fifties.

"Don't you kids forget that you are welcome to stay here any time. If you get that job, Cole, and I think you will because you're a very bright young fellow, you all can stay here until you find a better place to live. I know it's not big, but the upstairs of this bungalow has been sitting empty ever since your dad left, Chrissie. And there's also a sleep sofa in the basement."

"We just don't know what our plans are just yet, " I said. "But if Cole does get this position and we can move here . . . well, what about Mom and Dad? Doesn't Dad still come over every week or so?"

"Yes, of course, honey, but you know eventually I don't see a way around that situation. But you two decide what's best. I won't tell you what to do. I'm going to keep my big mouth shut for now, I promise." Her smile made me believe her.

"Lavender - or Chrissie - is still working up to these changes, Fiona, but I believe she's ready to handle whatever happens from now on," Cole said, putting his hand on my shoulder.

"Yeah, okay," I said pushing his hand off, "I can speak for myself. I'm a big girl. I've raised a daughter, I think I can manage . . ."

"Okay! Sorry!"

"You two are just like a married couple," Fiona laughed.

"Before we go I want to show you and Anais the lake. Do we have time?" I asked as we settled into the car.

"Which way do I go?" Cole said starting the engine. "Anais, did you buckle your seat belt?"

"Yes, Colette," came a weary voice from the back seat. In the past two days I'd overloaded my daughter with new information and my emotions about being back in Ohio.

"Well, we can't go to my favorite teenage hang-out because it's too close to George and Roberta's. But there used to be another secluded spot with access to the lake about a mile from my old street."

"Might you run into someone in your family?" Cole asked.

"My parents? Enjoying the great out-of-doors? No chance of that." I laughed.

I gazed out the window taking in all that had changed and all that had remained the same. Ani dozed in the back seat, but I kept waking her on exclaiming about one thing or another. Cole nodded politely each time I pointed out some small familiar place. Finally the blue vastness of Lake Erie came into view. Ani rubbed her eyes and sat up.

"There it is! The water looks like pure glass today. A great day for sailboats."

I directed Cole to pull off to the side of the road and we got out. We hiked down a short incline to a tiny unofficial beach area. A young woman and a small child waded in the water.

"Can we just sit here for a little bit?" I asked.

"Sure," Cole said, "This is lovely. Very peaceful."

I inhaled the smell of the water and listened to the screams of seagulls and the lapping waves until someone called out, "Chrissie?"

The young woman at the water's edge waved and grabbed the little child's hand and started walking towards us.

"Amber? Is that you? Oh my God!" I tripped over some roots and stumbled down the embankment and into the arms of my old friend.

"What are you doing here?" We both cried out simultaneously and then laughed and pulled out of our hug to look at each other.

"I live right down the street," Amber said, "This is my son, Tyler."

"Your son? When did that happen? Well, I guess I didn't stay in touch, did I? Oh, but I'm so happy to see you. I'm a mom, too. Well, I guess you remember that." I pointed up the hill to see Anais and Cole coming down to us.

"This is my best friend Cole and this is Anais, my daughter."

"Great to meet you both," Amber, of course, gave each of them a big hug.

"Now, what are you doing here?" she asked, scooping up her little Tyler in her arms.

"We might be moving back here. I haven't seen my parents since the night I left and came to your house. They still don't know about Ani and, well, it's a long story. But I do remember that I still owe you money. Did you ever get your guitar?"

"Oh, yeah," Amber giggled, "that Christmas I told my mom everything and she said, even though I'd lied she was proud of me for being so generous and helping a friend, so she bought me one after making me promise never to run away from home. I never played the guitar as well as you, though."

I spent the next half-hour filling Amber in on the last nine years. We were overjoyed to reunite and promised to be in touch. I spent the ride home reveling in the reunions of the past two days.

Cole

Three weeks later I was offered a job as assistant principal at a large elementary school in a town about ten minutes from Fiona's. It was already July, so there wasn't time to waste. As soon as Lavender and I made the final decision, we started packing and Lavender started crying and wouldn't stop.

I heard sniffling from the bathroom, but the door was ajar so I gave it a little shove and saw Lavender sitting on the toilet seat with wadded up tissues in her hand.

"What is it, honey?" I leaned against the bathroom door and handed her a fresh tissue.

"I . . . I'm just so happy, Cole. This could be the start of a whole new life for me. I don't know what's coming, but at least it's something!"

"Yes, it's something, all right. Now can you take a break from the tears and show me which boxes to put some of this stuff in?"

"I'll be out in a minute. Just give me a minute, okay?"

"Sure, sweetie. Take your time."

The next thing I heard was Lav and Ani arguing. Lavender was still in the bathroom and Ani had joined her.

"Shut up, Mom! Why do you have to ruin everything? Stop your crying! Are you a baby?"

"Please don't speak to me that way. I'm just feeling a little overwhelmed . . ."

The bathroom door slammed and shortly after that Anais's door slammed.

I packed a few more things and heard more crying from the bathroom.

I knocked and waited.

"What?" A small voice came from within. It sounded like the little redhead I'd met years ago on a busy sidewalk of New York.

I gently pushed the door open. "What is it now?"

"I . . . I'm going to miss Lizzy and . . . Lydia. How can I leave them?"

"Oh, Lord, I can't keep up with these tears or the reasons for them. I'm going to check on Anais."

"No, just leave her alone. She's just been obnoxious these past two days."

"Maybe she's trying to figure out why her mother has suddenly turned into Jekyll and Hyde."

We spent two weeks doing nothing but arguing and throwing stuff out and packing. It all got stuffed into a truck with the help of Lydia, Chip and Lizzy. I drove the truck and Lavender drove my car and we were off to a new start in northeastern Ohio. By September, we were moved into a small rental house, I was an assistant principal, Lavender had easily passed the GED test and was enrolled at the community college and we enrolled Anais at Brookfield Elementary School.

Anais

Fourth grade pretty much sucks. Mr. Tucker hates me. One time he overheard me call him Mr. Fucker and he said, "Why does such a smart girl say such stupid things?" Then he called my mom. She said he was a rude smart-ass to her on the phone, she didn't care what he thought, and that he'd just have to deal with me. Great, thanks, Mom. So with no meds and a teacher who didn't get me or my *unique gifts*, as Colette calls them, I got all D's and one F on my first report card, except my usual A in spelling. I do feel different when I'm on the Ritalin. I know I'm a lot quieter, so I usually don't say those stupid things, but I also don't always say what I want to say. I like being good in school and I like learning and being smart, but I don't want to act like someone I'm not either. It's a conundrum.

Tucker gives me checks all the time. It's five minutes off recess every time I blurt out a comment. I like recess because I need to run around like crazy so I can focus in the afternoon. But I can't seem to stop getting checks everyday. Mom gets calls and then yells at me for being bad at school. I remember one time Cole and Mom got into a big fight because Cole kept saying I had ADHD and I couldn't help it. Mom was crying and yelling, "Don't say that about Anais. There's nothing wrong with her!" I was listening from the other room and that's when I started wondering what *was* wrong with me?

Sometimes school is boring. I already know all the stupid vocabulary words and spelling words so I just start doing something else at language arts time. Usually Mr. Tucker walks over and finds me with a book in my lap – another freakin' check. He always notices when I'm not paying attention. Why doesn't he notice that I get all A's on my language arts papers?

Math sucks too. I don't get it. Cole tries to help me with my homework, but I usually end up crying and he feels bad. Why do we have to know stupid stuff like what a parallelogram is or $Y = -5$? I'm probably going to be a poet or a singer anyway.

My mom doesn't seem to pay as much attention to me and my schoolwork since she's in school too. She also has a part–time job because we need money. Sometimes we'll sit at the kitchen table doing our homework together and that's kind of cool. Cole gets home from work a lot later because he has longer hours being a principal and all.

Every Wednesday night since we moved to Ohio we've gone to Grandma Fiona's for dinner. She's an awesome cook. She makes homemade lasagna and fried chicken and I even like her meatloaf, which kids don't usually like. She makes garlic mashed potatoes almost every week, and there's always dessert like homemade apple pie and ice cream. She says she misses having a family around to cook for. Her husband, my great-grandfather, died a long time ago and she's been basically alone since then. But even though she's old, she does a lot of stuff for other people and she likes to spend time at her church where she has *beaucoup* friends, (that's French).

It's also cool because Grandma Fiona lives close to Lake Erie. Sometimes before dinner Cole and I walk down to the lake while Grandma and Mom are blabbing away about something. I like watching the sea gulls diving and bobbing for fish. The sailboats look really pretty when they have their colorful sails out. Cole says they're called spinnakers. Mom used to tell me lots of stories about how she hung out by the lake when she was pissed off at her parents. I can kind of see why she wanted to come back to Ohio. It's nice here. Grandma can walk along the lakeshore to her church too.

She practically begged Mom to come to her church, but at first Mom said churches had some bad memories for her. Grandma promised that she would be welcomed at her church, but for a long time I went with Grandma Fiona alone. I loved her church right away. I loved the Sunday school classes and the services and all the people were so nice and cool to me. I made some new friends there too.

I really like things like pinwheels and sparklers and fireflies. They are all colorful things and they move around too. I collect pinwheels, which is a hard thing to do because a lot of toy stores don't even have them. Also you can only buy them in the summer. I have collected 27 pinwheels. I would have more, but my mom will only let me buy one or maybe two at a time. What I do is stand them all up in tall glasses or vases or whatever I can find and then I turn on my fan and watch them all go crazy. Sometimes I have my pinwheel circus, that's what I call it, while I'm doing my homework. It helps me think. I don't really know why. It's okay for stuff like spelling homework or vocab or something, but math still stinks big time. Since I can't light sparklers in my room I either have the pinwheel circus or, in the summer, collect fireflies in a jar. Mom calls them lightning bugs. I guess that's because she's from Ohio. She also asks you if you want a pop instead of a soda.

My friend Mandy is in my class. She thinks pinwheels and fireflies are stupid, but other than that she's a pretty good friend. Sometimes she'll come over and help me catch fireflies even though she says it's a waste of time and it's kind of mean to them. I help her with writing assignments and reports.

Last Friday Mrs. McCabe, my math teacher, decided she would be real nice and make Mandy and I math buddies. She said it was because she noticed that we were such good friends – and she probably thought poor Anais has no friends. Anyway, I'm not that retarded. I knew she partnered us up because I'm bad at math and Mandy is good at it.

"Anais, I'll explain it again. A prime number is a number that has only two factors – one and itself. A composite number has more than two factors. Get it?" said Mandy. "So, is 33 a prime or composite?"

"Um, prime? One times 33." I said, thinking I didn't see 33 anywhere else on the times table chart in front of me that I call *multiplication for dummies.*

"No! What about three times eleven?" Mandy practically was yelling so everybody in the room could hear her.

"Shit," I commented. Of course, Mrs. McCabe was standing right behind me.

"What did you say young lady?" I don't know why you are suddenly a young lady instead of a girl when you do something wrong.

"Sorry, excuse me, I didn't mean to say that . . ." I said. Then I had everyone's attention as I stood at Mrs. McCabe's desk while she wrote an office referral. I left the room and walked to the principal's office quietly saying "shit" over and over.

"Anais, why are you here again?" asked Mrs. Wilson, the principal. "Not another inappropriate word?"

"Yes, sorry. I try not to say stuff, but it just pops out." I said.

"Was it math time?" she asked.

"Yes, but I didn't yell or anything this time." Sometimes I get so frustrated that I have a little tantrum and Mrs. Wilson has to call my mom at work. That's not cool.

"When are we going to start controlling ourselves?" Mrs. Wilson asked, and I had to try really hard not to ask her if she had the same problem.

"Now?" I suggested.

"I know math is tough. Maybe we should bring this concern to the team," Mrs. Wilson said.

"The team?"

"The pupil services team meets every week to discuss problems our students are having. We don't want you to continue having these academic and behavioral problems. Do you understand, Anais?"

"Yes, I think so." I started to cry. Why do I always have to be the one in trouble? Why can't I be like everybody else? Why can't I be good like Mandy? She never gets in trouble. I don't know why she even wants to be friends with a loser like me.

"Now it's nothing to cry about. Maybe we can help. We need to get those test scores up so we can meet adequate yearly progress." Mrs. Wilson said.

"What?" I sat on the floor and put my head in my hands. Mrs. Wilson handed me a tissue and I remembered to say thank you. "What's adequate yearly progress?"

"Oh, it's something the state requires us to meet. We need every student to be proficient in all subject areas. If not, parents may choose to send students to another school or the school building staff will be reorganized," Mrs. Wilson explained.

"Because I don't pass the math proficiency?"

"Well, yes, Anais." She was dialing the phone.

"Oh." I was hoping that Mrs. Wilson wasn't calling my mom to tell her how I was ruining Brookfield Elementary School.

"We'll see if your mother can come in for a team meeting, all right?"

"Yes." I knew what that meant. The team will tell my mom that I need Ritalin or something like that and she will freak out. She'll say my personality is just who I am and they need to deal with it, not the other way around. She'll say I'm not being challenged enough. I know all this because it happened at my school in New York. That time

Cole came with my mom and since he was a teacher he knew all the right things to say. My mom has a real issue with drugs – well, meds. So that's probably what's going to happen. I'm always causing trouble even though I don't mean to. Shit.

Lavender

Teachers and the principal are constantly calling me to the school. They always start out with a positive comment about how delightful Anais can be, or what a talented writer she is, but then comes the rub – she can't control her mouth, she disrupts the class, she impulsively starts conflicts with peers, she's flunking math, blah, blah, blah. Even though I did well in school I totally get being the different one. I sympathize and empathize and in my heart I am fucking proud of her too. I really don't want her to be ordinary any more than I have ever wanted, or even have been capable of being ordinary. What good is your life if you are just like the next person?

I'm all about public schools in America, but I also know that they want everyone to fit the image of the perfect student, like little clones. If all the kids in a middle school wore the same clothes, and spoke the King's English, and got all A's, and scored advanced on all their mind-numbing tests, and never expressed an opinion, the administrators and the teachers would all have perpetual orgasms. Too bad human beings aren't made that way. I always got decent grades in school because I loved to read. But what about the kids that hate reading or are just slow at it? Every day is a challenge. Every day they face failure and frustration.

For Anais it's math. You just can't get away from math even if you're going to be an artist or a musician. You could be the world's greatest piano player or write the great American novel, but if you don't get math from age 5 to 18 you are a failure for those twelve years of school. Think how that damages some kids' psyches, whether it's math or reading or writing or spelling or just being able to put your brain in gear before your mouth. I remember this one boy I went through school with. He just wanted to stand up instead of sitting all day. He wasn't disrupting anything by standing next to his desk. He'd ask to have his desk in the back and then he'd just stand all the time. And of course, year after year most of the teachers would have a hissy fit about it. Forcing him to sit for really no good reason except that every one else was sitting. I never got that.

Cole

"So Anais said shit again," Lavender said through tears of frustration. "It's not like the other kids haven't heard that word before."

"We've tried to give Anais as much structure as possible. It's the best possible atmosphere for an ADHD child. The teachers might not notice, but I have seen a lot of growth in her ability to get organized and focus on homework at night," I said, thinking of anything to comfort her. "You're doing a great job with her, Lav. You make sure there are no distractions and she has her own little space in the corner of the kitchen to do her work. You are always nearby to detect when a meltdown is about to occur."

"I know, but it's not enough for these teachers, is it? They still want the drugs and I'm not sure I want to go down that road again. I'm doing the best I can!"

"Lav, you know it helped her before, but it's a decision for you two to make. We always remain extremely calm and as upbeat as possible when it comes to math homework. I'll admit I have all but done some of the homework for her just to make it through the evening on occasion. My patience has limits too," I said, handing her another tissue. "We definitely play up all of her writing talent and continually encourage her in all the ways that will help her through life."

"It's so difficult not to say – oh well, just try to fake your way through math for twelve years and then maybe you can focus on what you're really good at. And by the way, try not to feel like a dummy every day during math class," Lavender said. "I was so determined not to let her go through the ordeal of being different in school like I did. But it's just happening all over again."

"I think you're being too hard on yourself, honey, and you're not giving that little girl enough credit. She can handle it."

"Yeah, she does seem to handle these situations better than I do, doesn't she?"

Anais

I got in a shitload . . . I mean a boatload of trouble for my mouth again. And Mrs. Wilson wasn't kidding when she said she was calling a team meeting about me. When I got home from school that day my mom wasn't really pissed, she just looked sad and worn out.

"Anais, what am I going to do with you?"

"I don't know, Mom. I'm sorry, really, but. . ."

"You know I love you more than anything. You know that, right?"

"Yes."

"And I have tried to let you grow and bloom into the special girl that you are. But somehow, Ani, we need to deal with these school problems. I am so tired of hearing the same things over and over, year after year, from all your teachers."

Then my mom started crying, so I got upset and I started crying too.

"What is wrong with me, Mom? Am I retarded?" Snot was coming out of my nose and Mom handed me a tissue.

"Of course you're not retarded." Mom put her arms around my shoulders. "Remember all the other meetings I've been to in the past few years? And do you remember taking lots of tests with the school psychologist, Dr. Gulata?"

"Yes."

"Well, last year they told me that you have a learning disability in math. I was so upset and so afraid that I did something to cause these problems for you that I sort of denied it, and I haven't gotten you the help I should have honey. I'm sorry."

"What? I've got what?" Now I'm crying harder. "There *is* something wrong with me. *Two* things are wrong with me, Mom?"

"Sweetie, I'm sorry I didn't tell you and I didn't face up to it myself. It was just my own stupid insecurities about being your too-young, messed-up mother that kept me from getting you some help."

"What kind of help? Is there a cure for a math learning disability?

"Well, no, there are no cures. You know there are some medicines for ADHD."

"Can I get some now? Will it help me be good?"

"Oh, Anais, you are good. You are *so* good. I want you to stay just the way you are. I really do." And my mom was hugging me so hard I could hardly breathe and we were both crying.

It turns out that I'm supposed to be in special ed! I can't believe it. I'm like the best writer and speller and reader in the Brookfield Elementary School and I have to be in special ed - just for math though. That stinks, but my special teacher Mrs. Milanowski, seems like she understands my math problems and she's going to try to find a way to help me. I get to take the tests with her now and she gives me examples and teaches me in different ways and stuff so I can do better. My mom keeps blaming herself for everything, but I really don't know why.

As far as my behavior, I was right. I might have to take the Ritalin again. That's what I heard Cole and Mom arguing about the other night.

"Cole, you can not make that decision for me – or for her. You seem to think you know everything about children just because you're a teacher. You are not her father."

"But I am her father in my heart – in hers too, I think," Cole said quietly. Mom shut up after that.

We had a family meeting and it was decided that instead of giving me medicine to help my ADHD I would go to the counselor, Dr. Gulata, at lunchtime.

"How is that going to help me keep my mouth shut in class?" I yelled at Cole and Mom at the dinner table. I started crying and pushed my plate of macaroni and cheese to the middle of the table, like they care if I starve to death. I don't know why I was crying. It just made me feel like there was one more weird thing about me.

"We just want to try this first, doll baby," Cole got out of his seat and put his hands on my shoulders.

"Either way I'm an outcast. Medicine or a shrink. Everyone's going to find out! Either I'm going to the nurse at lunchtime for medicine or the counselor. They'll probably put some stupid chart on my desk to help me to self-monitor my mouth. They did that to a kid in last year. You should just make an announcement on the PA – *Attention everyone Anais May is a freakazoid and a retard, just so you're all aware.*"

"Ani, that attitude is unacceptable," Cole said.

"What do you know about being a freak? Oh yeah, you're a half-black, half-white homo. . ."

"You are grounded for the whole weekend," said Mom. She was looking over at Cole to see what he was thinking and he was just nodding his head, but I swear he was trying not to smile.

I didn't care. I didn't have anything to do anyway. It's not like I have tons of people calling me because I'm so popular. During the weekend I got out all my scrapbooks and some of our photo albums to look at in my room. Now that we live in Ohio it's getting harder for me to remember New York. It seems like it was so much cooler of a place to live than Ohio. But I really do like it here. We have a family here, which we didn't have in New York all those years when I was little. I didn't know the difference, but I know my mom did. Now I look at the pictures of Cole and

Mom and me, and I remember some other people from back in the day. Like Cole and this guy Nick. I remember Nick being super nice to me and I always had fun at their apartment. But Mom had a boyfriend named Chance. I remember Mom crying a lot and I know I learned all the inappropriate words from that guy when I was too little to know them. I was only about four years old. Mom told me I got kicked out of Sunday school one time for always repeating bad words and she knew she was with the wrong role model for me. No kidding, Mom, really?

It's weird not having a regular life like my friends. Everyone thinks you have lived here all your life and have a regular mom and dad and you don't have any problems whatsoever. Everyone has brothers and sisters and they've known each other since, like kindergarten. They go on family vacations to Disney World and stuff all the time and I've never even been there. I don't care because I'm too old now.

My photo album doesn't have many pictures since I don't think my mom could afford a camera. But Chip and Lydia took some pictures of me and so did Cole. It seems like I was around a lot of strange people back then. When I was really little there were my mom's really weird girlfriends and some of her boyfriends. No real aunts or uncles, no grandmas or grandpas, no sisters or brothers or cousins. Whatever.

One time Cole and Mom and I went to the Gay Pride Parade in NYC. They have it every June and it is really fun to see. It goes all the way down Fifth Avenue for like, miles and miles. You can stay there all day and watch stuff. Cole took some pictures. At the beginning of the parade there were lots of groups of people with shirts on that said stuff like *We love our gay child* or *Proud parents of gays* That was nice because even though Cole's parents are cool I can't see them marching in a parade about it. Then a whole big part of the parade was churches that think it's okay to be gay and that God loves all Her creations. I would have to agree with that. Their posters and banners said stuff like *All are welcome* and *God loves everyone.* When those groups went by I remember looking at Cole and my mom and they both had tears in their eyes, but they were both trying to hide it from each other. Weird.

Then the last part of the parade was the freaky stuff with the seven-foot tall men dressed like they were going to beauty pageants or whatever. It went on and on and Mom always tells people it was very life affirming, whatever that means.

In my scrapbook are some letters and poems that Cole wrote to me when I was a rugrat. I found one that Cole wrote just for me when I was really little.

There is only one Anais in the whole wide world
one shining face with many a golden curl
one silly giggle one funny smile
Anais has her own special style
There is only one Anais like you in the world
Anais, my beautiful little girl.

And I wondered, did Cole really think of me as his own little girl? Even though my life is different from other kids, I'm just as lucky as they are to have people who love me. I already know it doesn't matter if someone is your blood relative, but most people don't get that at all. They still expect families to be all the same. I mean, every year my teachers say stuff like – invite your mom and dad to open house or invite your father to Doughnuts for Dads breakfast day, and I don't even tell Cole about it even though I know he'd come, because everyone will say – oh, is this your dad? Why is his skin a different color than yours? Why is his name different than yours? Blah, blah, blah...

So tonight while I'm grounded I'm going to do some writing, which helps me sort out my thoughts and ideas. Sometimes I have so many ideas in my head I just can't get them down on the paper fast enough though! I might write a story about an unusual family or maybe I'll write a poem for Cole since he's the one that taught me about poetry and he's the one that showed me that I could write. That seems like the least I could do.

Since my mom named me after Anais Nin I've decided I'm going to be a diarist like my namesake. My diary is the only place I can write what I'm really thinking and if anyone ever read it I would totally freak out! These days I mostly write about how ugly I am. I hate my curly hair and I try to get it straight with a curling iron, but that only lasts for about a minute. It's kind of long, below my shoulders, and everyone says it's pretty, but I want it to be straight like everybody else's. That's the style now. Not frizzy ringlets. At least it's still blond, so that's pretty cool. One night Cole did that thing we used to do when I was little and he said, "I'll love you until -- your hair is straight!" He and Mom laughed like a couple of hyenas, but I didn't think it was funny.

This cute boy in my class is starting to check me out. That's why I want my hair to be straight. It would be so much cooler. Some of my friends are afraid to talk to the boys, but I'm very loquacious – that's my new word – so I don't have a problem talking to anyone. Cole says I should use that to my advantage someday, whatever that means.

I'm going to try to be good from now on because my mom seems like she hasn't been feeling well. She gets tired a lot and she takes naps. She and Cole say she's fine, but she seems different, so I'm trying to be good, at least as good as Anais Fiona May can be.

Lavender

"Grandma, I know all churches are not the same, but I haven't exactly led a conventional, suburban life, and I've run into too many people who can't get past that," I said during my weekly discussion with Fiona about whether I would come to church with her and Ani the next morning.

"God is the only one you're beholden to. It doesn't matter what others think," Fiona said.

"I used to try to believe that too, but it *does* matter when people reject you or infer that you are not welcome. It hurts, and I'll admit, I try to avoid hurt whenever I can."

"Christine, I know that the church you were raised in had its faults. All churches do. They are just buildings full of faulty human beings. Your parents being two of them. Pastors are human beings too. Probably as much harm has been done in the name of religion as good. I admit that, but it's also a place to grow and to experience God's forgiveness. I believe that He can overcome whatever hurt you've experienced if you allow Him."

"I believe that too, Grandma. I believe He, or She, as Ani says, has helped me come this far. I couldn't have raised my daughter without God putting amazing, giving people in my life to help me. I see that now. I'm just not sure I want to risk being rejected again. My whole life has been built on rejections. The decisions I've made have been results of rejections." I paused. I felt too weary to keep explaining.

"Well, you just keep thinking about it. There's no hurry. God's always waiting, isn't He?"

"Grandma? You know that doesn't mean I don't believe. I've grown up enough to see how He's led me to safety all these years. I'm not foolish enough not to see all the gifts, too."

"I know, honey, it's written brightly all over you."

"But if Anais is happy there, then thank you because you're giving her something I can't right now. I'm sure she'll persuade me if you don't eventually. I don't know about Cole. He's been knocked down too much this year."

"And he's such a wonderful person too. It's a shame. What's wrong with people?" Fiona asked.

"He's more than wonderful. I wouldn't be here if it weren't for him. He had this move planned all along, even before I'd ever thought of it. He only does what he thinks is best for Anais and me. He always has. I don't really know why, or how I'll ever repay him."

"I don't think he needs repayment. Just keep letting him be your little girl's daddy. I have a feeling that's all he's ever wanted," Fiona said.

"Oh, that's no problem. He's a better father than any I've ever known." Then I realized what I had just said. "Sorry, but it's true."

"I know it is, honey. I'll see you tomorrow when you drop off Anais, all right then?"

"Yes, Grandma, good-night. I love you."

"Love you too."

Cole

Managing the daily lives of five hundred young children is a daunting responsibility. I say *lives* because school is so much more than academics. Schools are responsible for social skills and manners, healing wounded psyches, patching up torn relationships, guiding overwhelmed and under-qualified parents, diagnosing disabilities and raising test scores so the public believes that schools are doing their job.

As assistant principal I facilitate the problem solving team that meets weekly to address academic and emotional concerns of many of our students. These days are long and tedious and I come home feeling angry at clueless and neglectful parents. Some parents are doing all they can to survive, and can't come to scheduled meetings. Other parents are too hung over to wake up in time. Some just don't care. The school is a free babysitter for them. The school district I work in is diverse racially and socio-economically. But race and economic status does not necessarily determine parenting skills. There are many giving and amazing grandparents and foster parents taking on responsibilities above and beyond the norm.

I spend a great deal of my time making phone calls and writing letters in an effort to reach the parents we need to see. Children in crisis often use school as a safe place to vent their feelings and reach out for attention in negative ways. We make every effort to inform parents of the kind of day their child has had when a problem has occurred. Sending scared and angry children home at the end of the day is not pleasant for me. The behavior these children exhibit can be frightening in its intensity and power to disrupt an entire school building in terms of the amount of attention and personnel required to address the problem. By law, children with disabilities, including emotional disturbance are often required to be in regular classes, and although inclusion of children with disabilities is usually a positive thing, it is not a fit for everyone.

When I finally arrive home on many nights I have no patience left for Anais's bad day or Lavender's angst over her life.

"Cole, can we talk later, when Ani goes to bed?" Lavender asked as soon as I walked in the door.

"You know what? No." I removed my sports coat and tie and threw it on the chair. I am exhausted and I just want to watch some TV and go to bed. Is there any dinner left?"

"Yes, it's on the counter. Cole, I need to talk to you."

"Can't it wait? Is it about contacting your parents again, Lav? Because if it is, I have nothing else to say. You are the only one that can make that decision."

"No, I can't! I can't!" Lavender started crying.

"Did you ever think about what I'm going through right now? This job is difficult. I had to call the police this morning because one of our students brought a knife to school threatening another student on the playground. A fifth grader! That's like Anais deciding to murder someone. That took up my whole morning because the mother's phone was disconnected, so I had to drive to the child's house and wake the mother up from her mid-morning nap, and she threatened to sue me!"

"I'm sorry. I know this job change is tough, but. . . "

"Oh, I'm not finished," I continued from the kitchen, throwing my plate into the microwave. "The fourth grade teachers asked if they could take me out to lunch. I really didn't have time, but I was so exhausted from the morning that I said yes. It turns out they wanted me to meet someone!" I turned and glared at Lavender.

She stared back at me for a moment, "Meet someone?"

"Yes, a woman! It was a fix-up! A woman! How perfect was that! I give up my entire life for this job and now I'm supposed to renounce my sexual identity too. Maybe I will!" I was shouting now and Anais came out of her bedroom and stood next to her mother, their mouths hanging open. "Yeah, maybe that will make everyone happy."

Then a snort escaped from Anais's mouth and both of them started laughing.

"It's not that funny," I said as I shoved French fries into my mouth. "Have you ever had to change who you are to make others happy?"

"Hey, that's my life," Lavender said laughing. "I'm sorry you had such a bad day though."

"A kid really was trying to murder someone?" Anais said.

"Oh, I don't know. But any kind of weapon is cause for complete alarm nowadays. It's not like when I was a kid and all the boys had knives for cutting fishing lines or some other innocuous hobby." I sat down on the couch and put my arm around Lavender. "What's up, honey? Maybe you can take my mind off this ridiculous day."

"You know what you just said about changing to make others happy?"

"Yes."

"That's the thing I'm finished with, Cole. It's time to step up and be who I am, do what I have to do."

"That's what I'm talkin' about," I said pulling her close to me.

"What do you say, Ani? Ready to meet your grandparents?"

"I've been ready, Mom. How scary can they be?" Ani bounced up and down on the couch cushion. "If they can't see what a cool person you are, that's their loss. And I'm pretty cool too." Ani bounced right off the couch and onto the floor. "Oops."

Anaïs

I tell myself secrets – the things only God knows. They are like little hostages in my brain and sometimes it's really hard to hold them there. Somehow I know they are true even though no one ever said them to me and I never saw anything about them anywhere. It's like knowing something before it happens, but it's just a feeling. I've never told anyone, not even my Mom.

Mandy came over for a sleepover at my house and I decided to tell her, because one time I had something like a daydream about meeting a friend named Mandy. She said that I am prescient and I could be a fortune-teller. It's not really that I can tell the future. It's more like intuition and it only happens once in a while. Like I knew that someday I would live in Ohio, even before my mom told me about it. I used to imagine what kind of house we would live in and it turns out our house is just like the one I imagined, but maybe it's just a coincidence too. When I was six I knew all the presents I was getting for Christmas and in third grade I always knew which book we were going to read next, even before the teacher announced it. Weird, huh?

Now I am prescient about meeting my grandparents, but there are two feelings I'm getting, so I'm a little confused. I think there are a lot of things my mom hasn't told me, but I don't get secrets from the past, just the future, so I'm kind of clueless as to whether my feelings are right this time. Either way I don't want to tell Mom. I know this is a really big deal to her and she's pretty much scared shitless. Instead of Mom telling me to be proud of who I am and all that kind of crap parents say, now I'm telling *her* that!

I told Mandy about why we came to Ohio from New York and how my mom hasn't seen her parents since before I was born. We stayed up until 3:30 am and I told her everything I knew about the situation.

"So how are they going to meet?"

"Mom has a plan. Grandma Fiona is going to tell her son, which is my mom's dad that she has been in contact with us first. She's going to see how he reacts to that. Then if he wants to know more she will tell him that we are living nearby and set up a time for us to meet. Grandma Fiona says it would probably be best if we just meet George, that's my grandfather, first, and not Roberta, my other grandma. Then before we meet she will tell him that he has a granddaughter, that's me. I'm a big secret."

"You mean because your mom never got married?" Mandy asked, stuffing microwave popcorn into her face.

"Yeah, I guess that's a big frickin' deal to them or something."

"I can't believe your mom was a punk rock singer, that's so cool. She still looks like one a little bit. Her clothes are awesome."

"She gets them all from a thrift store and then she rips them up and makes them the way she wants them. Her friend Lizzy, in New York, gave her an old sewing machine and she kind of designs her own stuff. I've only seen pictures when she was in the band. She plays her guitar and sings sometimes, but it's not what I'd call punk rock."

"Do you think your Mom and Cole will ever get married?"

"No! I told you he's gay! Why would they get married?"

"Oh, yeah, that's weird," Mandy said, rubbing her eyes.

"Yeah, I don't really think about it, you know?"

"Yeah."

"Maybe we should get some sleep."

"OK, I can't believe it's after three in the morning . . . Ani? What are you feeling about your Mom and your grandparents meeting?"

"I don't think it's going to go the way my mom planned," I said as my eyes started closing. "I'll let you know." But Mandy was already asleep.

Lavender

I'm spending every waking minute on my schoolwork. I haven't chosen a major yet, so it's the required classes like English and math, and boy, have I forgotten a lot. It's more difficult than it was in high school -- the studying for tests, the papers to write. Everything takes much longer than I remember.

Grandma calls on a regular basis to ask about *the plan*. She's anxious to get it underway and talk to my father. I, on the other hand, use every excuse in the book to postpone it. School is the main excuse. I have chapters to read, a quiz to study for, a paper to proofread, but there are other excuses too. I'm just too tired. I'm coming down with a cold, or Anais has bounced up and down on my last nerve.

Lydia's calls give me encouragement, Cole has complete faith in me, Grandma acts like we're going to a party, Anais is fearless. It is only me that holds me back, that holds all of us back from moving on and moving forward. Running, hiding, secrets and regrets have been my life, and all I can remember.

My daughter amazes me every day in her ability to understand her life, her gifts, and her limitations. Much more than I am able to even now. I look in the mirror and see my past in the flaming red hair and the bold clothing that belies the meekness inside of me. The life I know the best is being Anais's mother. Being Lavender is still a progression that I question and fear every day. I do not regret having my daughter or devoting myself to doing the best I can for her. I am beginning to see the fruits of these years, the knowledge that she is already the person she will always be. I don't have to worry about her character or her spirit; that is set in stone. She will face obstacles and rejection as we all do, but she will be more of a person doing so. I was naive and weak, and as much as I yearned to lead, to be different, to hold my own ground, I have always given in to what was around me, what was presented to me. Some of it negative, but also many surprises and blessings.

There is some urgency now the older I get. We all have expectations of what our life should be at certain ages and I am far from those. I have no career, no house, no marriage. The other reason that I feel anxious is because I know there is something wrong in my body. My awareness comes and goes, but it is there. I cannot ignore it any longer. To do so would be more hiding, running, escaping life's unpleasantness.

I have not been to a doctor and I don't tell Cole about the episodes of weakness and numbness that brought me to this conclusion. I do not know anything about my family's medical history and I believe that's one of the first things a doctor may ask. I asked Grandma and she says she can't think of anything important. I know my mother is very unwilling to share anything she deems personal information, and even if there were something significant in her family background, my grandmother would most likely not know about it.

The plan Cole, Grandma and I hatched has become so monumental in my mind it's like looking forward to a life-saving operation or a wedding day - always anticipating, but never believing it will actually come. The plan is for Grandma to tell my dad on his Saturday visit that she has a surprise for him. She will say that she has been in contact with me, that I am in the area and would like to see him. She is leaving John out of it for now, so there is no trouble for him. If he seems happy and wants to see me she will go on to inform him that he has a granddaughter and set up a time to meet. If he is angry or rejects seeing me, Grandma says it is probably better to let him warm up to the idea and approach it again the following week. If nothing else, it's a safe plan for me.

I could just show up on their doorstep and have it over with I guess, but I'm a coward and I'm afraid of the effect on Anais if that happens. Thanks to me she's only heard negative things about her grandparents. However, she hasn't seemed to let that bias her against them. She is curious for herself and hopeful for me. She and Cole are probably sick to death of hearing about it, too.

In reality I know we could have found each other somehow over these many years if any of us had chosen to. Maybe I come by being an emotional coward honestly. The fact that my mother never wanted to see me again I can grasp, but I've never believed so of my dad. My only explanation is that he bowed down to my mother's wishes as usual.

~~~~~~

The Wednesday dinner at Fiona's was lively as we discussed and laughed about all the possible outcomes of our plan. The one we didn't discuss was the one that happened. At 6:36 pm as we enjoyed some of Grandma's homemade apple pie, my father walked in the door.

I heard his voice before I saw him. I looked over at Grandma. Her hand was over her mouth, her eyebrows raised and a smile peeked from behind her gnarled hand. For some reason Anais said, "I knew it!" And Cole said, "This is it, honey."

"Mom?" My dad's voice called through the side door, "I had to come over this way to . . ." He stopped and stared at the scene with no expression on his face. He looked from me to Cole to Ani one at a time for what seemed like five minutes each.

Finally I rose from my seat and stood by my chair gripping it so I wouldn't fall over, "Hi, Dad."

"Christine? Christine?" He put his arms out and I went into them. We stayed in a clutch, unmoving, unspeaking until Grandma said, "George, let go of her and look around you."

"Mother, what's going on here?" He said as he held me at arms length. He looked over at my little blond daughter and my bi-racial best friend with the most confused expression I've ever seen on a person.

"Dad, this is my daughter . . . your granddaughter, Anais. And this is my best friend, Cole Carson." I went to stand beside Ani. I was feeling protective, but she jumped up and said, "Hi, Grandpa, I've heard a lot about you." She hugged him quickly and said, "Say hi to Cole."

"Hi, Cole." Dad said and held out his hand to shake Cole's. He turned back to me.

"Christine. It's really you. Where have you been?" Dad sat in an empty chair and put his hands over his face, "Oh, God, I knew this day would come." He began to sob.

"It's okay, Dad. I'm okay." I looked over at Grandma for a sign as to what to do. She smiled and nodded her head. I didn't know if the day that had come was eagerly awaited or dreaded, but Grandma's face reassured me. After a few awkward moments Dad looked up, "Mother, why didn't you tell me about this?"

"Well, honey, we had a plan, but you blew it for us." She laughed. Her hands went into the air and landed on the top of her head.

"How long have you been here, Christine?"

"It's a very long story. I lived in New York and New Jersey up until we moved here because Cole got a job last summer . . ."

"You've been here since last summer? Why didn't you call us?" He looked at me frowning. Then he turned to Grandma. "Mom, how could you keep this from us?"

"It's not Grandma's fault, Dad. I made her keep it a secret until we, well, *I* was ready. I was afraid you wouldn't want to see me, and you didn't know about Anais . . ."

"Well, I . . . I don't know what to tell your mother, Christine."

"Her name's not Christine, it's Lavender," Anais said.

"What?" Dad looked over at Anais.

"Never mind, Ani, that will have to come later." Cole put his hands on Anais's shoulders.

"And you, Cole . . . you are?" My sense of relief began to dissipate.

"Sir?" Cole answered.

"You are this young lady's father?" He looked from Cole to my pale, blond daughter.

"No sir, I am a friend of theirs."

"He's much more than a friend. We've lived with Cole since Anais was five. I mean, he *is* a friend." Tears of frustration filled my eyes.

"George! Aren't you happy to see your daughter and granddaughter?" Grandma shouted while cutting more pieces of pie. "All the explanations can come later. There is plenty of time for that, for heaven's sake, what's wrong with you?" Grandma's eyes looked huge and wide behind the magnification of her thick glasses. "Besides that, Christine is a grown woman, she doesn't have to explain her life to you until she's good and ready!"

"Well, she wasn't a grown woman when she left home."

"She is now, George, so get used to it. Now sit down and have some pie and you can get to know these lovely ladies and this gentleman, just skip the interrogation, okay?" Grandma practically threw a plate of pie in front of him.

"Dad? Do you think Mom wants to see me?"

"I don't really know. It's been quite a while since we discussed that possibility." He stirred the apple filling around the edge of the pie plate without taking a bite. "It's all we ever used to talk about for years, Chrissie." He looked up at me blinking to erase the tears.

"I'm sorry, Dad. I was so young and I didn't know what to do. I thought you both hated me." Then the room went silent since Dad wasn't supposed to ask any of the questions I knew he wanted to ask.

Anais finally spoke. "He doesn't hate you, do you Grandpa?"

"No, I never hated you, you're my daughter."

"I know how that feels now, Dad, ever since I became a mom."

Dad looked up at Ani, "You've been a mom for quite a while. How old are you? What's your name again?"

"It's pronounced *Ahna-eese*, I'm almost ten."

"Ten? That means . . ."

"George, why don't you eat some pie? How about a coffee?"

"Sure, Mom. Thanks."

"Can I have another piece, Grandma Fiona?"

"Comin' right up, little one."

"Wait until your brother finds out about all this," Dad stirred sugar into his coffee. No one said a word. I glared at Anais to remind her to be quiet and she nodded her head. I couldn't bring myself to inform him of one more secret.

"Your brother missed you, Christine. He lost out on having a big sister. I think it was lonely for him after you left."

"I know, Dad. I feel guilty about that every day of my life, believe me."

"I wasn't trying to make you feel guilty. It's just that . . . it's been hard."

"George!" Fiona practically shouted. "How does it feel to be a Grandpa?"

Dad looked over at Anais and smiled weakly. "I'm a Grandpa, huh? Boy, this is a lot to take in all at once."

"Well, I'm a great-grandma, how do you think that feels?" I don't know what we would have done without Fiona to break the tension.

"Fiona, you don't even look old enough to be a grandmother to begin with," Cole said grinning at her.

Fiona leaned over and rubbed Cole's forearm. "This one's a keeper."

"I know you don't want me to interrogate my daughter, but I need to understand a few things. Christine, what have you been doing all these years? Why didn't you ever contact us?"

I yanked at the back of my hair and tossed it over my shoulder. I glanced over at Fiona and she nodded her head and winked at me.

"Dad, to be honest, I didn't think you'd ever want to see me again if you'd have known I was pregnant. I didn't want to give my baby away. I wanted someone to love me and look up to me. I wanted something of my own. Remember the night I left? You and Mom gave me a big lecture about boys and unwanted pregnancy. What choice did I have?"

"We could have worked something out. You know we don't believe in abortion."

"Neither did I, Dad. I wanted to keep her. Mom said I'd be sent away. I'd give her up." Tears made their way down my cheeks. "Look at her, Dad! Look at her! She's my daughter. She's my life. Don't you remember how that feels?"

"Yes, I do." Dad looked down into his lap. A few seconds passed silently.

"I was only seventeen." I momentarily became aware of my daughter's presence. I had not intended to have this conversation in front of her. Her wide fearful eyes were riveted on me. Her mouth partially open and uncharacteristically motionless.

"Ani, are you okay?"

"Mommy?"

"Come here, honey." The chair scraped loudly in the silence of the room and she moved into my arms. "It's okay. You know I couldn't live without you, don't you?"

"I had to live without *you*, Christine."

"George!" Fiona called out. "Now you're being unfair. Look at how you've frightened this little one. None of this was her doing."

"I apologize, Anais. When you grow up you'll understand, I'm sure."

"I don't know about that. I'm not sure I understand myself." I said, pulling Ani closer to me.

"There are things that you don't know Christine. Just remember that."

"How was I supposed to know that when I was a teenager? Why couldn't you love me unconditionally like you were supposed to?" Cole handed me a tissue.

"I didn't . . . ?" Dad got out of his seat. "Excuse me." He went into the bathroom.

"There's a lot of guilt and anger and confusion right now, but it will pass," Fiona offered.

"I know, Grandma. I think we need some time, I guess. I don't know."

Dad came back into the kitchen. "I'm sorry about that. I probably should let you all get some rest and I need to get home." He turned to me. "Christine, regardless of what you're probably thinking right now, I am very happy to see you."

"Me too, Dad. I'm sure we'll work all of this out. Are you going to tell Mom?"

"Of course I'm going to tell her, but I'm not sure what I should say."

"Tell her I would like to see her and have her meet her granddaughter, but if she doesn't want to I understand. I won't force myself back into her life. I know I've caused enough trouble."

"It wasn't all your fault. You were so young. There was so much we expected you to know that you were too young to know or understand. It took a long time but I think your mother realized some things after you were gone." Dad put his hand on my arm. "But Chrissie, I don't really know how she's going to take this. These years have taken a toll on your mother. Not just because of losing you though. She's battled some illness as well."

I wanted to ask about illnesses in the family, but I knew it would have to wait.

"I'm sorry to hear that. Will you let me know what she says? I'll write my phone number down for you. We only live over in Brookfield."

"You live in Brookfield?" My dad looked so sad then that I reached out to hug him and we said goodnight.

Cole

"What did you think of our first meeting, Cole?" Lavender asked as soon as we sat down in the car. "I think we really shocked him. I'm sure you'll get to know him better the next time we get together."

"Yeah, it was a tough night for you two."

"Ani, your Grandpa is a nice man." Lavender leaned over the front seat. "It's just that he was so surprised tonight. I'm sorry you had to hear all of that."

"Okay, Mom."

"I thought he was a little rough on you. Why are you defending him so much?"

"I'm sorry if I'm hopeful. Just because it was awkward doesn't mean I'm going to give up on this. I'd think you'd be happy for me, Cole."

"I just don't want you to get your hopes too high. There is still a long way to go here you know," I said.

"I know. Even though it was difficult I'm kind of glad it happened that way. Grandma didn't have to do the dirty work, and I didn't have a chance to back out, you know?"

"I knew that would happen," Anais said sleepily as she dozed in and out of the conversation.

"What do you mean, you knew it?" Lavender turned around to face the back seat, but Ani appeared to be asleep so she didn't pursue an answer. I wondered what she meant too.

"I'm happy for you, Lav, but you've been apart for an awfully long time. You don't really know each other anymore. Even if your mother is willing, I think it will take quite a bit of work to reestablish your relationship. Are you prepared for her to take on a motherly role again?"

"What do you mean again? She never was the motherly type as far as I'm concerned."

"I want you to promise me you will only tell them what you feel comfortable sharing. I don't want you to spend the rest of your life defending all your past choices, whether they were right or wrong."

"Don't you think they deserve an explanation of why I stayed away for so long?"

"Actually, no, I don't. As Fiona said, you are a grown woman. You have lived your life your own way. Are they going to explain all the choices and decisions they made that affected your life?"

"I'm positive *that* won't happen."

"In my opinion, you should call the shots here. You have proven that you can live your life with or without them. I know you'd rather reconcile, but if they're going to put you through hell for it . . . "

"Okay! Are you protective of me, or what? I'll tell you what. I'll think about what you've said. I'll be strong and show them I don't intend to defend my life, but I know them. They have a way of manipulating people to get what they want. Just ask John."

"Speaking of John. I'm glad your dad just assumed that this would be a surprise to John. If not, that might have sent him over the edge."

"But I feel bad for John, because eventually they are going to find out we've seen each other and he'll have hell to pay."

"He's all grown up too, Lav. He managed to survive all these years with them. I'm sure he can handle it."

Anais

I wasn't really asleep that night in the car. I was just so sick of listening to Mom and Cole talk about my stupid grandparents. At first it seemed kind of fun to meet family members I didn't know before. And I could use some normal things to say about my life that are like all my friends, like having grandparents. I really like John and Fiona, but Grandpa, I'm not sure. He was weird. He kept looking at me funny and I didn't think he was that nice to my mom. He practically ignored Cole. He also had a gross comb-over and wore dorky clothes. I know you shouldn't judge people by their looks and clothes, but sometimes you just can't help it.

Also, Mom seemed different. I don't know if it was because she was surprised the way it turned out or because of Grandpa. I didn't like the way she acted. I started wondering what kind of illness my grandmother had. My intuition tells me that it's a mental illness. Why wouldn't Grandpa just say what it was? I read a book about a girl with bi-polar disorder and it was really sad because it's a sickness and people can't help if they have it. But then other people treat them real mean and stuff and call them crazy. In the book the girl finally got some medication and she was a lot better. Doesn't that show that it's a sickness – if medicine helps it?

Cole handed me the phone and said, "It's your Dad." Such foreign words.

"Hello?"

"Christine, it's your father. How are you today?" His voice sounded formal and flat.

"I'm well, and you?"

"It was a difficult night with your mother but she's consented to see you."

"Consented is kind of a strange word to use to see your own daughter." I regretted those words the moment they left my lips. I had vowed to myself to not be confrontational.

"Nevertheless, I hope you will be able to stop over tomorrow if you have time."

"Tomorrow?"

"I thought you wanted to see your mother?"

"Oh, I do. Yes, I do. Tomorrow. What time?"

"It's Saturday. Are you free around two?" Dad asked.

I paused. I looked for Cole as if I could not answer that question without him. He had left the room. "Christine. I don't know what you want from us. All these years you could've contacted us and now . . ."

I inhaled slowly. "Dad, you could have found me if you had wanted to. You knew I was in New York City."

"New York City is a very big place."

"Yes, but you could have tried. Did you ever even try?" The phone against my ear was shaking and suddenly dropped to the floor. I fumbled to retrieve it.

"Dad, are you still there?"

"Maybe this is not what you really want. There is too much hesitation on your part," Dad said.

"On my part? Are you kidding me? I just dropped the phone, that's all. You're speaking to me as if I'm a stranger and you are setting up a business appointment. I asked you a question, Dad. Did you ever even try to find me?"

"No. Your mother would not allow it. She was too hurt."

"Why is everything about what *she* wants? What she feels? What about you? Did *you* want to find me?" Neither of us spoke for an agonizing minute. I waited for his answer.

"What I wanted was not important," he said quietly.

"It was to me. It still is. I was a teenager. Didn't I deserve to be defended or at least understood? Didn't anyone care how hurt *I* was? I didn't know everything. I needed you, Dad."

"Christine. You don't understand a lot of things."

"That's right, I don't! I'd really like to understand. Why didn't you ever defend me, stick up for my rights as an individual when I was just a child? I don't know why I'm nothing like her. I never even wanted to be . . ."

"There are just things you'll never understand."

"I'll never understand because you'll never explain them to me. Now that I'm a mother I understand my childhood even less. Most of the time I accepted it the way it was. I had no choice. But now – with Ani – how could you take all the joy out of a child's life? Why would anyone want to do that?"

"I'm sure that's not what your mother intended to do."

"Oh my God, are you kidding me?" Cole walked back into the room and handed me a tissue. There were tears of frustration now.

"Listen, if tomorrow is my big chance, I'll be there at two. I'll see you then, okay?" I did not try to hide my sniffling.

"Yes, we'll be waiting."

The next day, the next step, was something I had to do on my own, without help from Cole or John or Grandma. The voices in my head were in full control driving back to the white colonial house. It's blank, unadorned, square presence on the street made it blend into the snowy background like it didn't even exist. I searched for a sign of life; a wreath on the door, a light in the window, but there was nothing. I stopped the car by the side of the road several houses away. I turned off the engine and sat quietly, numbly, trying to put the voices to rest before I continued.

Mom? I got invited to the Homecoming dance. Can I go?

Were you invited by that boy, Jeremy?

Yes. You've met him and his parents. Please, Mom. I've never been asked to anything before.

You're really too young, Christine.

I'm sixteen! The school sponsors these dances you know. Everyone else's parents think their daughters are old enough to date. It's what kids do in high school. Didn't you ever go to a dance?

What I did is not your business. Times are different now. How do we know what goes on there?

Like I said, it's a school event. All I need is some money for a dress. Jeremy has his license. He'll pick me up and bring me home.

I'll have to think about it. But you should spend your own money on a dress if that's what you want.

I don't have any money, Mom, you know that! I haven't had any babysitting jobs and you made me put the last of my money into my savings account. Can I get some out now?

For a dress? You'd probably buy the most inappropriate one in the store. I don't think so. That money is for your future.

What future? Being a prisoner here? What will I need money for? I'm not allowed to do anything!

My brain was suffused with negative and terrifying thoughts. The fear of the unknown: unknown words, unknown emotions, unknown outcome and future – all about to be discovered after years of wondering. *What have you got to lose?* I heard Lydia's kind voice. I don't know, maybe my mind? Then I heard my daughter's voice: *You can do it Mom. They're just people like us.* And Cole: *You've raised a child of your own and done a great job. You're not their little girl – you're their equal if not more. Don't apologize for yourself or your life.*

I saw my hand knocking on the front door of the place I used to call home. Dad opened the door to allow me to walk through and put his arm around my shoulder.

"Hi, Dad. How – how are you?" I pulled at my hair and flipped it around to the front of my shoulders.

"Hello, honey. I'm doing fine. Your mom is in the living room."

"Is this going to be okay to do now? I mean, what do you think?" I heard the old meekness creeping back into my voice.

"I think it will be fine," Dad said in an unconvincing voice. I turned the corner of the foyer into the beige living room.

My mother arose from her chair without looking at me. She slowly raised her head and said, "Hello, Christine. How are you?"

I saw Roberta look me over in one glance. From my black boots to the rip on the knee of my jeans to the slouch hat atop my red and black streaked curls. I walked towards her and hugged her stiff torso briefly. She smelled like mothballs, and looked the same in all ways except her face. It looked like a grape withered on the vine, small, tight and dry. She wore the same type of skirt and sweater set, pantyhose and brown shoes. Her hair was short and severe.

"Let's all sit down. I'll get some nice hot tea," Dad said.

"Oh, thanks, Dad." I felt panic-stricken watching him leave the room.

"Mom, how are you? Dad said you'd been ill. Are you all right now?"

"I wonder why that matters to you, Christine."

My head and my heart dropped. "Mom, it does matter to me. I'm here, aren't I? I know this isn't easy for any of us but can't you try to forgive me? When I left here I was young and scared, and the things you said to me made me feel I needed to go. It was a long time ago and I'm grown up now."

"Oh, so it was all our fault?"

"No, of course not, but aren't you even a little glad to see me?" I paused to stop myself from apologizing again. "We all have been hurt in the past. Maybe we can work out some of these things later. I know you and Dad have a lot of questions . . ."

"Yes, I am glad to see you. I just wish you had contacted us years ago. I don't understand what we did to deserve this." Roberta's face showed no emotion. She certainly wasn't about to shed any tears like my father did. My father walked back in with a tray of hot tea and cookies.

"Listen, can we decide who's to blame some other time? Did Dad tell you about your granddaughter?" I tried to smile.

"That's the cruelest part of all, keeping us from a granddaughter." My mother stared right into my face.

"Mom, I'm s . . ." I stopped myself.

"I mean," Roberta continued, "every woman looks forward to having a grandchild. Sometimes it's like a second chance. It was one thing to have you leave us,

Christine, but then having a baby. Your brother would never do such a thing to us."

"But wait until you meet her. She's a wonderful little girl. She's brought me so much joy and, well, now I understand about being a mother."

"You've been a mother for many years, I understand. Ever since you left us."

"Yes, that's true, but . . ." My mind went blank. My arms felt numb. I closed my eyes at the weakness flooding my heart and body. So tired.

I stood up, every inch of my body shaking inside and out. "I feel like you don't want me here, Mom. Did you ever think that's why I never came back? Instead of being glad that I survived and made a life for myself and have successfully raised a daughter of my own, you just want to place blame and show your anger. I get it."

"Christine, sit down, let's talk about this," Dad said.

"No, Dad. At least you were happy to see me. She hasn't changed at all. If it's so cruel to keep your granddaughter a secret why aren't you willing to be reasonable and have the opportunity to meet her? Do you think I'm going to bring her over here so she can experience the same rejection you showed me?" I grabbed my coat off of the chair and struggled to put it on with shaking hands. I turned around quickly and lost my balance. The chair broke my fall and I stood back up to leave.

"Christine, wait!" Dad got up to follow me.

"Wait? I waited all these years and nothing has changed!" I sat down in the chair by the front door and put my head in my hands. I did not want to cry. I sensed that this had all happened before. I was seventeen again. But this time I did not want to give up so easily.

I looked up at my mother. Her face had softened slightly. She was smoothing out her skirt and then looked up at me.

"We've all waited for this day in some respect," I said. "I don't want these feelings to eat us up more than they already have. It was hard to come here. I'm sure it's just as hard for both of you." I felt like I was babbling in my effort to not have to leave. I knew I would be sorry if I did. I'd have to start this process all over again, and that thought was unbearable.

"I have feelings too you know," my mother said quietly.

"I know, Mom. That's what I'm trying to tell you. I understand how it is to be a mother. It changes you. Of course, you have feelings about all this but . . . well, I can't go back and change the past, can I? I've grown up a lot. I was hoping we could all move forward – as adults."

"You hurt your brother too. He didn't deserve a broken family," Roberta said.

"A broken family? I know. I know," I said, feeling too drained to think of anything else to say to defend myself.

I stood up and looked at my mother. "If you're not ready to see me, or meet Anais, or face any of this, I guess there's nothing I can do about it. I'll go on with my life either way. Dad knows where to find me if you change your mind. At least he welcomed me back and still wants to be my father, right, Dad?" George silently nodded his head. He looked over at Roberta as if he hoped she might say something, but she did not.

"I'll see you at Grandma's, Dad. I'm sorry it turned out this way, for your sake."

Cole didn't have to ask me how it went, but he was at the door with a hug. The phone rang and it was my dad.

"I'm so sorry about today, honey. I know we don't deserve it, but maybe if you give your mom some time to get over the shock of seeing you . . . "

"Why do you always defend her, Dad? She could barely look at me, let alone act happy to see me. Do you think this is any easier for me? At least I made the effort. stopped talking as I felt my hope evaporate. A profound weakness swept over me. There was nothing else to say.

"Yes, you made a good effort. I'd like to see you and my granddaughter again if that's okay."

"Sure, any time. We'll talk later."

I still needed a family history of health information from my parents. I really couldn't be angry with my Dad. He firmly held his place in the middle just as he always had. Now I could see his position and feel sympathy for him, but not her.

Hope and the loss of hope seem tangible at certain times in life. There is a grief process when hope leaves you. It takes visions of the future and erases them without a moments notice. You are left with nothingness and a sense of something beyond sadness. Why I had built such a false dream castle in my mind I'll never know. I felt a great sense of loss when I left Chance, but this was different. This was my future *and* my past.

Cole

There must have been a spark of hope left when Lavender consented to have dinner with her parents at Fiona's two weeks later. Anais and I did our best to get out of it, but Lavender needed the support and we all agreed that Roberta should at least meet Anais. Nothing said or done in the past few weeks would make a child want to acquiesce to this experience, so several arguments and tantrums ensued. In my mind Fiona was either a saint or a glutton for punishment. It was certainly an act of love towards her son and granddaughter.

Roberta was cold, formal and unforgiving. She sat straight-backed in her chair and said little to anyone during the dinner. Her complete focus seemed to be on Anais. George was amiable and upbeat. He and Fiona kept the conversation going and Lavender began to enjoy herself. If we could have erased Roberta from the picture, it would have been a nice family portrait. Although Lavender's parents had been informed that John had already met us, he was away on a business trip, so that complication was saved for a later date.

"Anais, do you like having an unusual name. I wonder how your mother ever thought of it," Roberta asked.

"I'm named after a writer, Anais Nin. I like it, because I like being different and I'm also a writer, so it's kind of cool being named after one."

"Oh, really. I've never heard of her."

"She mostly wrote eroticism," Anais added, a lasagna noodle hanging from her mouth.

"What did you say young lady?" Roberta said.

"Oh, I'm sure she doesn't even know what that means," Dad said forcing a laugh.

"Yes, I do . . . " Anais started with her mouth full, but I interrupted.

"Anais is truly a gifted writer. She won the Power of the Pen contest this year."

"That's nice. And what do you do, Cole?" Roberta asked.

"I'm a principal in an elementary school. I used to teach high school English in New Jersey. I enjoyed my years there, but I do love the young children."

"I'm sure you do," said Roberta flatly. I quickly turned to see Lavender shooting a look at Fiona, both of them rolling their eyes.

"Is there something wrong?" asked Roberta.

"No." Lavender turned to put her arm around Anais. "So what do you think of my daughter, Mom?" A quite brave and reckless question I thought.

"Well, she's lovely, very outspoken I'd say. You were so quiet at her age. Where did she get that blond hair, I wonder?"

Lavender shot back immediately, "I don't know, Mom, where did I get my red hair?"

"Fiona, let me help you with the dishes." Roberta rose from the table, silently stacked up some plates and left the room.

"Good comeback, Mom," said Ani, trying to lick her dish while I smacked her lightly on the back of the head.

Anaïs

My prescience is telling me that my new Grandmother kind of likes me, even though she can't show it. I don't like her because she's mean to my mom and Cole. She also wears dorky clothes like Grandpa. Mom says they have plenty of money but they never spend it on fun stuff like clothes or eating out. If I had a lot of money I'd be at the mall every day, eating pizza and buying cute outfits.

I'm not going to any mall for a while because I'm grounded for like, a week. Mom had enough of my tantrums about going to dinner at Grandma Fiona's. She said it was hard enough for her without me making it harder and why couldn't I understand that? How am I supposed to understand everything? Of course, I am extremely gifted in certain ways and prescient too, even though the only person I've told that to is Mandy.

Mom said she thinks that her relationship with her mother has gone as far as it's going to, but I'm not sure about that. I'm feeling like there's more coming. Like something's going to happen, but I really don't know what.

Now every Wednesday when we go to Grandma Fiona's for dinner my grandpa is there too. He and Mom are happy talking about back in the day when Mom was little. I think they did what Jesus would do, Grandpa forgave my mom and she forgave him. Uncle John shows up when he can too, so it feels more like a regular family now, even though everyone knows that my other Grandma doesn't really want to participate. I say, so what? Her loss, right? It's starting to be fun and Grandpa and Cole are like, good friends now.

Cole called me a conundrum today. He thought he was so cool and I'd have to ask him what conundrum means, but I already knew. I'm getting sick of his cute names for me. So now I'm holding myself hostage in my closet. I make myself a hostage when I know I'm about to freak. The school headshrinker, Dr. Gulata, told me to find a safe place to calm myself down, so I threw all my shoes in a laundry basket and put my beanbag chair in my closet. I've got a flashlight, my diary, three pink pens and two purple ones and a box of cheese crackers for an emergency hunger attack.

The reason he called me a conundrum was because I spent five minutes on a fractions worksheet, got mad and ripped it in half. But then I spent over two hours on my social studies poster about the Ohio inventor, Garrett Morgan. I don't know why that's a shock to him. I get out of doing my math homework by telling Mom and Cole that Mrs. Milanowski will help me with it in the resource room tomorrow, which she usually does. They're not very good at hiding their relief at not having to help me themselves anymore, even Cole the expert teacher.

I'm probably going to pass math this grading period because of Mrs. Milanowski, but that didn't help me when it came to the math proficiency test. On the day of math testing I felt like I had been placed in an advanced Chinese class, then I'm told – oh, just try your best – even though I don't know *beginning* Chinese! And by the way, even though Mrs. M. always helps you with your work, she can't help you now! You're on your own, baby! Do a great job. Yeah, right.

Dr. Gulata says I should work on loving myself the way I am and feel good about all the things I'm good at. How can I when I am a failure everyday at school? It's not just math. You should see what a goof I am sometimes with the other kids, even when I'm doing something I'm good at.

"Anais, would you please read pages 87 to 88 for us in our new story?" said Mr. Tucker.

"Sure," I said quietly. Inside I'm saying Anais, *don't make a fool of yourself this time.* I start to read and I can't help it. I give the characters different sounding voices because that's the way you're supposed to read a story! That's the way Cole always read to me when I was little. Pretty soon I hear laughing.

"Class, let's listen respectfully please. Anais is doing a good job of creating the characters for us," Mr. Tucker said. But it's too late. Tanya is practically falling off her seat trying to get bratty Brittany's attention so she'll laugh too.

"Shut up!" I hear myself shouting.

"Anais, I can handle the class. You need to continue reading, please."

"Why should I? Everyone's just going to keep laughing," I said.

"Anais, that's enough disruption. Would someone else volunteer to read now?"asked Mr. Tucker, "Maybe you'll be an actress when you grow up."

Then the entire class started cracking up. Thanks, Mr. Fucker. I slammed my book shut and walked out of the room. I heard him calling me to come back, but I kept going. I went to the bathroom and sat in a stall for about ten minutes until I knew reading would be over and the classes would be switching for social studies. I just wanted to call Mom and go home, but I knew she wouldn't pick me up again. Why do I do things I don't want to do? It's a conundrum.

My grades really got better once Mrs. Milanowski started helping me in the resource room, which is just another name for the place where dummies go. I know I'm not supposed to think that anymore, and everyone has been busting their butts to make me believe that I'm really smart and a learning disability is just a way of learning differently than other regular kids. I guess that's true because I really did start getting fractions once Mrs. Milanowski explained it to me in different ways and let me use what they call manipulatives to see what she was talking about. It also helped that I was not in the room with kids who were always making fun of me and stuff. And Mrs. M. would explain it to me a million times if I asked her to. She was really cool that way. She never got pissed at me as long as I was trying.

So I was feeling a little better about school and I really did try the last half of the year to get my act together. Dr. Gulata helped me with strategies to calm myself down, and how to think about things in a good way sometimes. Mom and Cole were constantly rewarding me like I was a genius or something. I got a new bike and a CD player for my room. They also said if I got on the Honor Roll I could redecorate my room any way that I wanted to. They might be sorry they promised that.

So it's the last day of school and Mom and Cole show up all dressed up. I see them in the back of the auditorium all smiling and everything. But it's not that big of a deal. I guess they weren't sure I was going to pass.

I joined the choir this year and we sang two songs and then we all said the Pledge of Allegiance. Mrs. Wilson made a lame speech about how special we all are and then she said it was time for the awards portion of the ceremony. I sat back in my seat and started daydreaming about summer and all the books I was going to read. Then I thought I heard my name. Sarah and Ben both elbowed me at the same time from different sides. I yelled "Ow, what the. . ." Everyone started laughing and Ben said "Get up there, Mrs. Wilson called your name."

"She did?" I looked up and Mrs. Wilson was motioning to me with her curled index finger to come up to the podium. I tripped over Sarah's big feet and put my hand in Brittany's face to steady myself but I finally made it up to Mrs. W. and I noticed the audience clapping.

"What did I do?" I asked Mrs. Wilson. My voice went through the microphone and everyone laughed again.

"What you did, young lady, was an excellent job of improving your grades this year and so I am presenting you with the award for the most improved student. Here is your certificate."

"Thank you." I tried to look out and see Mom and Cole. I found them and saw my grandpa sitting with them. He looked really happy.

"Would you like to say anything, Anais?"

"Well, I always like to say something, you know that, Mrs. W." The audience laughed again. "I'd like to thank Mrs. Milanowski for helping me this year and my Mom and Cole. . . my dad." Then I kind of felt like I was going to cry, so I stumbled my way back to my chair and lots of the other kids were going *good job, way to go* and stuff like that. It felt pretty good and I was glad that I tried so hard.

The auditorium was super hot and all the kids were squirming around. One thing I've learned is that in fourth grade kids get a lot smellier. I was using my fancy certificate as a fan when Mrs. Wilson called my name again. Of course, again, I was not paying attention. When I got up to the podium Mrs. Wilson gave me another certificate for achievement in writing. It turns out I had the highest score on the Ohio writing achievement test out of all the fourth graders in the whole district. Maybe I'm not such a loser after all.

After the ceremony was over Mom and Cole and Grandpa all hugged me and were smiling and stuff.

"Anais, I'm so proud to be your grandpa today. You are quite talented. I hope you'll let me read some things you've written."

"Sure, anytime, Grandpa. I like having a grandpa!" Everyone laughed.

"How about if we all go out for ice cream? My treat. Anyone know a good place?" Grandpa said.

"We do. I'll lead the way, Mr. May," Cole said.

"You can call me George from now on."

We went to an ice cream place that was close to the school. I ordered a big old banana split. We sat outside at a picnic table and had fun laughing and talking. I felt really happy because one, I finished school and two, I had fun with my new Grandpa, and three, I never saw my mom so happy.

"Dad, can you tell me anything about our family medical history?"

"Why do you need to know? Is something wrong?"

We sat at the local coffee shop on a wintry Saturday morning. I had just dropped Anais off at swimming lessons at the Y. Dad takes every opportunity to spend time with me these days and his fondness for Anais and Cole is more than I could have hoped for.

"Well, over the years I haven't taken very good care of myself. For years I had no money or health insurance, and any money I had went to Ani's check-ups of course. I need to find a doctor here and get a full physical. I'm sure they'll want to know any pertinent information, so I thought I'd ask."

"But you're okay, aren't you, honey?"

"Yeah, well, sometimes I don't feel quite right, I thought I should check it out."

"Of course you should. Well, let's see. Your grandma is healthy as a horse as you can see. I've been battling high cholesterol for about ten years. I'm on some medication and I try to eat right, but my doctor is not very happy about my levels recently. Maybe I'll be switching medications."

"Is cholesterol an inherited thing?" I stirred milk into my tea.

"I think it might be. I know heart disease runs in families. It's not your heart, is it?"

I laughed, "No, Dad, I think my heart is okay. At least medically speaking." It was comforting and new to have a parent worry about me. I soaked it up. "Anything else?"

"Well, of course, there are some things in a person's background that you can't know for sure." He poured a second packet of sugar in his tea.

"What do you mean? What about Mom's side?"

"I can't think of anything that would affect you." He looked distractedly out the window. "Look at the wind blowing those trees around. Did you have wind like this in New Jersey?"

"Yeah, I'd say the weather is very similar there. It looked a lot like Ohio. I think it's the lake breeze here though."

"Never been out of this state much. Your mother doesn't like to travel, you know."

"I know. Dad, is that all you can tell me about medical history?"

"That's all I can think of, honey."

"Are you okay, Daddy?" I suddenly felt six years old.

"Oh, sure. Well, I had a small heart attack a couple years ago."

"You did?" Tears filled my eyes and immediately spilled down my face without warning. "I'm so sorry. I didn't know. I should've. . ."

"Hey, it's okay. It was a very mild attack. I'm still here. We're here together. That's what matters now, isn't it?" Dad pulled a tissue out of his pocket, and put it in my hand.

When I told the doctor about the periods of numbness, the loss of balance and occasional fall, and the few weeks that my vision had blurred, she only nodded her head and said, "Uh-huh." She asked about other symptoms such as fatigue, dizziness, depression, and cognitive difficulties. I tried to joke about the last one saying I was never the brightest light bulb in the pack, but she didn't laugh.

"What could it be?" I asked

"I hesitate to make diagnoses without further tests."

"What kind of tests?"

"I am going to schedule you for an MRI. Do you have health insurance? It's very expensive." I tried to read her face for a hint of the seriousness of my condition, but there was no expression for me to read. I was starting to feel a little panic.

"I'm going to college right now, but I do have some student health insurance. What is the MRI for?"

"It's going to give me a look at your spine and your brain. After you have the MRI call my office and set up an appointment with me to discuss the results." She said in her business-like way. I told myself if it was life threatening surely she would be more compassionate.

"I would also like you to see an ophthalmologist. Here is a recommendation." She handed me a card.

"I'm not having the blurred vision anymore. That was over a year ago, actually. I just thought I'd mention it," I said.

"I'm glad you did. It may help us understand what's wrong here. Have you always lived in this part of the country?"

"I lived here until I was seventeen and then I lived in the New York City area until this past year."

"Is there anyone in your family with an inherited neurological disorder or a neuromuscular disease?" The doctor continued typing on the computer keyboard in front of her. I attempted to lean over to see what she was typing, but I could not see the screen because I was seated on the examining table.

"Not that I know of." My voice sounded small and weak, even to me. This doctor's bedside manner was making me feel like a child who is only supposed to speak when spoken to.

She stood up in front of me, "I need to give you a neurological exam." She asked me to do a variety of physical tasks like pushing on her hands with my hands, squeezing two of her fingers, touching my finger to my nose with my eyes open and then closed. She used a pin and a feather to test the sensations on different parts of my body and a reflex mallet.

"Stand up please. Walk across the room on your toes. Good. Now on your heels. Stand with your arms at your sides and close your eyes." I performed robotically.

She looked into my eyes with a light and said nothing. She had me read from a card.

"I will see you in about two weeks. Try not to worry. We'll know more at that point. It was nice to meet you." She walked out the door leaving me with only my unspoken questions and fears.

Cole

Lavender looked like a puppy dog that's just been whipped into submission when she walked through the door. She told me about the exam and the doctor's cold responses and unwillingness to even give her an idea of what could be wrong. She fell into a silent pout for about a day, ignoring her schoolwork and keeping her distance from everyone. I realized that whatever these physical symptoms were, she had been hiding the bulk of them from me for a long time. For the past year or two I had joked about her clumsiness and how she was so old she needed glasses. Now I felt horrible about making light of all of it. I told her I would help to pay for any tests or treatment that her minimal health insurance wouldn't cover. That just made her cry.

"If I had made something of myself, if I had already gone to college and graduated and had a career I wouldn't need my best friend to continually bail me out of life's dilemmas."

"It's only temporary. You're well on your way to completing your education and choosing a career. It's going to take a little more time, though." I attempted to change the subject. "With most of your required courses out of the way, have you thought about a major?"

"Of course I've thought about it. But it's just one more thing I can't seem to make a decision about. Maybe I'll go back to being a punk rock singer, how about that?"

"That's very funny, sweetheart. Let's try to think outside the box."

"The only thing I've ever really enjoyed was working at Lizzy's with the plants and the lavender." She blew her nose.

"Well, what about the business end of the farm? Lizzy turned some of that over to you, didn't she?"

"Yes, I was pretty good at it too."

"Maybe there is a business you can start or run. Get a business degree."

"Oh, sure, I've got tons of money saved to start a business."

"There are loans for that, you know. Think about it."

The phone rang and as Lavender moved across the room to answer it I noticed her grab onto the couch on the way for balance. How had I not noticed these things before? I went about straightening up the living room of books, magazines and schoolwork during Lavender's short conversation.

"It was my mother. Can you believe it? She actually called me. She wants to spend an afternoon with Anais and me, take us to lunch and shopping."

"Wow, that's a turn of events. What did you say?"

"I said yes, of course."

Anais

I'm supposed to be cleaning my room, and Cole says I can't come out until it's finished. That's so lame of him. Why does he care if my room is clean? I like it messed up like this. It's got all my stuff and I know where everything is - well, usually. My room is about as big as doghouse. Where am I supposed to put all this junk anyway? Cole threw a few cardboard boxes in my room and said, "Maybe these will help." Yeah, thanks a lot.

In the hallway ceiling outside my room there are some stairs that you can pull down and go up into the attic. Once, when I was mad at my mom I went up there, pulled the stairs back up and stayed there for like, an hour. My mom was freaking, because she had no idea where I was. That was hilarious. Anyway, I filled the boxes up with some stuff from when I was in third or fourth grade and I decided to try to put them in the attic. While I was up there I noticed a box that had my name on it, so I decided to check it out. I thought it would be baby toys or drawings I did when I was little, but it was a box full of paperwork.

There were all kinds of forms and reports and stuff. One was called a School Age Evaluation Team Report from when I was in first grade. The first few pages were background information. I noticed in the spot for father it said *unknown.* I've asked my mom a thousand times who my father is. When I was little she would just say I didn't have one, but Cole was just like a father. That was okay with me until I knew about the facts of life, and realized that everyone had a father, and that my mom must have had sex with a lot of men if she didn't know which one of them might be my father. That's kind of disgusting. So one time when we were having a fight I asked her why she had sex with so many boys. She didn't answer me and she didn't speak to me the rest of the day. But now, seeing that word *unknown* on this report, it just makes me sad, because somewhere out there I do have a dad.

The next page in the report had a checklist of concerns for the referral: attention span, activity level, acting out, peer relationships, adult relationships – all checked off. Under that it said: *Ms. May believes that smoking, taking drugs and alcohol during her pregnancy has contributed to Anais's difficulties in school.* What? My mom was stoned while she was preggers with me? No wonder I'm an idiot. I like the way she lectures me all the time about smoking, drugs and alcohol and she did it herself. What a hypocrite!

Then I come to a page of test scores. There is something called verbal IQ, performance IQ, and full scale IQ. I guess the verbal score means talking because it was the highest. It was 135. There were a lot of other scores and stuff that I had no clue what they meant, except one called listening comprehension, which was 90. I'm thinking that's bad compared to 135.

On the last page there is a summary that says: *Anais is diagnosed with ADHD as evidenced by her hyperactivity and short attention span in first grade. She has difficulty completing academic assignments, staying on task, and following directions. When challenged, Anais throws tantrums and becomes disruptive. Other elevated scores are noted in the areas of rule breaking behaviors and aggressive behaviors. Standardized tests show that Anais has above average intelligence, and scored particularly high in the verbal subtests. Anais is already reading at a third grade level. Anais's math scores are somewhat lower in the basic concepts of addition, subtraction, telling time and counting money. Anais is having difficulty maintaining appropriate relationships with peers and adults. She often becomes frustrated with peers and initiates arguments. She is often unwilling to share and cooperate, which her mother attributes to being an only child and somewhat isolated at home. Anais's fine motor skills lie within the above average range. Although test scores do not indicate a learning disability in math at this time, the team recommends further testing in second grade.*

Recommendations: The Clairemont Elementary School problem solving team recommends that Ms. May seek medical intervention for Anais's ADHD as well as counseling. Classroom teachers should set up a behavior intervention plan with a daily reward system. Consultation services will be arranged with Mrs. Stevens, the special education teacher. Ms. Evans, the social worker will write Social Stories with Anais on a regular basis to address social concerns with peers.

Wow. I knew I was a loser, but I didn't know it was that bad! I don't remember much back then, but I do remember a lady taking me to her miniscule office and we would write stories together about stuff like taking turns to talk and making friends. I thought it was fun, because I loved writing and making stuff up. I didn't know it was because I was a social outcast.

There was a piece of paper attached to the last page and someone had written:

Ms. May is against any type of medical intervention for personal reasons. She believes drugs were the cause of these problems and should not be used to solve them. Ms. May also claims not to have medical insurance and cannot afford the recommendations made by the team. Ms. May requests that the school use their own resources to help Anais and she will work with her at home as well.

I decided not to say anything about what I'd found – at least not yet. There were about a million thoughts flying around in my brain that I needed to think about. Most of what I'd read was no big surprise, but the unknown dad was making me feel really sad all of a sudden.

When Mom told me I had to spend Saturday with my dorky grandmother, I almost freaked. But since I just finished being grounded I decided to chill. I just hoped no one I know would see me at the mall.

It started out okay. We were just walking through the mall and Grandma was trying to be nice, but it seemed hard for her. I felt a little bit sorry for her. When she smiled it looked like it hurt her face. She kept asking me stupid questions about what kind of music I listened to, or rather, what did my mother *allow* me to listen to. Like she really knew any of the groups anyway. She commented on the fact that my jeans had a hole in the knee and I tried to explain that I bought them that way, but she didn't get that at all. She said that was the most ridiculous thing she'd ever heard. I doubt that.

We walked by some high school kids and she said, "Look at those hoodlums."

I'm like, what?

"Mom, those aren't hoodlums," my mom said. "That's just the way kids dress now."

"Well, I certainly hope you don't let Anais dress like that."

"I think she should be able to dress the way she wants to, within reason," my mom said.

"You haven't changed at all, have you Christine? Here's where we're having lunch. It looks like we'll have to wait. I'll put our name on the list."

"Mom?" I looked at my mom like *get me out of here!* My mom said let's just give it a chance. Okay whatever, but I'm ordering a hamburger, cheese fries, coke *and* dessert!

We sat on a bench waiting for a table and no one said anything for a few minutes. Mom tried to ask Grandma about some people she knew back in the day, but Grandma said she didn't "associate" with them anymore.

Lunch was okay. Grandma didn't like what I ordered because it is so unhealthy, but I don't care. We were waiting for dessert, so I went to the bathroom. When I came back I heard Mom saying *please don't tell me how to raise my own daughter*, and I was like, oh no. When I got to the table they both stopped talking. After that we walked through the mall some more. Mom bought me a new t-shirt and Grandma bought me a book.

~~~~~~~

Tonight the bats are darting around the streetlight outside my window and it's firefly time again. I've got a jar of them sitting next to me in the dark. I'm about to let them go though. When I was little I used to keep them in the jar and then wonder why they died. I guess it seems stupid that I'm still catching fireflies to light up my room at night, but it's comforting to me. It reminds me of summer nights in New Jersey when it was just Mom and Cole and me.

I think I'm ready for school in the fall. I learned a lot this year. I fought being the "special ed" kid for a while, but it really did help me to find out the ways I could learn the best. Having ADHD really sucks most of the time. Like, I keep starting to clean up this pig sty of a bedroom and I go for about ten minutes and then something catches my interest and next thing you know I've been sitting on the floor for two hours reading some book I found under the bed or writing in my journal about fireflies or playing a game on the computer Mom and Cole got me for getting good grades. Mom calls me for dinner and I look up and my room is still a mess.

Everyone says how come you can focus on a book or a game and not math or listening to a teacher, and I say that's just the way ADHD is. I can spend hours doing a jigsaw puzzle. It's like my mind just fastens on to something and gets stuck there. But something that's boring or I don't get – well, I just drift away without even realizing it. I've always got to be doing something, which I don't think is necessarily bad. And I'm the "drama queen" for always reacting to everything before I think about whether it's worth reacting to or not. Dr. Gulata is working with me on that because it tends to get me in a lot of trouble with outbursts in class. I still talk too much and so I try to get some of my thoughts out in writing, which is much less annoying to everyone around me.

Mom and Cole and I belong to a church now and it's pretty cool because everyone there likes me and accepts me the way I am. The adults are always telling me that God gave me a lot of gifts that I need to use. They also don't ask retarded questions about why Mom and Cole and I are a family. It's all good with them. Even Pastor Brian says God must have put us all together for a reason.

One Sunday Pastor Brian was reading the scripture for the morning and this is what it said – *I do the things I don't mean to do and I don't do the things I mean to do.* I was actually paying attention and when I heard him read that I thought "Yes! That's me!" Unfortunately I thought it out loud and everyone started laughing. I looked over at Mom and she was just shaking her head. Pastor Brian said, "I like your enthusiasm Anais!" But again, I did something I didn't mean to do.

Anyways, I'm praying that God will help me with this stuff. She knows that I need to grow up and be more responsible because my mom really needs me now.

I never argue about going to church like most kids. Sometimes I go the Sunday school class and sometimes I sit in the service with Mom and Cole. I have friends there that don't go to my school and that's the only time I get to see them.

There was this teacher, Annie, who is awesome and made Sunday school fun. We'd act out Bible stories and she'd always give me a part because I'm so dramatic. She was always telling me how cool my family is and she admired my mom's style. Whatever. I know that. No one had to tell her that Cole isn't my dad. Plus, we have different names, so it's kind of obvious. But Annie adopted a baby so she had to quit teaching for a while. Then this lady Helene took over. She was all right until one Sunday she had us doing these Father's Day projects, so naturally I made mine for Cole. We were supposed to write a poem about all the ways our dads helped us and stuff, and how that was like God's love for us. She had special paper to print it out on the computer.

"Oh, no, I don't think you should use your father's first name for the poem," Helene said looking over my shoulder.

"I don't call him Dad. He's not my real dad, but he's the only dad I've ever had. We've lived together since I was in kindergarten," I had to explain for like, the millionth time.

"You have? Well, that doesn't seem right. Why doesn't he marry your mother? Grown-ups should not live together outside of marriage. That's in the Bible."

"I guess because they're friends. Cole doesn't really like girls that way," I said as I was continuing to write the final draft of my poem. My friend Ashley and I made eye contact and we were both trying not to crack up.

"I see, well . . ." and Helene just sort of wandered away. I looked over at Ashley and she just couldn't hold it in anymore. Helene looked over at us, and then just walked away. A lot of people in our town know Cole since he's a principal, and everyone loves him because he's just a cool person.

This is really sad, though. After that some people in the church got their panties in a twist about Cole and said that the denomination had rules about his so-called lifestyle. Some butthead sent a letter to Cole saying basically that maybe he should find another place to go to church! Can you believe that? What would Jesus do, guys? Don't they remember the part where Jesus has dinner with the outcasts and misfits and he was cool with them? Jesus came to show us how to live, anyone knows that. It made me really mad because Cole was upset and also I wouldn't get to see Ashley much anymore. Why are some people such shitheads when they don't even know what they're talking about? How about reading the part in the bible where it says *love your neighbor as yourself?*

Pastor Brian visited us one night and he felt bad about the whole thing, but he was kind of stuck in the middle. He told us we didn't have to leave the church and that we were valued members. But Cole said he didn't want to attend a church that didn't want him there and that he wouldn't feel comfortable anymore. Cole doesn't like to make a fuss about stuff like this.

So now we're going to find a new church that accepts everyone just like Jesus did. Mom suggested that we find a non-denominational church that doesn't have so many rules and doctrine, whatever that is. She told me that she'd make sure that I get to see my friends too. And Cole said to remember that it wasn't God that rejected us, it was just human beings.

Lavender

My mother never had hobbies like normal people. Her sole hobby has been to see how much she can control other people. I thought maybe this would have mellowed with time, but it hasn't. She is still more interested in appearances than reality. As a child I gave my mom fake flowers one Mother's Day because I knew she would like the fact that they looked real but actually were not.

My parents' house still appears as if no one lives there. It could be a model house that you visit, but have to use your imagination to tell what it would be like to live in it. Sometimes I am angry with my dad for sacrificing so much of himself for my mother. I resent that he let her boss him around and minimize the life experiences and happiness that John and I could have had in our childhood. I know he knew better, after all, he was raised by Fiona. Other times I feel sad for him. He seems beaten down and resigned. He's retired now, and after all the years of working to support his family he should be enjoying time at home, but it seems he mostly wants to escape it. I am grateful for the time I have with him now after so much time I lost. If nothing else I know I did the right thing by coming home to reestablish our relationship and give Anais a grandpa.

When you're a kid, you don't pay attention to your parents' lives or care to know much about their past. It isn't until coming back home that I've realized I know nothing about my mother's life. Her parents are both gone and she has one sister, my Aunt Barbara, who lives about an hour away. They never were close as far as I know. She dropped out of college to marry my dad and she has been a housewife ever since then. I remember photographs in albums of some typical family outings when I was very young, even before John was born. A trip to the Cleveland

Zoo or swimming in Lake Erie at Mentor Headlands State Park, family friends over on the Fourth of July. I haven't seen the photos for many years, but I know my mother was smiling in some of them.

Grandma Fiona brought out an album one Wednesday night. It had pictures of Mom holding John and I as babies. She looked different. Not just younger, but more peaceful. Her expressions were soft and tranquil, unscarred. I thought about the fact that my mother never had told me any stories about my birth or my infancy. I was six when John was born. I vaguely remember the excitement of the baby coming home and feeling protective as the big sister.

John's memories and experiences are less extreme than mine. He says he doesn't remember things being as bad as I describe them. I think being six years apart in age, and different genders, our experiences wouldn't typically be the same anyway. Mom had completely different expectations for John and me. She was much harsher with me, but as a teenager I attributed that to the fact that John was so much younger. I thought *his time will come*, but now I don't think it ever did.

Now being with Mom is still like walking around with a lit firecracker in your hand. I can already see that she can't wait to get her hands on my daughter. Our first argument was on the day we went to lunch together. Anais went to the bathroom.

"Why do you allow her to wear those ripped clothes? She looks like a pauper," Roberta said watching Anais walk away from the table.

"I guess I'm not as concerned about the way she looks as who she is – and she's an amazing girl. I'm proud of her."

"Well, people will judge you by your children you know."

"I realize that is something that always concerned you, Mom, but I want Ani to be her own person, not a little me. Anyway, I'm used to being unjustly judged."

"What is that supposed to mean? I didn't judge you. I tried to raise you properly."

I felt weakened by the effort of the discussion. "I'm sure you did, Mom, but Anais is my child, not yours. Let's end this conversation now. I don't want her to be involved and she's coming back. I was hoping our relationship would not revolve around how much you could influence her."

"I'm only trying to help."

"Just please don't tell me how to raise my daughter."

"Anais," Roberta said as Ani sat back down in the booth. "I will buy you some new clothes if you wear what I suggest."

"No thanks, I like the clothes I have."

My daughter is much feistier and surer of herself than I was at her age. I had no one on my side, but Ani has had people in her life to give her acceptance and confidence even when she's faced some exceptional challenges. The angels I prayed for have been there for her - Lydia, Chip, now Fiona and Dad and always, always, Cole.

School exams and stressful visits with my mother have given me reasons to put off making that MRI appointment. I'll do it soon though because I have a blurry spot in both my eyes and part of my left side is numb.

2005

Cole

When I arrived home all I saw was Lavender dropping to her knees with the phone in her hand. My first thought was that it was another fall, another symptom, but then I heard "Oh, God, no!" and a horrible choking sound. I ran and sat on the floor next to her.

"What is it? What's wrong?" I thought of Anais and automatically turned around, my eyes searching the living room, but then I saw her standing a few feet away.

"Mommy?" Ani ran over to join us. Lavender only said, "Dad."

She handed the phone to me and it was Fiona.

"Chrissie? Chrissie?"

"It's me, Fiona. What happened?"

"George, he's . . . he's gone. Oh, Lord, my son is gone," Fiona wailed into the telephone.

"Fiona, please, tell me what happened." I could feel the pounding of my chest through my shirt. I gripped the phone in one hand and tried to reach out to Lavender with the other. Anais knelt on the floor in front of her mother, their foreheads touching as Ani handed Lavender tissues.

"He was such a good son," Fiona blew her nose into the phone. "He came over to shovel the driveway. I told him not to. I . . . I . . . I promised I'd get a snowblower this year, but he insisted."

"Fiona, please, what happened?" I got down on the floor next to the girls.

"He had a heart attack, Cole. I looked out the window and saw him laying on the driveway - in the snow - the damned shovel still in his hand. I ran out to him. I should've called 911 first, but . . ." she sobbed.

"Fiona, we'll be right there. Will you be all right until we get there?"

"Yes, my neighbor, Helen, saw the whole thing and ran over to help. She's still here."

"Ask her to stay until we get there, okay?" I grabbed Lavender's and Ani's coats out of the closet.

"Yes, I'll do that. Cole?"

"Yes?"

"I called the paramedics, but it was too late. He was out in the cold, in the snow. He was alone."

"He knew you were there, Fiona. We're on our way." Lavender and Anais cried all the way to Fiona's. In the rearview mirror I could see Ani's eyes wide with fear over seeing her mother's grief. I was Ani's age when I lost my grandmother. The pervasive fog of death is a sense you never forget. The hollow helplessness and the stunning fear of the one thing we can never understand is haunting. When we arrived at Fiona's there was already a sea of people from her church and the neighborhood in the living room comforting her. The four of us fell into a single clutch of arms and tears.

John arrived with Roberta from the hospital. Lavender immediately hugged her mother and refused to let go even though Roberta's arms hung at her sides -- her face unreadable. Anais did the same, then her eyes searched for me. I nodded my head in approval.

George's sister, Kathy, arrived and she and Lavender reunited affectionately. During the evening people came and went, each one needing an account of George's passing. Lavender was inconsolable and just kept repeating *why now*? Ani appeared to be completely overwhelmed the entire time, and unusually quiet. I made an effort to not let her get lost in the chaos.

"Roberta, I'm so sorry." I took her cold hand in mine. "I didn't know George very long, but I know he'll be greatly missed." She pulled back slightly, but then allowed me to continue. "I know Lav – Christine is going to struggle with all the time lost with her father, but I'm so glad we came back . . ." I suddenly felt foolish. As if I were advocating for Lavender's feelings when this woman had just lost her husband.

Roberta eased her hand out of mine and crossed her arms in front of her. "I'm sure we'll all face regrets now that George is gone. Thank you for your concerns."

"Oh, well I . . . I'm truly sorry for your loss." I did not know what else to say.

The calling hours at the funeral home and the memorial service were more of the same. Lavender's uninhibited tears, her mother stoic and silent, Anais confused and observant. Fiona accepted every hug and kiss and comment with graciousness and warmth. The number of people that came to honor George and surround Fiona stunned me. Roberta sat in the shadows quietly mourning in her own way. People spoke to her as briefly as possible and then moved away.

Two days after the funeral Roberta left to stay at her sister's house for an undetermined amount of time, leaving Lavender, John and Fiona to grieve as a family.

Anais

I liked having a Grandpa. I think I already loved him because he really tried to get to know me and he cared about my mom.

I've never seen a dead person before. No one remembered to tell me that when you get to the funeral home you actually *see* the person in the casket. My mom told me I could go over and say goodbye to Grandpa and I thought I was going to throw up. I could see a little bit of his face from across the room. I stood by the door for a while until Cole came up and asked if I wanted to go with him. When we got over there, Mom was standing there crying and talking to Grandpa like he was still alive, so Cole and I waited for a few minutes. Then Mom turned around and held out her arms to us, but she couldn't even talk because she was crying so hard. The worst part was after the service when just the family stayed in the room and we all had to go up and say goodbye. I was really crying then. That was the first time I saw my grandmother cry too. I thought it was weird that she didn't cry very much, but Cole said some people just don't express themselves with tears. Grandma Fiona said, "I love you George. You were a wonderful son and I'll see you when I get to heaven."

I wondered about heaven. At Grandma Fiona's church they say that if we believe in God we'll go to heaven, even if we did some bad things on Earth. She'll forgive us if we ask. I think that heaven will be different for everyone. Whatever you wanted life to be down here on Earth, but it never was, that's what heaven will be. I hope Grandpa is happy there.

Lavender

"I know you, Lav," Cole said, "You're fixated on regret and guilt. But what you should focus on is the good decision you made to come home. You made your dad very happy. You should be proud of that."

"But there was so much wasted time. Time I could've spent with him." I began to cry again. "When I was seventeen my parents were a group package to me. I didn't see how different my dad was. I should've given him another chance way before now. Why did this have to happen now?"

"If you only feel regret then you're just creating the same life for yourself that you had before we came to Ohio. You'll never find peace, honey."

"I'm sure you're right, as usual. Listen, I'm meeting John at Mom and Dad's house. We're going to go through Dad's things while my mom is gone. She told Aunt Barbara she didn't want to deal with it at all."

"Then you're going to your MRI appointment?"

"Yes, I am. I'll see you later."

The wind whipped the springtime snow into my face as I got out of the car. I used to love the snow, but now it was an enemy. The reason my dad was dead. I hated the snow. John was already upstairs in Dad's bedroom. The house was freezing and the stairs creaked as I climbed them. I hadn't been upstairs since coming back to Ohio.

"Separate bedrooms? When did that happen?" I asked.

"A long time ago. It sure wasn't Dad's idea," John said. On the bed were stacks of simple, solid colored shirts and pants. All of Dad's shoes were in a box next to the bed. Two suits still hung in the closet covered in plastic. I thought I remembered one of them from years ago. I looked around the room. It was plain and sparse and lacking any sort of color or patterns. The bed was neatly made and the dressers cleared off except for four photographs; my parents' wedding day, John's high school graduation, my high school picture and a small school picture of Anais I had recently given him.

"John, I'm sorry you have to do this. Do you want me to take over?" John looked up from the dresser drawer he was shuffling through. He had tears in his eyes.

"I can't believe he's gone."

"I know." I moved to his side and put my arm around his waist.

"You really made him happy, Chrissie. He told me he was proud of you and that he was amazed that you raised Anais all on your own."

"He said that?" I sat on the bed and pulled a tissue out of my pocket as the tears returned. "Oh, God, there are so many things we should have known about each other. Now it's too late. I don't know what I was thinking all of the years I was away – that Mom and Dad and Grandma would be here forever? Just waiting for me to come back? How could I have been that stupid? That selfish."

John sat next to me, but said nothing. We both stared at Dad's dresser for a few minutes.

"What's your favorite memory of Dad?" I asked.

"Well, I'm not sure I have a favorite. I guess all the times we'd play ball out in the backyard." John paused, "When I was sixteen Mom didn't think I was mature enough to have a driver's license. One night I overheard Dad tell her that driving is an important milestone for a boy and he was not going to let her take that away from me."

"Wow, he really stuck up for you, huh?"

"Yeah, actually he did that a lot."

"He did? I guess it was different for you. I mean, maybe because you were the son or something." John went back to the chest of drawers and pulled out a wooden box.

"What's that?"

"I don't know. I've never seen it before.   It's locked."

"Have you seen a key or anything?"

"No, but it looks easy enough to break into." John took a pocketknife from the dresser and pried the little box open. It held a small, faded photograph.

"It looks like this was taken with one of those old Polaroid cameras. The kind that you could get the picture instantly," John said.

"Yeah, I sort of remember those. Who is it?" I took the photo from his hand. It was a picture of a young woman holding an infant.

John said, "That's not mom is it?"

"No, definitely not," I turned the photo over and written in pencil it said: *Lisa and Christine Feb. 1976.*

John and I stood silently for a moment.

John spoke first, "Chrissie, that's you."

"I know, but who is the woman? Who is Lisa? Do we have any relatives named Lisa?"

"No. Look at her though."

"Yeah?"

"She's got red hair."

"She's got . . red hair," I repeated the words slowly to myself. "Why would a red haired woman be holding me on what looks like a few days after I was born?"

"Look at the background. It's a hospital."

"Maybe it was one of the nurses. Like before Mom and I left the hospital they wanted a picture of one of their nurses." I looked up at John. My heart felt like a superball, whiz-banging and ricocheting around in my chest, bruising me from within.

"Why would Dad have a picture of a nurse from thirty years ago locked up in a wooden box. Come on Chrissie. Think about it."

"I was thinking about it, but I don't think I want to now." My body fell backwards and I collapsed on my father's neatly stacked clothes. I covered my face with my hands. A burning sensation crept up my throat, more tears stung under my eyelids.

"Oh, God!" I sat back up, pushing my tangled hair off my face.

"Chris . . ."

"Shut up, John! Don't say anything! I mean it. Just shut up!" I clutched handfuls of my hair and pulled as hard as I could. "This is fucking bullshit!" I pulled a pillow off the bed and crushed it into my face, sobbing. John just stood there with the photograph in his hand.

"Maybe there's a reason . . . I mean. . . we don't know who this Lisa is . . ."

"I said shut up!" I screamed from the middle of the pillow. After a few minutes of a stunned stupor I looked up from the pillow, now wet with mucus, and black with mascara. John was emptying Dad's sock drawer. I went outside and found some cigarettes in the glove compartment of the car. I leaned up against the house, the snow melting against my bare ankles, and smoked two cigarettes. The smoke blurred my focus as the snow covered my hair with a net of whiteness. I coughed and choked on the drainage flowing out of my sinuses, my brain frozen and blank as the world around me.

"Chrissie, come on in. You're gonna freeze." John pulled on my arm and I let him lead me into the house.

"Here, I made you some tea. Do you want to talk about this?"

"Thanks." I put my pale blue hands around the steaming teacup. One of my silver rings slid off my finger onto the table. "It's funny the way your hands seem to shrink when they're cold, isn't it?" John faced the kitchen window and squinted at the brightness of the snow. "Sorry for yelling at you. It's not your fault."

"I was thinking," John wiped off the counter, "Maybe we should ask Grandma who Lisa is. Maybe she'd know."

"Yeah, I guess I'll have to face reality some time now, won't I?"

"Maybe there's an explanation . . . "

"Like what, Johnny? What sort of explanation do you think there is?"

"I don't know. This whole thing with you, Chrissie. I mean . . . it's been hard. Ever since we got back in touch - you say all these things about Mom and Dad and your horrible life, and, well, I know they weren't perfect, but what are you so angry about?"

"You know what? I don't know! Maybe I made up my whole childhood! Maybe I'm fucking crazy, how's that?" John turned his back to me and went upstairs. I drank the rest of my tea, washed the cup out and went upstairs to find him.

"Johnny," I leaned against the doorway to Dad's bedroom as John continued his silent packing. I noticed how meticulously he packed each item, just like Roberta would have done. "Have you ever felt like your whole world was disintegrating before your eyes? Like everything you thought you knew was a lie? Like you understood absolutely nothing about your own life?"

John faced me in anger, "No, I've had a perfect life, you know. No one has ever suffered the way you have, big sister."

I stared at the flawless hardwood floor beneath my feet for a few minutes.

"Okay, I deserved that. Listen, I don't want to alienate you."

"I'm grieving too." For the first time I noticed his unshaven face and the darkness circling his eyes. He smelled like overused deodorant, so unlike his typical perfect grooming.

"I know. And I'm a selfish bitch." I moved towards the closet and brought out the remaining boxes and items. "Fiona. Grandma. She's said things to me like someday I'd understand and she believes in keeping promises. Promises like keeping secrets. That's what she was talking about."

"Well, we can't ask Dad, but we can sure as hell ask her," John said, finally looking at me. "Do you want to do that? Because if you do, I'll go with you."

"I'll call her and see if we can go over when we're finished here."

"This is a nice surprise, my two favorite grandchildren. Take those coats off and I'll get some tea." Fiona wore a crocheted yellow and orange poncho and red stretch pants. Jazz from a radio floated into the kitchen from another room and the house smelled like slightly burnt toast.

"How are you doing Grandma?" John asked.

"Oh, I'm managing. How's your mother?" John and I glanced at each other.

"She isn't communicating with anyone right now. Barb is pretty worried about her. I asked if we could come out to visit, but she said she needed more time," John said.

"You'd think she'd want her children around her most of all. I have to say, I've never understood your mother," Fiona set teacups on the table. She turned to get the cream and sugar.

"Are you sure about that?" I asked.

"What do you mean, dear?"

"Are you sure that you don't understand my mother?" I made a huge effort not to express emotion. None of this was Grandma's fault and I did not intend to burden her with my reactions.

John cut in. "Grandma, we found something in Dad's dresser. Do you know anything about this?" He handed her the photograph.

"Well, let me see." She took her glasses off her forehead and adjusted them on her nose. John and I watched as her eyes focused on the old photo. She turned it over and read out loud, *Lisa and Christine Feb. 1976.*

"Where did you say this came from?"

"Dad's dresser. It was locked up in a little wooden box," John said.

"Well, I'm sure he had a reason for locking it up. You shouldn't go into people's personal things, Johnny." Fiona got up and began putting cookies on a china plate.

"Grandma, Dad's gone. John and I are packing up his things so Mom doesn't have to do it when she comes home," I said. "I don't think whatever secrets Dad had really matter . . . "

"I'm just not sure now . . . will you two excuse me for a minute? You have some of these cookies." Fiona left the room.

"What do you think is going on?" John whispered.

"I don't know. She seems a little confused and upset. Maybe we should have waited a while to do this. I don't want to cause her any more heartache."

"Grandma, are you okay?" John yelled in the direction of the hallway bathroom.

"Oh, yes, just a minute, you two."

Fiona reappeared with a forced smile on her face.

"My goodness, this is something isn't it? You finding that picture? You know I'm quite forgetful these days and, well, 1976 was along time ago, wasn't it?"

"Grandma, do you know who Lisa is? The woman in the picture?" I asked.

Fiona sat across from John and I at the table. Her gnarled hands busied themselves smoothing out the flowered cotton tablecloth repeatedly. I could feel John's eyes on me, telling me to be patient, not to rush her.

"Well, I had to go and collect my thoughts and make sure I'm right about this," she paused. "It's been so long and I had to go in private and say a little prayer for guidance.

"Grandma, whatever you need to tell me is all right. I'm going to be okay with it, I promise. Just tell me who Lisa is," I reached my hands across the table and put them over hers.

"Christine, I'm not going to lie to you. That's your biological mother. I'm sorry you had to find out like this. I promised your parents I would never tell you." Her eyes filled with tears and I tightened my grip on her hands. "I vehemently disagreed with them. I believed you always had the right to know. But now that your father's gone, I have no more secrets to keep. I did it for him, not your mother." She pulled her hands away, removed a linen handkerchief from her pocket and dabbed at her eyes.

I took the photo off of the table, "My mother." I could feel John and Grandma staring at me. "I'm adopted?" I stared at the photo in silence. I looked up, "What about my father?"

"That's the good news. George was, and always will be your real father."

"Then who's Lisa?" John asked.

"You two are adults now, so I guess it won't hurt to explain all this to you." Grandma sat down and started pouring the tea into our cups. There was nothing in my brain even trying to guess what she was about to say.

"You know your mother, Roberta. Well, I'm sorry kids, but I never did see what your father saw in her. She seemed to take the joy out of everything. Shortly after they were married your mother got pregnant which was a shock to me because George didn't seem too happy in that department if you know what I mean."

"How would you know that?"

"Oh, he would just say little things here or there and I caught on. Putting two and two together with your mother's personality it wasn't too hard to figure out. Anyway, I'm sorry to tell you but they had a baby girl that died in childbirth."

"Oh my God," I said.

"Yes, it was a terrible tragedy. Your mother had an emergency C-section. I don't recall now what all the complications were but they told her she it was unlikely that she would conceive again."

"Wait a minute," John said, "Am *I* adopted or something."

"No, you're not Johnny. I'm getting to that part. So your mother fell into quite a depression and I didn't blame her. She lost a baby and the hope of another one. George was devastated too. Their marriage went through a real rough patch. After about six months, according to George, your mother still wouldn't let him touch her. He was suffering too and he had no one to turn to, so he had a little indiscretion, I'm afraid."

"Dad? Dad had an affair?" I clapped my hand over my mouth.

"Yes, he did and I'm not proud of him for it, but I also understand the state he was in at the time."

"Wow, Dad had an affair," John murmured to himself.

"I'm sure you're starting to get the picture here. The girl he had an affair with was a college student and she was going to put the baby up for adoption. George confessed everything to your mother and asked if she would consider raising the baby as her own. She was so desperate to be a mother that she said yes immediately. She hardly cared that George had strayed."

"My real mother's name is Lisa. Do you know anything else about her?"

"Not a thing. I don't even know her last name. Was there any hospital paperwork or adoption papers anywhere in George's things?"

"No, but we're not finished going through everything," John said.

Grandma reached across the table and gently rubbed my forearm, "Christine, honey, I know you had a rough time with your mother, but she was a good mother to you at first. She really tried, but she was never the warm, fuzzy type. Then lo and behold, six years later she was pregnant again! It was a surprise to everyone, including her doctor, but it happens. So Johnny, that's your story. You were a real little miracle."

"I never even knew that part. Mom and Dad didn't share personal things with us," John said.

"I know. In my mind, that's nothing to be ashamed of, certainly," Grandma added.

"I'm sure I'm going to have a million more questions, but I need time to absorb some of this. I'm just overwhelmed at the moment. I'm afraid my head's going to pop," I said getting up from the table. "Wait, do you know if Lisa ever saw me again or tried to keep in touch with Dad?"

"No, like I said, I never knew a thing about her. Once you were here we all treated you as if you were ours to begin with."

"Except Roberta . . ." I started, but then let it go.

"Do you think we should tell Mom that we know?" John asked.

"I think that should wait until she's up to it. We've all been through a lot these past few weeks," Grandma said.

I tried to imagine my mother's grief over losing a child. What had it felt like to be told that your baby, a daughter, was dead before her life had even begun? I remembered the fullness of Anais's life in my body. How I had been comforted by the knowledge of her inside me.

How I loved her even then. A mother can't imagine life without her baby even before it is born.

Visions of a tiny Anais fluttered through my mind's eye. How she filled my days with diapers and crying and holding and burping. Then days of toys and toddling and falling, of new words and wonder. Then years of struggle and pride and of all the times she'd made me laugh. The one good thing I had done in my life. Could I have ever loved another child as much? Is the blood bond the most powerful force between a mother and daughter? I kept hearing my brother ask me why I was so angry.

That night I dreamed of Roberta. She was young and happy. In the dream she was standing on a windy cliff – the kind I'd pictured in *Wuthering Heights*. She was holding a baby close to her body, her head thrown back to the wind, and then suddenly the baby was blown from her arms and dropped down to the crashing sea. I awoke to my voice crying, "No! Come back. My baby, come back."

Cole

I found Lavender rocking furiously in her rocking chair, smoking a cigarette. She had pulled the chair up to the window, which was cracked open to let smoke out. Staring out at the small snow covered backyard, she didn't appear to have even heard me come in. I could hear Anais's muffled music playing in her bedroom.

"Lav, you okay? How did the MRI go?"

"The MRI? Oh my gosh, I totally forgot to go!" She nervously dunked the cigarette into an empty mug on the windowsill.

"You can't put this off forever. Don't you want to know what's. . ."

"It's not that. I really forgot because something happened today. Look at this." She handed me the photograph and told me the whole story.

"It turns out I *am* like my mother," she said with tears in her eyes. "Look, she has red hair like me, and she had a baby when she was a teenager and not married. And look at what she's wearing, Cole. That could be something I found at the thrift store to wear to a show. If only Dad was here to tell me more about her. Grandma didn't know anything."

"Oh my God, Lav. I don't know what to say. Did you ever have even a hint about this?"

"No, would you ever think that one of your parents wasn't your real parent?"

"Maybe you can find her. We can look up the Ohio adoption laws on the Internet."

"I've been in such a stupor trying to absorb all this that I hadn't thought of that yet. Do you think we could?" I nodded my head. "This explains so much about my relationship with Roberta; why she never could accept who I was, why she tried so hard to make me be like her, why she favored John. I'm only beginning to understand her." Lavender turned back towards the window. "Fiona said my mom was happier when I was a baby, but then she must have started to resent me. Wouldn't you resent a child that represented a betrayal? Someone else's daughter? Especially if she wasn't your own?"

"I guess so. It's pretty hard to put myself in that position," I said.

"But you love Anais as if she were yours, don't you?"

"Of course I do. You know that."

"Then why couldn't my mother do that? It wasn't my fault that my father had an affair. It was really *her* fault."

"I don't think the circumstances of something that happened almost thirty years ago can really be understood by us."

"I know, you're right. I wonder if she asked God why her daughter couldn't have been the one to live and not me."

"I hope you're not going to say that to her, are you?"

"I don't know what I can say to her. She still is the woman that raised me. Maybe she did the best she could. I can't imagine carrying a baby for nine months and having it die. I loved Anais from the minute I knew she existed."

The next morning I went to the computer to search for adoption information. From what I read there were efforts to change Ohio laws so that adopted persons would be allowed access to health and background information. As far as finding a biological parent, the parent had to voluntarily sign a release form that would be on file before the adopted person would be able to contact them or get any information about them.

"As if I'm not in enough mental chaos, now this," Lavender handed me an official looking legal paper.

"What's this?" I asked noticing a smile that I hadn't seen for weeks.

"Apparently my dad had a little money of his own stashed away. He must have hidden this account from my mother, because John told me that all of my Dad's finances were taken care of."

"This says that the money in this account goes to you and John with no stipulations on how it is spent. Wow, Lav, you've got some money for the first time in your life. Congratulations!"

"I know! Too bad I don't deserve it, but I guess I can find something to do with it."

"What are you thinking of?"

"Well, I haven't had much time to think, but I was wondering if Mr. Jackson would consider selling this house to us?"

"To us? You mean we would buy it together? Does this mean we have to get married?" I asked putting my arm lovingly around her shoulders.

"Aw, now you just want me for my money, but if you insist. You know I've always been in love with you." She kissed me on the cheek.

"This house is perfect for us. But what if one of us actually does get romantically involved?"

"I think," Lavender said, "should that happen – which by the way I haven't given up on for either of us – that we'll work it out as friends. Let's agree that each of us will have the opportunity to buy the other person out if it ever comes to that." She stuck out her hand and we shook on it.

Anais

I miss Grandpa, but it was really cool of him to give us some money. I'm pretty sure if it was up to Grandma that wouldn't have happened. I don't see what's so big about owning a house, but Mom and Cole are all about it right now. That's all they ever talk about. It's kind of bad because now I'm hearing about all these projects we're going to do like painting and scraping off wallpaper. I don't like the word *we* when they talk about the work. Cole loves to decorate but he's never had his own home to do it in, so I guess I don't blame him.

Spring is almost here and Mom is totally obsessed with the garden she's going to plant in the backyard. There are no trees in the back so it's sunny for a garden. Ever since Mom worked at that nursery with Lizzy she's really been into plants. There are little things growing in every window in the house. I don't know what most of them are and I don't really care. Mom says it's good for the soul to have living, growing things around us. I don't spend much time worrying about my soul.

Mom told me about the fact that my Grandma adopted her. She didn't really want to explain the whole story to me, but I kept asking how Grandpa could be her real parent but not Grandma, so she finally said, "I guess you are mature enough to understand this." The fact that people have babies when they're not married is no biggie to me. Hello? I have no clue who my real dad is! Sometimes I think about the fact that there is some guy out there who is my father, especially now that we're in Ohio where Mom grew up. I don't ask my mom though, because she gets so upset about everything now with Grandpa dying and finding out Grandma isn't her real mom. Besides, Cole is a good enough dad for me. I've heard kids say stuff about my weird family, but I've decided I'd rather have a misfit family than no family at all.

Mandy is still my best friend even though sometimes I think she doesn't really want to be. Mandy tries to back me up when I get teased, but why should she? I mean, she's just about perfect. No one can even find anything to diss her about. Both of us have blond hair, but hers is really straight, and mine sort of goes wherever it wants to and it's all frizzy on warm days. I also have a ginormous scar across my forehead from when I jumped off a jungle gym when I was little, and Mandy's face is perfect. She gets like thirty dollars a week for allowance so she has some really cute clothes, too.

"Psst, Ani, this was in the bathroom," Mandy whispered. She handed me a folded up piece of notebook paper with my name on it, but it was spelled Anise. I opened it and in red marker it said AFTER SCHOOL WE'RE GOING TO BEAT THE SHIT OUT OF YOU REETARD. YOU HAVE A BLACK FATHER.

"Who wrote this?" I whispered back to Mandy. She shrugged her shoulders and had this sad look on her face. Her eyebrows looked like upside down V's. I felt like I was going to throw up a little bit. I hoped it was a joke, but I was pretty sure it wasn't. I pointed out the spelling of retard to Mandy and we both started cracking up.

Our teacher gave us a dirty look, and pointed to the boring videotape we were supposed to be watching. I smiled at him and nodded my head. At least he didn't ask me to share the note with the class.

After class, Mandy said, "What are you going to do?"

"Nothing, I guess. Run home? Maybe I should call Cole to pick me up, but what if it's just a joke and then I really do look like a retard running away from nothing?"

We kept walking, practically having to yell at each other over the noise of the hallways.

"I don't think it's a very funny joke. Who would do that?"

"Yeah, and what am I getting beat up for? Because Cole has a different skin color from mine?"

"I don't know. Just because people don't like you doesn't mean they should beat you up."

"What do you mean, people don't like me? What people?"

"Well, I didn't mean you . . . I just meant like, when people don't like each other and they do mean stuff to them. I have to stop in the bathroom, you better go in the room so you're not late."

"Okay."

"Oh, and Ani? I can't walk home with you today because I have play practice."

"Great." I said feeling like dead meat.

It's almost always hard for me to focus, especially in classes I hate, like science, but now I had to think about getting beat up. And I didn't even know who wanted to beat me up. I didn't want to be a big baby and tell an adult, so during science I decided I would just start walking home like I usually do. I walk along a busy street most of the way home, so it seemed like I'd be safe.

At 3:10 I put all my crap in my backpack, zipped it up and walked to the door of the school. I stood there for about five minutes just looking around. A couple of times a kid would bump into me like they were doing it on purpose and this one kid, Grant, said, "What are you waiting for?" which I thought was weird and I said, "None of your business idiot!"

I walked really fast for about two blocks and then Grant and Lacy jumped out from behind some bushes with their friends Alyssa and Kyle.

"It's the ree-tard!" He yelled and they stood around me in a circle even though I tried to keep walking.

"Leave me alone. I mean it!"

"Aren't you in the retard class with my dumb brother?"

"I don't know – get out of my way, come on."

"You have a stupid name, you know that?" Kyle said.

"And you think you're so smart in language arts, but you're not!" Alyssa said.

"And your father is gay and black!"

"He's not my father . . ."

The whole inside of my body felt like it was shaking. My stomach muscles kept pinching together and moving around. I held my backpack in front of me as if that were going to protect me. Grant grabbed my backpack and threw it into somebody's front yard. Someone else shoved me towards Lacy and she shoved me back the other way.

"What's going on here?" A man's voice said. He was holding my backpack.

"Who does this belong to?"

"Me," I said holding out my hand to him.

"I think you children should all get home now."

The kids all just walked away without saying anything. They didn't seem afraid of the man, but they left.

"Are you all right, young lady?"

"Yes, thanks for helping me. I'd better go."

"Why don't you wait here for a little while until they're gone."

"Yeah, I'll just sit here on your grass for a while."

"Why were they bothering you?"

"I don't know. Because I'm not like them, I guess, and my family is not like theirs either."

"Well, why would you want to be like them?" the man said smiling down at me.

"Yeah," I said, but I was thinking maybe I would like to be a little more like the other kids sometimes.

Being prescient I decided I wasn't going to tell Mom or Cole about the bullying incident, and I definitely won't tell the principal because then I *will* get the shit beat out of me! It's actually kind of interesting to me why some kids want to beat me up when they don't even know me.

It must be like when Cole and I argue about something because I think I know more about it than he does. That happens all the time and he never lets me get away with it. It makes me mad that he thinks he's so smart, and I want to feel smarter than him sometimes. Maybe that's how those kids are – they want to feel bigger or stronger than me. It's not like I'm not totally scared of them, but I'm not going to stay home from school or something stupid like that. That would just show them they're right. And as far as my family, they have no idea what they're talking about.

As a diarist I think I'll be able to use some of these experiences to write about someday. I don't want to write about the way kids treat me though. I'm pretty sure my mom would never read my diary, but if she did she would be all upset. I like seeing my mom happy now. I'm really trying to be good and not screw things up for her like I always have.

Seeing my mom go through a lot of stuff and being a part of an unusual family has taught me some things. Some of my friends, even Mandy, don't seem to know a lot about things that I know about. They just have their perfect little lives with both their parents, and they have a lot of money.

I was talking to Cole about it. I told him that my friends never have to think about family problems or not having money to do things, but I do and sometimes it sucks. Cole said that at least I understand reality and I will be able to make it through anything life brings me because

I saw my mom do it. I didn't argue with him that time, because I think he's right.

I just thought of a good one for Cole: I'll love you until - Anais is the most popular girl in the school.

"The results of the MRI and the report from the ophthalmologist are as I suspected," the doctor said holding a folder of information. She looked up from her papers and I gripped the side of the chair.

"Yes?" The doctor continued to examine the folder. Why did I have to prod her?

"Ms. May I believe you have a mild form of multiple sclerosis. There are several lesions on your spine and brain. You have also experienced optic neuritis. There is not a true definitive test for MS, but when we look at all of these factors that would be my diagnosis at this time."

I waited a few seconds for more information. "I . . I'm sorry. I'm not familiar with multiple sclerosis. Am I going to die from it? What's going to happen to me?"

"It is not fatal. You appear to be in a remission at this point. Have you had any symptoms lately?"

"No, I've been feeling fine actually."

"That's good. You may experience relapses, as lesions are present."

"Lesions?"

"Lesions show up as spots on the spine and brain. These indicate that the myelin surrounding the nerves has deteriorated. This is what causes the episodes of numbness, loss of balance and blurred vision. You may be without symptoms for long periods of time or you may experience more severe symptoms such as loss of sight or difficulty walking."

"Oh my God. I have a daughter. I'm in school now."

"Yes, well I suggest that you just go on with your life as usual. If there are more severe symptoms we may need to try some medication that involves daily or weekly injections. I would like to see you in about six months and we'll see how you're doing. If you have concerns before then, please contact me. If you will take these out to the front desk my nurse will give you some information about MS and the local support groups."

She handed me a folder and opened the door.

"Wait! Can I ask you something?" The doctor stopped in the doorway.

"Is this inherited?"

"It is not a genetic disease but it sometimes runs in families. It is also prevalent in this area of the country, leading some researchers to believe it may have environmental components."

"Oh, thank you, because I just found out that I am adopted . . ."

"Well that may be something you want to check in to. Try to keep your stress level low. I'll see you in six months, Ms. May." She closed the door behind her.

"Keep my stress level low?" I said to myself. I sat motionless for several minutes before I was sure my legs could lift me out of the chair. Only my mind seemed numb.

That spring and summer the one thing that could keep my mind off the failure of my body, grief over Dad, and the shock of knowing I had another mother somewhere, was my new garden. I was taking two summer classes, but I still made the time to spend hours in the midst of lavender, daisies, purple-blue delphinium, butterfly weed, yellow yarrow and anything else I could get my hands on. Weeding, watering, and pruning the small plants put my mind in a quiet mode. It lessened the voices and the questions. The summer was warm, but not scorching, the rain regular and the plants flourished. Going out to inspect their progress washed away the visions of what was, what could have been, what might be coming. In the garden I was incapable of attempting to make any sort of decision. The garden was my present tense, the moment happening and nothing else.

As the summer progressed I added a bluebird house, a birdbath, and an angel statue, all found at local garage sales. I saw four kinds of butterflies and sometimes hummingbirds as I sat in a plastic lawn chair nearby. On rare days when I was alone, when Anais was at swimming lessons, or at a friends, it was a praying garden.

By fall, I understood that my garden was to be a lavender garden. I was drawn to read about drying it for sachets, distilling oil from it, cooking with it, making tea, soaps, lotions from it.

I had a lavender garden.

I also understood why I was going to school. The community college offered an Associate of Applied Science in horticulture, landscape operations, garden center operations or landscape design. The catalog was, to me, like the big toy advertisement books were to kids at Christmas with horticultural botany, plant production, soil technology, plant pathology, greenhouse operation. I wouldn't be saving the world, but I found a passion, a career, stability for my daughter's future, and possibly, my place in the world.

As the lavender in the garden faded and the petals of the flowers dropped to the ground I began to gain the strength to confront Roberta about the truth that lived inside of me every waking moment. My feelings about her as my mother, my judgment of her austere and constrained ways often bordered on compassion and sympathy. I saw her more objectively - as a wounded woman. I grew towards the moment of truth as another woman, not the frightened, rejected child I had always been around her. But small puffs of anger would suddenly arise out of nowhere. I couldn't completely dismiss the fact that I had suffered for something I had no control over. My emotions teetered precariously between the two.

Roberta had isolated herself at her sister's house for several months after my father's death. After she moved back home she never said anything to John or me about taking care of my dad's belongings or about the revelation of the hidden money he had left to John and me. She appeared to resume her normal life with very little discussion or change. She spent most of her time volunteering in the church office.

"Thanks for coming with me, John. I really need the moral support," I said driving towards Roberta's house, the place of my abandoned life dreams.

"This is something they kept from both of us. I kind of feel betrayed too," John said. "I hope she can handle being confronted by both of us though."

"This feels about as comfortable as juggling knives, you know?" I pulled into the driveway. "Time with Mom never gets easier." We knocked on the door like unexpected visitors.

My mother opened the front door and immediately looked me over. The truth had caused me to recently feel that familiar tug on my own identity. I had repierced my eyebrow and started dying my hair different colors again. It was like an old addiction resurfacing. Was I daring her to reject me again? I asked myself as I removed my coat to reveal the sleeveless shirt that displayed my "freedom band."

"You look very nice today, John," she said, nodding her approval at John's impeccable outfit. "Is that a new sweater?"

"Yes, Mom, thanks," John leaned over and kissed Roberta lightly on the cheek.

Roberta's dining room table had coffee and tea and snacks set out on a white linen tablecloth. There was a faint odor of mothballs and I noticed she already had on one of her winter wool skirts. "So what is this visit all about?" She poured the hot drinks into china teacups and we took them into the living room.

"We don't need a reason to visit, do we, Mom?" I asked.

"No, it's just that John sounded like there was something on his mind when he called."

John looked my way and gave an encouraging wink. It was difficult to create small talk with Roberta so I inhaled deeply and began.

"Mom, you know that Johnny and I went through Dad's things after he died."

"Yes, I never thanked you both for that. I do appreciate it. I'm sure it wasn't pleasant for either of you." She blew over the top of the teacup without looking up.

Out the window the nimbus clouds opened and rain began battering the gray landscape.

"We've had a lot of rain for this time of year, don't you think?" Roberta got up and brought a tray of cheese and crackers over to the coffee table. I felt my courage waning and knew I had to continue.

"Mom?" I waited for her to acknowledge me.

"Yes, what is it?"

"Mom, we found something and . . . well, we were wondering if you knew anything about it." I handed her the photograph.

Roberta stared at the picture for a few seconds, handed it back to me and said, "I don't know who these people are, I'm afraid." The words dropped out of her mouth like stones. Her face expressionless. My body froze as if in a straightjacket of disappointment.

"Mom," John said. "Are you sure, because Grandma. . ."

"Your grandmother is a demented old woman. Whatever she told you is a lie!"

"What is it you think she told us?" My voice raised to a higher pitch.

"Christine, what is it you want from me?"

"I want the truth! Something you've never bothered to give me, have you? Don't you think I have a right to know about my own life? *Mom?*

"Why are you speaking to me like this? What have I done now that has ruined your life? I only raised you, took care of you, put up with your teenage rebellion. I suffered when you left, Christine. You left *me*, remember? I didn't leave you."

"Yes, but you didn't give birth to me, did you?" The sky was collapsing on me and my little freckled hands weren't strong enough to push it back up. I began to cry. Roberta got up and began to leave the room.

"Mom! Come back here!" John stood up. Roberta turned, stunned at John's forcefulness. "We know the truth. Why won't you admit to it? Chrissie needs to hear it from you. She just wants to understand – you owe her that."

"I don't believe I owe her anything. She left this home willingly. That was her choice." Her words impaled me. I felt lifeless. I wanted to leave.

"But it was her choice to return. What about forgiveness, Mom? Isn't that what our faith is about?"

"Don't you lecture me about faith. I go to church every Sunday."

"Just because you spend time in church doesn't mean you spend time with God," John blurted out and then sat down, defeated.

"How dare you speak to me that way, John." But then Roberta sat back down on the pristine white couch. Enveloped in silence, the three of us felt the sting of the moment, knowing none of us could escape now.

My mother sat with her head bowed and said nothing. Minutes passed as we all looked around for something to distract our thoughts. I prepared myself for more anger and indignation, but when Roberta looked up her softened expression reflected sorrow and regret.

"This is the day I've feared for almost thirty years. But now it is here and I can't change that. Christine, it wasn't until you came back and I saw how much George loved and needed you that I began to understand I had spent years blaming you for something you had nothing to do with. Something that was not your fault. When I was away after George's death, I had to grieve, but I also had to face why you left and how difficult it must have been for you to return. I realize you made your father very happy." My mother started to weep.

"Mom, it's okay . . ." I started.

"No, Christine, let me finish while I can." She took out a pink tissue and touched the corners of her eyes. "When I found out that George had a baby girl I pushed all the feelings I should have had about that out of my mind and instead only thought about the fact that I was going to have a daughter after all. I wanted you so much. I stopped grieving for the baby I lost and I made you take her place. But you were taking the place of a perfect child in my mind, you were taking the place of a child George and I had created and that's not who you were." Roberta raised her head towards me. "I am sorry for that, Christine. That was too much of a burden for an innocent child to carry."

John got up and went to Roberta's side, but I was too stunned to move. I had never heard my mother apologize in my entire life.

"As you grew, your red hair and freckles kept reminding me that you were not my child. I asked God to help me love you and treat you as my own but . . . I failed time after time." She turned her body into my brother's. "Then you came along, John. A miracle, an answer to my prayers. The feelings I had giving birth to you just intensified my confusion at raising you Christine." Then the silence was only punctuated with my mother's sniffing and me blowing my nose for what seemed like minutes. "I can see that you are a wonderful mother to Anais and I am proud of you for that. You sacrificed as I couldn't."

"Mom, I don't know what to say." I said wiping my face off.

"I think I'm actually relieved. Lies just hurt people, but somehow I never applied that to you, or to me. The secret has harmed all of us. I blamed your father for the conflicting feelings I constantly had, I blamed him for putting me in that situation and for making me become someone I didn't want to be. For years I just hated myself. Now that he's gone it's much harder to feel angry with him." Roberta looked at me with blurred eyes, "And you, Christine, you did just fine without me all these years."

Then I moved to the other side of her and the three of us had a brief awkward hug. I moved back to the chair I had been sitting in and just stared at this woman I didn't know at all.

"Mom, I'm sorry I . . ."

"No, let's just leave it as it is. No more apologies. I'd like it if we could be friends, Christine."

"Friends?"

"I think what Mom is trying to say is that your relationship will probably be different now that you both know the truth," John said.

"You don't need to speak for her, Johnny. She's making herself very clear." I closed my eyes for a moment wishing that the last few minutes was a dream. The disappointment clutched in my throat. I coughed and opened my eyes.

"You know Mom – *Roberta* - that would be great, let's be friends, but maybe I'd still like to have a mother, and a grandmother for Anais. You just said that none of this was my fault! Why do you get to *be* a mother, but I don't get to *have* one?" I got up and started putting my jean jacket on.

"Christine, stop acting like . . ."

I put my hand out in front of me, "Please don't say it, please. John, can we go now?"

"Maybe you two should talk a little more. Do you want to leave it this way?"

I took a deep breath and focused on the black silhouette of trees in the neighbor's yard. I turned back to Roberta.

"Okay, listen. Mom, I appreciate your honesty and your apology, I really do. I understand a lot more about my life now, and really, I can't imagine losing a child and I will hopefully never know what that was like. But I lost out on a childhood because of it. I wanted to be close to you, and when I came back home I still had my little foolish childhood dreams that that could still happen, so I'm feeling a little disappointed right now. But if you want to be friends, well, if that's the best I can get, then all right. I'm going to go now. I need to think about all of this."

"Yes, I think that's best," Roberta said.

"Chrissie, give it some time. At least Mom was truthful," John said in the car.

"I thought our talk was going so well, but then all of a sudden this very familiar feeling overwhelmed me – the feeling of being rejected – again. It was a 'I'm back where I started' moment."

"I know you're disappointed right now. I think it took a lot for her to offer you friendship."

"I don't think I need a friend like her."

Cole

Lavender and I decided not to share any more of the adoption drama with Anais. Sometimes we find ourselves talking to her as if she's one of the adults. She often has insights that are remarkable, sometimes senses what's happening before it happens and has already formed a preadolescent opinion on it. Maybe the fact that we allowed her to hear and see so much of our struggling for so long has given her more understanding. Oddly enough, that night at dinner, she asked us when she was going to be able to see her Grandma Roberta again.

"I know she makes you mad sometimes, Mom, but she *is* still my Grandma. Maybe she'll like me when she really gets to know me!" Anais said, smiling and chewing on pizza at the same time.

"I'm sure she likes you, honey. I'm just not sure if we're going to have much time to spend together with school for both of us and working on this house," Lavender said.

"Do we have to work on the house every weekend?"

"For a while. Now that we're in the middle of these projects, we need to finish what we started, don't we?" I said.

"Yes, boss." Ani rolled her eyes. "But don't you think you should make time for your own mother, I mean, I know she's not your real mother, but she's still your mother, right? Like Cole isn't my real dad, but I'll always see him."

"Yes, smarty. She's the only mother I have at the moment anyway." Lavender said. "We'll see. Right now, I think homework is what you should be more worried about."

After Anais left the room I said, "It seems like she is as hungry for family as you are, sweetie. Maybe you should think about that."

"I've been a little distracted by something else I'm hungry for, if you know what I mean." Lavender looked over at me with a smirk on her face.

"No, I don't know what you mean," I picked up a stack of dishes.

"A guy, Cole. There's a guy I like at school," she whispered.

"What do you need a guy for? You've got me."

"Oh, so funny. Actually he's one of my instructors. His name is Matthew Grant."

"Does he have a crush on you too?"

"A crush? What are we, in junior high? In fact, yes I think he does like me. He asked me out for coffee tomorrow after class."

"You don't like coffee. Are instructors allowed to date students?"

"I don't think it's a big deal. It's a community college, not Harvard, and he's just a part-time teacher there. He actually owns that little garden center over on Bank Street."

We continued cleaning up the kitchen together silently until I said, "I know what you mean. It gets lonely. We have each other, and I thank God for that everyday. But someday I'd like to experience the true love thing, you know?"

"Me too."

Anais

Ideas are popping like popcorn in my head. It's like God telling me to do something about this situation with Mom and Grandma Roberta. I know I said she wore dorky clothes, but I do too sometimes. Usually I have better things to think about than fashion – not like the other girls in my class.

When Mom was out with her new boyfriend Grandma Roberta called. I answered the phone and she tried to start this big, long conversation with me about school and books I'm reading and stuff like that. I told her I was still having a lot of trouble with math and that I have a learning disability, but that I'm really smart in reading and writing and especially spelling. Grandma said that back in the day she thought about being a math teacher before she married Grandpa. She actually likes math – double weird.

I usually don't think before I say something so all of a sudden I said, "Can you help me with math, Grandma?"

"I'd be delighted to, but I don't know how your mother would feel about that. Maybe we should ask her first."

"She and Cole will be happy because they won't have to help me anymore," I said.

That was the first time I ever heard her laugh. "Well, you ask your mother and then call me back and let me know. Maybe I can come over after school sometime and help you with your homework."

"That would be awesome, thanks. I'll call you back later."

"That's fine. I'll be home all evening."

When Mom got home I told her what Grandma said and she didn't seem that happy about it but she said we could give it a try.

Lavender

It was just hot drinks in brown mugs at Starbucks but it felt like something I almost remembered from long ago - the adjacency to a man. Matthew and I talked and flirted and sipped our coffee and tea for almost two hours. The first surprising impressions of Matthew were of intelligence, maturity and an unbiased connection. I was never a girl to see a guy, sense his attention and immediately envision myself in a wedding dress being carried across the threshold of a white picket-fenced house. And I didn't see that now. I just sensed a renewing of my mind, like an extra gift under the Christmas tree that you didn't expect – maybe something to keep and treasure. Like a perennial plant that unexpectedly sprouts out in a new place in the spring, a few feet away from the parent plant, you can sit back and watch it grow.

Cole and I have discussed our dependence on each other many times. Sitting on the couch watching some psychologist on a talk show describing co-dependent relationships, we'll look at each other and go, "Yep, that's us!" and laugh.

Reuniting with my family, actually *having* a family, a home, a daughter, a career goal, and believing I might still find a loving relationship has given me strength beyond my friendship with Cole. I am becoming the individual I tried so hard to create years ago. I don't need to be a girl in her mini-skirts, fishnets, boots laced to the knee, tattooed, pierced, purple hair slashing her way across a stage. I am my own girl now.

I am still amazed that Anais is in the world with me. She has been my little oracle, the one following and leading me, my earthly redemption. But now I am more than her mother, more than Cole's dependent scared punk-chick friend. For all that I have been - I am a mother, a daughter, a granddaughter, a sister, a soon-to-be plant expert, a homeowner, and whatever else I can create out of myself. I cannot be a reduced form of a woman anymore and I don't want a reduced life. I want it all.

I am not panicked at the sight and sound of this new man. There is equality, and our past living is at once trivial and paramount in bringing us to this place and time. When I see his eyebrows crushed together in interest at something I've said, or I see him walk away, his soil-stained hands pushed into his pockets like a little boy with summer treasures, I know there is something to wait for.

Cole has been seeing someone too, and I believe he has waited for me to be ready to allow him that space and time. And as we are reaching out of our lives, away from each other, we also cling to all that we have had together, all that we have survived together. But my dream of acceptance was always within my reach. It was Cole.

Cole

My life-dreams have always been like most others, a career, a home, and a family. Lavender believes she has overused my friendship and depended on me too much. But Lavender gave me the chance to be a father, to love a little girl with all my heart. When we moved to Ohio I became aware of the possibility that someday a young man might appear in our lives and that young man would be Anais's biological father. That is not something I wish for. I fear my reactions and emotions should that ever occur. To my knowledge neither of my girls are interested in that right now, but there could come a day.

I want to be the one to hug her at high school graduation, to walk that little girl down a church aisle one day. I've repeatedly had dreams that she called me Daddy. I've relied on their love and acceptance and received more than I've given.

I mistakenly believed that I had experienced true love in the past, but as time went on it held no warm memories for me. I have only experienced that love through the girls. My happiest days have been with them, no questions, no doubts, just *we love you, Cole*.

I've watched Lavender bloom into something new, and it gives me peace. I can rest in knowing she and Anais are capable of taking care of themselves. John recently introduced me to a friend's older brother and we have cautiously begun to get to know each other, no fireworks, no urgency, just the enjoyment of being together for now. It is time.

Anais

Grandma came over after school to help me with my math homework. She brought homemade chocolate chip cookies and I poured us two glasses of milk. I poured slowly so I wouldn't spill it like I usually do. We were sitting at the kitchen table when Mom got home.

"Mom, Grandma made chocolate chip cookies for me," I said.

"That's nice. I don't remember you making cookies when I was little, Mom," my mom said in kind of a rude way.

"I heard Anais say that they were her favorite," Grandma said.

"They are! Did I do this one right?" I showed Grandma how I multiplied the fractions and then reduced the answer to lowest terms.

"That looks right to me, good for you!"

Then Mom threw her stuff down on the kitchen counter and practically ran out of the room.

"Well, your mother must have had a bad day," Grandma said. "Let me talk to her for a minute. You try those last two problems."

I could hear them sort of arguing, but not yelling. I couldn't hear what they were saying though. Grandma came back into the kitchen and I heard Mom's bedroom door slam. I finished my homework and I was putting everything in my backpack for the next day.

"That backpack looks pretty worn out. How about if we go out and find you a new one?" Grandma asked.

"Awesome! Let me go tell Mom." When I tried to open Mom's door it was locked.

"Mom! What the hell! Oops, sorry. I mean, open the door, would you?"

"What do you want?"

"Grandma wants to take me to the store to get a new backpack, is that okay?"

"Don't you have to finish your homework?"

"It's already done, can I go?"

"Well . . . I'm not sure when Cole will be home, and he's going to make dinner."

"We won't be gone long. Come on, Mom."

"All right, go, have a great time," she said, but she didn't sound like she really meant that and she still wouldn't open the door, which was bizarre to me.

Lavender

I loved school so much that it didn't even seem like work. It pulled me out of the years of self-inflicted belief in my own stupidity. Occasionally I would wallow in unpleasant reminders that I was nearing the age of thirty and just beginning a life for myself, but then I would look around the community college campus and see that I wasn't alone. Everyone in my life encouraged me. Even Roberta had no negative comments, and to me, that was encouraging. No one questioned my love of horticulture and no one knew where it came from, including me.

I opened a brand new textbook and it felt like opening many things at once, a book of opportunities. Previewing the book, I flipped through and landed on a photograph of a path that was worn through a wooded area. It was the kind of path that took years of foot traffic to create. It was yards away from an asphalt sidewalk and a road farther in the distance. The caption said it was a desire path. I remembered Lizzie telling me I was on my desire path.

I pondered my long-ago decision to give myself the name Lavender. At seventeen all my thinking was arbitrary, based on emotion, but now seemed so strategic and prophetic. It made me believe that God had been working behind the scenes all of the time. There was a plan. I had not taken the paved concrete streets, but had walked along my own desire path. The path I created for myself. A path that had not existed for anyone but me. My Doc Martens and Converse sneakers trod a path from Ohio to New York to New Jersey and back, from rejection to acceptance, from confusion to understanding.

Cole watches me like a heron stalking a fish, quietly and relentlessly. For the past few months the left side of my body has been partially numb. I took great efforts to hide it, but he knows me too well.

"Lavender, I'll help with the cleaning today. Don't you have school work to do?" Cole said.

"You know I don't. Since when are you so excited to do the cleaning?"

"Since I've seen you having symptoms again."

" Oh . . . It's not too bad. Just a little numbness," I said lowering myself onto the couch.

"How long has this been going on, honey?"

"A couple months, but I've been so busy. I don't have time and I don't want to go back to the doctor. She said this would probably happen. It's called relapsing-remitting. Maybe it will remit again," I looked up at Cole and tried to smile.

"Well, that's your call. Just let me know what I can do."

"Thanks. Wow. You're actually treating me like an adult. What's up with that?"

Cole sat down on the couch next to me and put his hand on my knee. "I want you to know how proud I am of you. You are all grown up now, Lav. Don't hold back, okay? Not for me or even for Anais. You go for it all, promise me."

"What are you talking about?"

"I think we're both holding back on our new relationships. Why do you think that's so? We're so used to filling those gaps for each other, but it's all right to need more. To need and want what we were born to need and want. Matthew really cares for you, but I see you starting to distance yourself from him. What are you afraid of?"

"What am I *not* afraid of is the easier question. What if this MS gets really bad? What if I can't walk someday or something like that? What if he and Anais don't get along? What about us, Cole?"

"Nothing will ever change between us. If we move on in our lives, new people, new places to live, it's all right. That's what we've been working for, isn't it?"

"You and Anais are my family," I put my hands on top of his. "I'm sorry it took me so long to realize that I had everything I needed all along."

"No, you didn't, honey and neither have I. We're friends, best friends, and that doesn't ever have to change. But life will change eventually. Lovers, jobs, homes. Ani is going to grow up. It's not going to stay this way forever. Look what you've made it through this year – everything you were so afraid of."

"When I'm finished with my classes this spring, Matthew said I could do my internship at his garden center. I've been thinking about what I want to do after that." I got up and started sweeping the hardwood floors of the dining room and Cole didn't stop me.

"What's that?"

"I want to have a business selling and making products from lavender."

Cole laughed, "Lavender products, what does that mean?"

"Don't laugh. It's legitimate. Lavender can be used for cooking, making tea, soaps, lotions, perfumes, things like that."

"Is that right?"

"Yes, that's right, and I love lavender."

"Yes, you do. Finally! And so do I," Cole grinned at me. "Well, I have a date tonight, so I'm going to take a shower and spend a whole lot of time trying to decide what to wear."

"That's great. I'm glad you two have been having such a good time together," I said slowly bending down to sweep the dirt into a dustpan. Cole came over and took it from me and held it to the floor. I stopped, holding the broom to my chest. "Cole? I understand what you're trying to tell me. We both need other people in our lives. We need love and there are people here, now, waiting for us. Good people."

"Yes, that's what I've been trying to say." He stood up and then bent over to hug me and left the room. I finished my sweeping and then flopped onto the couch to rest. I heard Anais rousing from her Saturday morning slumber. I felt a peace I hadn't felt for a long time. I reached for the phone and called my mother.

"Mom, how would you like to spend some time with Anais tonight?"

"Yes, that would be fine. Do you have a date?"

"Yes, I'm hoping I do, but I wanted to see if you could watch Ani for me first."

"Bring her over any time. Would you like me to keep her overnight?"

"Mom, that would be great, would you? I'll pick her up tomorrow morning before you go to church."

"No need to do that, I'd love to show off my granddaughter at church, if she'll come with me."

I couldn't answer because I was crying. I coughed to cover up the choking and finally said, "Okay. Thanks Mom."

I cried for about ten minutes, blew my nose and called Matthew.

Dinner was at a small Italian restaurant in town. Matthew gave me a brief red wine tasting lesson and then we dug into our spaghetti.

"My Aunt Marian used to make soap from lavender," Matthew said.

"You're kidding? I thought it was kind of a new thing – the lavender – like a fad or something." I cut my spaghetti with the side of my fork so I would not have it dribbling out of my mouth in a completely unsexy way.

"No, I don't think it's a fad. It's a lot of work to create those kinds of products by hand, but I remember she really enjoyed it." Matthew swirled the maroon liquid around in his glass and sniffed it quickly before taking a sip. My biggest expertise was in chugging beer.

"Do you know anything about the products you can make from it?" I asked.

"I remember my cousins and I hanging around trying to help my aunt when we were kids. I don't think we were much help though. There were five of them plus my sister and me. There was more screaming and running around and messing things up more than anything." He looked up at me grinning that little boy grin. " But I might remember a thing or two. I will help you get started in any way I can."

"Well, I want this to be something I do on my own for a change, but I'll take any advice you can give me." He reached across the table, gently took my hand and kissed it.

"Whatever you say, Lavender. It's your life. It's your future career."

The protective coating around my heart was melting with every word this man said. I felt a light turning on inside of me. I stared at the lock of brown hair that fell over his forehead, the muscles of his jaws chewing his food with great enjoyment. He looked up, raising his eyebrows as if to say "What?" But he said nothing. Just smiled. Just sipped his wine. Just looked like he'd never been anywhere but here, across the table from me.

After dinner Matthew and I came back to the house and Cole had not come home. We wordlessly entered the house and threw our coats on a chair. I took his cold hands between mine and rubbed them, then led him into my bedroom. We watched each other undress from opposite sides of the bed. Matthew grasped and threw the covers to the footboard and we laid on the bare white sheet facing each other. He gently ran his fingers over my body, then kissed every place he had touched. Soon there was turning, clutching, entwining. He knelt and lifted me onto his lap. We turned our faces to the mirror opposite my bed and watched us for the first time. I saw the *oh* of my mouth, the pleasure-pain in his eyes. My brazen fingers dug into his flesh as I willingly dipped my body into his and gazed at our unison movements.

I remembered sex, but I did not remember being made love to. When tears rolled out of my eyes, he didn't ask why, but licked them off my chin and kissed my eyelids. I fell asleep with my head in the hollow of his shoulder and when I woke in the morning we were still alone. Matthew smiled at me, said "Good morning" and made love to me again.

Cole

Lavender and I didn't need to describe our dates to each other. Everything was conveyed in our gestures, our demeanors, our expressions. We talked about the new people in our lives, but avoided the word love. Still touched by past hurts and misconceptions, we both moved slowly through the age-old dance of new relationships. Lavender's questions were of health and concern for her daughter. I held questions that involved my career and life outside my home. I only mentioned the girls to my colleagues as dear friends, never divulging that we lived together.

Teachers in an elementary school building tend to be obsessive about their students and effectiveness. State and district testing absorbs great amounts of energy and time during the workday. My sociable staff often spent time together outside of work hours. I was set apart as an administrator, and happily let it remain that way. I thought it more professional anyway. Teachers do tend to gather in the main office after school to debrief and unwind.

"I think I might know someone that Mr. Carson would like to meet," I heard one of the second grade teachers say. She was speaking to another teacher, but loud enough to be certain I would hear her. They looked my way smiling. She walked towards me.

"Cole, I have a lovely cousin about your age. She teaches on the west side. What do you say? Would you like me to write down her phone number?"

"Whoa!" I held up my hands, trying to laugh in a natural way, " Been there, done that, if you know what I mean!" Those around began chuckling and someone started describing a blind date, and the attention was diverted.

My administrative assistant said, " Don't you hate it when people try to do that? Especially when they don't know what the hell they're talking about." She smiled at me and I gratefully smiled back.

Spending each day with children gave me a perspective on Anais. I couldn't be a more proud or biased parent. I found her verbal abilities and insights superior to most others her age. She still struggled with her ADHD and learning disability in math. At times there were tantrums of frustration, yet, the vast majority of the time Anais accepted her quirks and differences as simply a part of who she is. She has an uncanny ability to accept others' differences also.

"Apparently," Lavender said, "Anais had a great time with her grandmother the other night.

"You sound surprised."

"I'm dumbfounded. I never had a good time with that woman! At least not one I remember. What's she trying to do, turn Ani into the daughter she never had?"

"I highly doubt that anyone could turn Anais into anything, even if they wanted to."

"Well, that's true, but what's her motivation? Why is she being so nice? She never treated me to chocolate chip cookies or new backpacks or fun and games like she has been doing with my daughter."

"Maybe it's her way of showing you she's sorry. Maybe this is the only way she can think of to make up for the mother she wasn't for you."

"I guess I don't trust her. She was always so manipulative, so rigid in her ways."

"She told you and John that she thought a lot of things through after your dad died. People can change you know."

"I know, I just never would have thought that of her."

"We always said that we thought Ani should have more people in her life. Now she has two grandmothers and an uncle. When is she going to meet Matthew?"

"Soon. I'm pretty sure they're going to like each other. They are both open and welcoming types of people. I think the only thing I'm afraid of is all the questions a preteen girl is going to have about her mother's love life, especially *this* preteen girl!"

Anais

Mom's boyfriend is awesome! When he came over Saturday night I was watching one of my favorite TV shows and he knew all about it and he was like, laughing at all the stuff I was laughing at. He looked through my CD's and he said he had some of them too. It's really sad, but Mom still likes her old-school punk music and sits around playing those songs on her guitar.

Mom ordered pizza and we watched a movie together and it was pretty cool. Mom asked me to go out and make some popcorn and when I came back they were making out on the couch.

I covered my eyes, "Like, do you guys want to get a room or something?"

"Where did you hear that saying?" Mom asked.

"Everybody says that, Mom."

"So, do you want to get a room?" Matthew said to my mom.

"Now that's gross," I said, sitting in front of them so I wouldn't have to watch whatever they were doing. But we had a fun night watching the movie and then Matthew played a video game with me and I went to bed. I tried to listen to them from my room, but they were mostly whispering or kissing or something, so I'm not sure what's going on. It would be cool with me if my mom fell in love with Matthew because I think he really likes her and would make her happy.

On Sunday I got to meet Cole's boyfriend. He wasn't as cool as Matt, but he seemed nice. They only stayed for lunch and then they took off for the day.

Mom asked me if I'd like to spend more time sleeping over Grandma Roberta's or Grandma Fiona's. I said, "Sure, Mom." Like I don't know why.

Lavender

When Chip and Lydia learned that I had completed my Associate's Degree of Applied Science in Horticulture they were so proud and excited that they planned a trip to Ohio to see us. It had been over two years since we'd seen each other, but their presence in my life still meant so much to me.

"I think that's them!" Anais shouted as she ran to the window.

I opened the door and Ani bolted out and hugged them as comfortably as if we'd left last week. There were more hugs and exclamations and we all moved inside for a tour of our little bungalow and then out back to see my garden.

"This is beautiful, Lavender. You really have a green thumb, don't you? Have you kept in touch with Lizzy? Sent her pictures?"

"We have kept in touch. If it weren't for her coming into my life I would have never found this love of growing things," I said.

"I'm sure that was the plan," Lydia said.

"And look at this little sprout," Chip said, putting his arm around Anais. "All grown up!"

It wasn't until after lunch was over and we were sitting under the back awning in the summer shade that I asked about Chance.

"He's been sober for a year now. We're real proud of him. He found another job with computers and he has a new girlfriend," Lydia said.

"I'm so glad. You know, I've realized that, even without the drinking, I don't think Chance and I would have made it. We didn't really know ourselves then, or what we wanted from life. But sometimes I wish it could have worked out. . ." Like a home video in fast forward I could see my time with Chance; the rush of his recklessness, the enormity of our sexuality, the hopes of a future, my broken heart when I knew I would not be a part of Chip and Lydia's family.

I poured some more iced tea into their glasses. "I have someone in my life now and so does Cole. In fact, Cole is going to be moving out and Matthew is moving in soon." I waited for their reaction.

"That's wonderful, honey. Will there be a wedding in the future for us to come to?"

"I'm not sure about that yet. It's taken a lot of courage for Cole and I just to get to this point. It's going to be the first time we've lived apart in seven years. Can you believe that?"

"You've definitely been a blessing to each other," Lydia said, "and we understand, you have to go your own way."

Lydia and Chip stayed overnight in Anais's room and the next day we had a picnic. Lydia helped me prepare the hamburgers and corn and baked beans while Cole went to pick up Fiona. I invited my mother, but she said she couldn't make it. John was in the area on business and he came later. Matthew showed up with fresh, handpicked strawberries. The conversation and laughter moved us through the evening until lightning bugs twinkled around us. I took a tray full of dishes into the kitchen and stood looking out the window at a sight I never thought I'd see. A family in my own back yard. My grandmother and brother, my daughter, the Slaters, my best friend - and Matt.

"Yes, Chip and Lydia were like a mom and dad to Lavender, and grandparents to Ani. Well, they still are." Cole was speaking to Matthew, then turned to the Slaters. "I don't know how Lavender would have survived that time in New Jersey without your love and kindness. It was the first time Ani could experience a real family, I think."

"Oh, Cole," Lydia said, "You are her family, her daddy. You've given her so much – such a wonderful man." Lydia patted Cole's hand. "But thank you for all your kind words. We love these two as if they are our own."

Then my mother walked into my back yard. I heard her through the open window.

"Well it looks as if everyone is having a wonderful time here without me."

"Mom," John said. "I thought you said you couldn't come."

"I don't want to interrupt this cozy family gathering." She stood tall and straight-backed as ever. Clutching her purse to her side, her clothing covering every possible inch of skin on a warm summer night.

"Grandma, sit down." Anais pointed to a worn out lawn chair.

"No thank you, Anais. It seems as if there are enough people here now." Her gaze moved across the gathering of my loved ones. I quickly stepped out the side door as if I hadn't heard anything.

"Hi, Mom. Come sit down. I thought you were busy tonight." I could see that she had heard the conversation going on at the picnic table.

Everyone was staring at Roberta and her pinched, somber face.

Fiona spoke up, "Roberta what in the world are you here for if you don't want to join us? Did you expect everyone to be sitting around bemoaning the fact that your sour old face wasn't here?"

"Grandma . . ." John tried to interrupt.

"Johnny, I'm an old woman and I've been waiting to have my say – and now, well, the truth is out and there's no time like the present! Do you know why *we're* here, Roberta? Because we love this little family and we intend to show them all the love that you didn't. You chose to make Chrissie your daughter and then you treated her like an unwelcome stranger her whole life. Of course she ran away!" Fiona's hands flew up in the air. "Who wouldn't? But did you try to find her? Make it up to her? No, and it kept her from the rest of us all these years. You should be damned proud of how this child turned out in spite of her weak excuse for a mother."

Roberta did not move or open her mouth to defend herself. The shock of Fiona's tirade left everyone silent. I moved my head slightly to glance at Cole who was gnawing on a fingernail and the faint melody of *My Girl* emanated from his throat, but clearly enjoying the entire scene. Anais's mouth hung wide open and the Slaters were mostly looking into their laps and casually sipping their drinks as though nothing was happening. Matthew got up, moved next to me and grabbed my hand.

"Grandma, I think that's enough." John put his hand on her shoulder as if that would close her mouth.

"I'm not finished. I lost a son, my dear son, and you never said one kind word to me about him. I watched you take all the joy from his life for years. But he stayed by your side, Roberta. He was a much better husband than you ever deserved. I thank God he's in a better place - the God you've always used as an excuse to judge everyone around you. Even I cannot believe what you said about this fine young man," Fiona turned to Cole.

"What did she say about Cole?" Anais asked, her face collapsing into a frown.

"Never mind, little one. I wouldn't have the heart to repeat it. But *my* God loves all His creations and He is the only one fit to judge any of us!"

"Fiona, you've made your point. I'm sorry I've ruined everyone's evening."

Roberta turned and walked through the darkness of the driveway to her car. John went after her, but when he came back without her he shrugged his shoulders and said nothing.

On Sunday morning Chip and Lydia came to church with Anais and me. The scripture reading was Romans 12:2. It made more sense to me than anything at church ever had before:

Do not conform any longer to the pattern of this world, but be transformed by the renewing of your mind. Then you will be able to test and approve what God's will is, his good, pleasing and perfect will.

The final transformation of my mind, the missing piece of that perfect will was a woman named Lisa. I could petition the Ohio probate court for adoption information, and if, at some point Lisa had filed a form granting the release of her name and whereabouts, I could find her. She could have found me, since she knew my father and where I grew up, and obviously chose not to do that. Could she have put my birth out of her mind forever, or could she be waiting for me to find her? If it was the latter, I already respected her beyond words.

Multiple sclerosis is not known to be a genetic disease, but I have read accounts of two or three people in a family having it. I still wanted to know my own background and heritage. I still needed to know if I am anything like my biological mother beyond the fact that we were redheaded unwed teenage mothers. It won't change things now, but I've been obsessed with imagining how different my life might have been with her. Would she have understood me, accepted me, encouraged me? Would I have gone to college at eighteen and become someone she could have been proud of? These words swim in my head every night before I sleep. Yet, the last thought always is – if my life had turned out differently – I wouldn't have

Anais. If you have the chance to change the bad in your life it would almost always change the good too.

In a cleansing orgy I decided to begin cleaning out remnants of my old life before Matthew moved in. I burrowed into the one crowded closet I had like a mole in the ground. I threw shoeboxes and bags and piles of loose clothing out into the center of the room and across the bed. I yanked down towers of punk t-shirts, hats, sweaters and jeans that sat on a top shelf. I had boxes of memorabilia and notebooks. I didn't want to throw it all away. I wanted to review where I'd been, how far I'd come - and remember.

In the piles of vintage, Salvation Army, worn-out garments I spotted the dress I had worn right before Ani was born. The empire waist mini-dress. I stood up, stripped off my jeans and shirt and put it on. I looked in the mirror and then dove back into the closet and pulled out a misshapen laundry basket, dumped it on the floor and saw my old purple hat and red boots in the mess. In a minute I was looking at eighteen-year-old Lavender in the mirror. I smiled and remembered myself up on the stage with the Joeygirls, kicking at the crowd and bellowing into the microphone. Momentarily I felt fear move through me remembering the terror of the unknown, the loneliness and confusion at being that person in that place in New York City. I softly sang the song I knew so well – *I found a reason to keep living, oh and the reason dear, is you. I found a reason to keep singing and the reason, dear, is you.* That was one thing that had never changed.

I decided to make a memory box of clothes, the outfits that had defined me at certain times in my life. I went out to the garage and found a big box and carefully folded up some of the punk t's, the plaid mini-skirts, the one pair of fishnets that had survived, the hair ribbons, a couple pair of knee-high boots and my purple hat. I took off the mini-dress and laid it gently in the box. I closed the box and put some tape across the top and labeled it **Clothes I loved**, and put it aside.

I took a sturdy shoebox and put only the most precious items inside; my striped knit scarf, pictures of New York, a clipping of the one review Joeygirls had in the newspaper, matches from some of the bars and clubs we played at, a small notebook of cute things Anais said when she was a toddler that I had written down, a necklace Chance gave me one Christmas – and lastly the picture of Chance right before the car accident. I labeled that box **Things I loved.**

I found a box of photos that mostly other people had taken and given to me. I decided to keep them out and organize them into scrapbooks. But there was one picture of me leaning up against a brick wall smoking. I put that in the **Things I loved** box because I had finally quit smoking for good. I shoved all the boxes back into the closet and fell across the bed feeling full and satisfied. I prayed *God thank you for all these memories, good or bad they were, and always will be, my life. The life you've given me. I never imagined that my path would lead me back here, to family, to Matt, but thank you. Thank you.*

I got up and stuffed a couple garbage bags full of items that were too embarrassing to keep, then went to the kitchen to make some tea. I thought about Roberta and whether I should contact her after the uncomfortable scene in the back yard, but what I would say? I knew Fiona meant well and was doing what she had always done – defend me to my own parents. Even though I felt a wisp of sympathy for Roberta I still didn't understand her inability to deal with the fact that I am home and I have other people in my life now. I took my tea and walked out to the mailbox to get the mail. In the pile of junk mail I spotted a handwritten envelope – from Roberta. I set my tea on the table and sat down on the couch to prepare myself.

Dear Christine,

I am sorry I cannot yet say this to you face to face. I hope someday I will have the courage to do so. We both know the truth about our lives, your childhood and my years as your mother. When Fiona scolded me the other night I was humiliated, but I also heard some of what she was saying. Everyone else heard it as well and therefore I cannot pretend anything different. I have no defense for myself except to retell the hurt I felt at losing my daughter at birth, and then you. After thirty years I have come to understand that it is no longer a good excuse for the woman I became. I regret every day since your father's death the life that I gave him. He did not deserve it and neither did you.

I am asking for your forgiveness Christine. I realize it is a lot to ask. I know you are in the process of finding your birth mother and I truly hope that it is a successful endeavor for you. However, I am the woman that has known you longer than anyone. I hope that you will consider that in the future.

I ask for one more thing, and I understand if you do not agree. I would very much like to be a real grandmother to Anais. She has already brought me more joy than I deserve. I cannot go back and change the mistakes I made with you, but I can learn to be a loving grandmother for her if you will allow me that chance.

Love, Mom

I held the letter to my chest, put my head back on the couch cushion and sobbed. God had answered the prayer I had been too afraid to pray. My tears of grief

319

mingled with tears of joy for all that had been and all that could be. I choked and cried until the wetness of my face had run down my neck and onto my shirt. I had the feeling you get when you're at the dentist getting x-rays and the heavy chest protector is lifted off of you. It's over. It's lightness and relief. You don't have to sit still anymore. Of course, no one can change mistakes of the past. To be unable to forgive would be to keep wishing that the past had somehow been different.

The day that Cole moved out and Matt moved in wasn't nearly as difficult as I thought it would be. It was simply the next step in the progression of my life - our lives - as natural as seeing light come in the windows each morning. Love with Matthew was the easiest adventure I had gone on so far and we both knew we were doing the right thing. Cole was happier than I'd ever seen him and would be only fifteen minutes away from us. Anais was ebullient in telling her friends she had a family now, and two dads.

I recognize and acknowledge all that has gone before me and understand that dreams change and grow with time. I sit by the garden each day and see the deepening of colors, broadening of leaves, thickening and swelling of buds, and I feel so small before the beauty. Not a meek, worthless smallness, but small in the glow of gratitude and belief in all I cannot see or comprehend. In gratitude for the desire path that brought me to this place.

2006

Cole

Anais and I have a lunch date almost every Saturday and then she'll do her best to talk me into stopping at the mall for a possible purchase. Since I moved out I've felt like the absentee father assuaging his guilt, and I usually indulge her with some trinket, CD or trendy piece of clothing, which is paramount at her age.

The store for teens almost blinded me in its color variations. The music was loud enough to make the racks vibrate.

"Why do people get married?" Anais asked as she pushed hangers across the metal floor racks.

"Humans are social beings. Generally speaking, I would say it makes us happy to be in a deep relationship with one person who knows us very well." I held up a hideous pair of pink pants. "I think your mom is finally getting to experience that now."

"Would it make you happy? I mean, do you want to get married, Cole?"

"Yes, I believe it would make me happy, but it's against the law."

"What the f . . .!"

I help up my index finger to indicate that she should not end her sentence.

"You can't marry someone? Even if you love him?" She looked at me with confusion on her sweet face.

"No, well, not yet anyway."

"That's against the law."

"Why do you say that, dollbaby?"

"We're learning about the Declaration of Independence in school. It says all men – *and women* I want to say, are created equal and we all have the right to presue happiness."

"Pursue – yes, it says that. Thomas Jefferson wrote it, but he also owned slaves at the time. Unfortunately, it's an ideal, not a law."

"That sucks. Why should Mom be able to pre-, uh, pursue her happiness and you can't?"

"That's a question I hope will be answered in your lifetime. You know, at one time my own parents wouldn't have been allowed to marry in certain states."

"Why not?" Anais stopped her shopping and looked up at me.

"Because they are different races."

"That's stupid. My social studies teacher said that people get married to have babies."

"It's true that marriage is for the formation of a family, but as we both know, a family can be made up of any kind of people." Anais smiled at me.

"And if it was only babies, then Grandma Roberta could never get remarried because she's too old, right?"

"That's right sugar-pie-honey-bunch."

"Oh, Colette, look at this awesome top. Can I have it?"

"Yes, let's get going," I glanced at the ridiculous price tag and moved towards the cash register. "It looks like a storm is coming."

The rain blew across the street in horizontal slashes as we drove into the driveway. Lavender came running out into the driveway to meet us, ignoring the water soaking her red curls into soggy clumps.

"What are you doing? Get in the car!" I yelled out the window.

"Are you crazy, Mom?"

Lavender was waving a now wet envelope in the air in front of her. "I got it! It came!"

"What came? Shut the door!"

"My mother! She filed a release form almost twelve years ago. I guess when I would've been eighteen. I can find her! I'm going to meet my real mother!"

"Oh, honey, that's great news. Is that what it says in your sopping wet envelope?"

"Oops, yeah, can you believe it?"

"That's cool, Mom," Anais said, "Mom? Am I gonna have *another* Grandmother?"

"You might." Lavender tried to pull the soaked piece of paper out of the envelope.

"Before you show us, let's go inside." I pulled an umbrella from under the seat.

Lavender put the kettle on for tea and brought out some towels to dry us off.

"Okay, now let's see this piece of paper that's changing your life," I put my hand out. "Authorization for Release." I read aloud. "I guess your mother thought that once you were an adult you'd have the right to find her."

"If only I had known that back then."

"It's bogus, Mom. You'd tell me if I was adopted wouldn't you?"

"Of course I would. The truth is always best."

"Maybe Lisa could have been in our family all this time, right Mom? Ouch! Damn that's hot!"

"Ani, watch your mouth. Why can't you wait until the tea cools off?"

"Yes, Colette."

"So what is the next step?" I asked.

"It says I have to petition the Ohio probate court and then the information she filed will be released to me through the court. I wonder how long that will take? What if she doesn't live in the same place she did then?"

Lavender asked. "It also says that just this year, adoptive persons have been given access to health and background information." She looked up from the paper. "So I could still find out medical information even if I couldn't find my mother."

"It seems like it should have been that way all along, doesn't it?" I asked.

I loved these moments with my girls no matter what was going on. Our lives had expanded to include new people and it wasn't as awful as I'd expected. I would miss the little things: the way Lavender and I would finish each other's crossword puzzles, the nights we'd stay up for a midnight snack discussing our concerns for Anais, the days we used to walk in Central Park like a family. But now my ramparts have fallen and my arms are open. I know I will always be a part of them. I don't have to doubt that anymore. And I'll love them – until the end of forever.

Lavender

Love and loss and heartache are inevitable experiences for most people. Expectations and perspectives change. Despite the healing wounds and miasma of old lives and lovers, Matthew and I were miraculously brought together in a common thread of time. He is the numerator and I am the denominator, and we mean something completely different when you put us together. I have learned what can still grow in the fallow ground of my heart and soul, and my flesh is reawakened.

Matthew walked with me every step of the way to find my mother Lisa, from filling out paperwork, through the long waiting and trips to the courthouse in downtown Cleveland. As we left the courthouse Matthew took my hand.

"You have a birthday coming up," Matthew said.

"Yeah, a big one. I can't believe I'm going to be thirty."

"I'd like to take you out for a special evening if that would be all right with you."

I didn't say anything for a minute.

"Lavender? It is okay, isn't it?"

"Yes, it's just that it will be the first time a man has taken me out for my birthday. That's kind of pathetic isn't it?"

"No, you just waited for the right man, that's all."

I went out the next day and bought a whole new outfit for my birthday dinner. I'm thirty years old and it's the first time I've done that. There would be no ripped punk t-shirt or redesigned vintage dress for this occasion. There would be no smoking breaks out in the cold since I had not smoked for three months. I bought a red silk blouse and black pants, stiletto boots, black leather jacket and a silver handbag. I hoped that Cole would do my hair, pulling the top back in a new silver clip, letting the red curls hang down over my shoulders the way Matt likes it.

As I drove home from the mall the snow circled down in front of me slower than gravity would allow. Yellow lights shone from houses, a few people were already out shoveling driveways, tree branches were painted white from giant boughs to the tiniest toothpick tips. I rolled down my window to listen to the silence and smell the cold. Honking geese made a gray arrow in the sky above me. I pulled into the driveway of my house, my home. The warmth of lights shone out the windows, but Matt's car was gone and Anais had been with Cole for the afternoon.

Now I can venture into the world. I could not be Matthew's partner until I became my own. My singular desire path has led to this home, this night, this moment. Like a baby bird chipping away at the fragile shell of an egg, I broke out, and left the shelter of my runaway life, and my protector, Cole.

I sat at the kitchen table, looking out at the dormant lavender garden – the place where my desire path ended. I envisioned it in springtime, imagining the bushy pale green-gray leaves and the fragrance of dark purple spikes. I could feel Matthew's arms envelope me from behind and his head rest on my damp, sunburned shoulder. I remembered John, Anais, Cole and the Slaters laughing at the picnic table.

Then car doors slammed. Anais and Cole came into my view, throwing snowballs, yelping and laughing. Cole singing *"Ain't No Mountain High Enough"* while racing around the yard after Ani. I smiled and heard the side door open and close and Matthew was there, behind me, his arms encircling me, his tender face next to mine.

CPSIA information can be obtained at www.ICGtesting.com
262375BV00002B/7/P